M000202412

Keep Tahoe

Blue

NICOLE PYLAND

Keep Tahoe Blue

Tahoe Series Book #1

Kellan Cobb had to get out of San Francisco. She'd just watched her ex-girlfriend meet the woman of her dreams. Her broken heart needed a break from it all, and Lake Tahoe was calling her name.

Reese Lee has a secret. Only her twin sister knows the one thing Reese hasn't even told the closest people around her. When she meets Kellan at a fun weekend game of beach football, she knows there's something interesting about the tourist. She's never had a problem wining, dining, and sometimes bedding the tourists that strolled into the lake town. But with Kellan, she might just see the possibility of more.

Kellan is determined to address the loneliness in her heart. Reese is determined to keep her secret for fear it would change the way people see her. As the two women try to navigate their attraction, they each have to give up something their holding onto that could prevent them from finding what they've both been looking for all along.

This is a work of fiction. Any names or characters, businesses or places, events or incidents, are fictitious. Any resemblance to actual persons, living or dead, or actual events is purely coincidental. No part of this book may be reproduced or transmitted in any form or by any means, electronic or mechanical, including photocopying, recording or by any information storage and retrieval system, without written permission from the author.

To contact the author or for any additional information visit: **https://nicolepyland.com**

You can also subscribe to the reader's newsletter to be the first to receive updates about upcoming books and more: **https://nicolepyland.com/newsletter**

BY THE AUTHOR

Stand-alone books:

All the Love Songs

The Fire

The Moments

The Disappeared

Chicago Series:

- Introduction – Fresh Start
- Book #1 – The Best Lines
- Book #2 – Just Tell Her
- Book #3 – Love Walked into The Lantern
- Series Finale – What Happened After

San Francisco Series:

- Book #1 – Checking the Right Box

Copyright © 2019 Nicole Pyland
All rights reserved.
ISBN-13: 978-1-949308-11-2

CONTENTS

CHAPTER 1

HER HEART WAS BROKEN. It had been shattered into a thousand pieces that she was now attempting to pick up and glue back together on an impromptu and much-needed trip away from the city. As she drove, it was as if each of those pieces was stuck to the wet pavement on the deserted highway, and she couldn't pick them up fast enough. That was life though, Kellan reasoned. People leave pieces of themselves all over the roads they travel. She'd been through heartbreak before and was certain she'd left little pieces of her heart and soul with each of her former partners. Keira might have been the worst of all though.

Keira had been a friend for only a short time before they'd started dating. While Kellan had fallen hard and fast for her, Keira hadn't had the same experience. They'd become friends again after a time. Kellan had silently held onto the chance that they'd get back together one day. But when Keira met Emma not long after they'd ended their relationship, Kellan's hope all but disappeared.

Keira was in love. And Kellan couldn't stand around and watch the two of them continue to fall deeper. She couldn't join them at the Exploratorium After Dark each month or go to drinks with them each week at their local lesbian bar. It hurt too much right now to stay in San Francisco and have her heart hit by a wrecking ball every time they walked into a room together. Kellan packed up her things, and after telling Keira and their shared friends what she needed, she'd hit the road to Tahoe.

She'd rented a cabin in South Lake but off the main drag. It was nearing autumn. Most tourists would be heading home until the winter ski season. She was looking forward to the peace and quiet of the tiny cabin that she'd been able to rent for two weeks. She'd spend that time hiking and staring out at the crystal-clear water. She'd go back to the city rejuvenated and with a fresh layer of glue holding her heart together.

Tahoe was a faraway place to Kellan growing up, despite how close she was to it, living in the Bay Area. They couldn't afford vacations of any kind when she was a kid. She couldn't afford them all that much now either with her student loans still very much unpaid after veterinary school. She'd taken short weekend trips with friends or a girlfriend, and they'd shared a place and the expenses. This was her first solo trip to the lake after about ten with other people. It was the first one that she'd taken specifically to get away from those friends and former girlfriends.

"Kellan Cobb?" A woman of about fifty with long snow-white hair stood outside the cabin when Kellan climbed out of her old Jeep.

"That's me," Kellan replied and stretched. "Jane?"

"I've got the keys here for you." Jane climbed down from the porch of the cabin and toward Kellan, who had parked in the short driveway just off the main road that wrapped around the lake.

"Thank you." Kellan accepted the keys from the woman and ran her hand through her shoulder-length dirty blonde hair.

"You can drop the keys at the main rental office on your way out of town," Jane stated like she'd done this a hundred times before.

"Okay," Kellan replied and watched as Jane headed back toward the main road. "Nice welcoming committee."

It didn't take her long to grab her two bags from the back and her backpack from the passenger's seat. She'd packed light for a two-week trip, considering her hiking boots and outdoor equipment took up much of the space. She wasn't certain she could trek as long and hard as she used to, when she'd go just outside the city and tackle the mountain trails, but at thirty-three and being a city dweller that walked most days, she could handle most of the intermediate trails in the area.

Her phone chimed after she sat her bags on the ground. She considered not pulling it out of her pocket to check the text from Keira. She knew it was from Keira without looking because Keira had her own text tone. Kellan pulled her phone out to read the message. She'd asked Keira for time away from their friendship to try to sort out her feelings and move on from their failed relationship. Keira had been respectful of that but had sent a text that morning requesting the Kellan let her know when she arrived so she knew she was safe. Kellan replied that she'd arrived, planned to get settled in, and was turning off her phone. Then, she did just that.

The cabin was a standard log cabin, but she'd ensured it came with amenities. It rested over a hundred yards away from the lake itself and had a thin layer of trees and a small hill she'd have to climb down to get to the beach, but that was one of the reasons she'd chosen it. It wasn't too public but near a small market that was about half a mile away and across the street. The sky was gray and cloudless, and a slight drizzle had begun. She grabbed her bags and lifted them onto the wood-planked porch. A creak startled her for a moment before she realized it was only the age of the wood and her steps causing the only sound she could hear, outside of the birds in the trees surrounding the sides and back of the cabin. She unlocked the front door and pushed it open. Immediately, she was overtaken by the smell of wood and fire, and possibly a candle of some kind. No, it wasn't a candle. It was pine. It was the smell of the trees through the open back windows.

She breathed and tried to remember the last time she'd smelled nature like this. It had been with Keira, on their fourth date. Kellan had all but forced Keira, a self-proclaimed indoor girl, to go to Redwood State Park with her and spend the day amongst the tall trees. The trip had not gone well.

Kellan's cabin had one bedroom and one bathroom. She dropped her stuff onto the floor next to the queen-sized bed with a burgundy and white quilt and six matching pillows. The headboard was likely pine, as well as the matching dresser and bedside tables. There was a mirror attached to the dresser, and after dropping her bags down, she looked up and at herself. She let out a deep sigh. The bags under her blue eyes only proved how exhausted she was. She'd been working non-stop since she'd finally graduated from vet school.

She hadn't told any of her friends about the second job she'd taken to help pay off her loans. Rent in San Francisco was expensive. She was starting out behind everyone else because she'd taken so long to graduate. Her face and the exhaustion evident from working herself so hard turned away from the mirror and headed back out to the living room, where she recognized the television and a small movie collection she'd seen in the photo on the rental company's site.

She thought that she might buy some wine one day this week, or maybe something stronger, and have a movie night. She had plans for the days she'd be here. But as for the nights, she hadn't thought through how to occupy herself beyond grabbing a solo bite to eat in town or watching something stream on her laptop. It seemed like it wasn't that long ago when she'd had movie nights with Keira. And as she flopped onto the comfortable sofa, Kellan recalled what it had been like to watch a movie with her precocious ex.

"Kell, you said this wasn't a scary movie," Keira had said as she snuggled into Kellan's side on her sofa.

"I said no such thing. I said it was a thriller." Kellan had laughed when Keira closed her eyes away from the screen and into her side.

"Thriller doesn't mean scary."

"It's not scary, Keira. You're just scared of everything." Kellan had laughed again and kissed the top of Keira's head.

This was their tenth date. Kellan had remembered every single one that had come before it, and she was more than excited that Keira was this close to her. She could breathe her in and wrap an arm around her shoulders.

"I'm not scared of everything; just a lot of stuff," Keira had commented and lifted her face to look up at Kellan, who smiled down at her. "Did you do this on purpose? Get me to cuddle up to you like this so you could take advantage of me?"

"Maybe." Kellan had laughed again.

"I knew it." Keira had shifted back. "If you want something, you should just ask for it, Kellan."

"Yeah?" Kellan's eyebrows had lifted in unison. "So, if I wanted to skip the rest of the movie and go to the bedroom, you'd be for that idea?"

"I have an early day tomorrow, Kell," Keira had reminded her. "I wasn't planning on staying over tonight."

"You don't have to stay over. We can occupy ourselves for a while, and then you can head back to your place." She had teased kisses along Keira's collarbone.

"We should probably just finish the movie. I'll stay over Friday night or something."

"It's not about you staying over, Keira." Kellan had pulled back and removed her arm from around Keira.

"You realize we haven't had sex in like two weeks, right?"

"Two weeks?" Keira had appeared to be considering this as if she'd been unsure.

"We met at the wedding. You managed to seduce me into your bed, and we had one wild night together. Then – nothing."

"Because we just did the friend thing after that."

"Until you told me you wanted to go out. We did. And now, here we are. We've had sex after two of our dates, and you never stay over. And I don't stay over at your place."

"We're not there yet," Keira had defended.

"We're not where yet?" Kellan had questioned.

"We're not a couple or anything, Kell. We're just dating."

"I'm aware of that, Keira. Trust me, I am more than aware that I am way ahead of you in this thing." Kellan had stood then and grabbed at the two wine glasses on her coffee table.

"What's that supposed to mean?"

"It means that I'm ready for things that you aren't." Kellan had dropped the half-finished glasses off at her counter and turned back to see Keira staring at her. "It's fine." She'd deflated at the look on Keira's face. "I had a long day at work, and I probably should have canceled this date."

"Kell, what's going on?"

"Nothing, Keira."

Kellan had lied that night. Something *was* going on with her. She was already in love with Keira. She knew that Keira wasn't in love with her. She'd seen Keira's face that night, staring at her with a look of horror; like she was ready to end whatever they were doing and run out the door. And Kellan hadn't been ready for that, so she'd lied.

CHAPTER 2

"REESE, YOU HAVE TO take better care of yourself."

"I know, Doc," Reese replied and slid her jacket back on over her long-sleeved t-shirt. "I've taken precautions and done the best I can."

"I know, dear." The doctor that Reese had known since birth finished writing on Reese's chart. "You just have to watch out."

"I tried. But they're four, Doc. There are more of them than there are of me. Sometimes, I have to chase one of them down. I ran into the corner of the desk."

"And you almost broke a rib, Reese," the doctor reminded her and sat the chart down on the counter next to the exam table. "You're lucky it's just a bad bruise and nothing more. How about I call that specialist at Stanford?"

"I don't need a specialist." Reese zipped up the jacket, remembering it was raining when she'd made her way into the clinic. "I'm fine."

"So you keep saying."

"I am. I'm careful. Remy moved in with me. She's

helpful." She stuck her hands in her pockets. "I need to get to the store. I'm cooking dinner for her tonight as a thank you."

"One of these days, you might actually listen to me."

"I do listen to you. I came in today, didn't I?" She smiled and gave her favorite doctor a wink.

"Three days later than you should have," the doctor chastised.

"Better late than never?"

"In your case – yes, but still better on time than late, Reese Lee."

"Yes, Doc." Reese laughed.

She'd known she should have checked in with the doc sooner, but the bruise hadn't appeared that bad at first. And it was only Remy's not so gentle push that she visit the doctor earlier than usual that made her go. She normally only saw the doctor once a month.

"All good?" Remy asked once Reese arrived home two hours later. "Anything we need to worry about?"

"God, you're worse than mom and dad!" Reese placed two reusable grocery bags on the counter. "I'm fine. Bruised ribs. That's all."

"Mom and dad aren't here to do this anymore, which means the big sister has to step in." Remy approached and tussled Reese's short brown hair.

"You're four minutes older than me," she said to her twin.

"Still older." Remy lifted herself onto the counter next to the bags while she watched Reese unzip her jacket. "Did she recommend the specialist again?"

"Doesn't she always?" Reese hung the jacket on the coat hanger by the door.

"Maybe you should listen this time," she suggested.

"Rem, we've talked about this."

"I know." Remy began pulling items from the grocery bag.

"I've seen a hundred doctors."

"Not recently. Mom used to make you go, and she's been gone for over a year now."

"You don't need to remind me how long mom's been gone, Rem. I remember."

"I know." She jumped off the counter and handed Reese the bag of potatoes to put away. "I also know you're tired of hearing about this."

"I am, yes."

"Why didn't I get it?" Remy asked.

Reese moved to the refrigerator to open it so Remy could put the milk away, but she closed it at that serious question from her sister and best friend.

"Rem, come on."

"It's just a question, Reese. We're identical twins. Shouldn't we have identical diseases?"

"I don't think that's how it works, Rem." Reese gave her sister a straight-lipped smile.

"I wish it was me."

"No, you don't. I don't either."

"I do, actually." She passed Reese the milk. "Because at least I'd listen to my fucking doctor." She squinted at Reese before giving her a playful smile. "What's for dinner?"

***

Reese had wrapped up the PM session of her class and made her way to the South Lake Tahoe visitor's center of which she was an employee. She'd had a particularly long day with her combined preschool and kindergarten class. Half of her students did not want a nap. There was a crayon theft that left Joey in timeout and Anthony telling little Joey that they weren't friends anymore.

She'd gotten little sleep last night after she and Remy had spoken yet again about her problem. Hearing her sister say time and again that she wished it had been her was hard for Reese to hear. Remy was her other half.

There were two major differences between Reese and Remy outside of the fact that Remy had dyed her hair blonde when they'd gone off to college together. She'd kept it that way ever since. Remy was straight and had a boyfriend, Ryan, that she'd been with for the past six months. Reese had only ever had one boyfriend, and that had been when she was fifteen and a freshman at high school. It hadn't taken long for her to realize he was not what she'd wanted. She'd come out to her sister as soon as she'd figured out she was gay. They'd had a long conversation about that between the two of them, trying to figure out – if they were identical in DNA and in many of their experiences – how Remy had turned out straight while Reese preferred women. The other major difference was Reese's little problem.

Reese worked at the visitor's center twice a week as a volunteer. Her mother had done it for years, and when she'd passed, Reese felt like she needed to pick up the slack. Tourism was a vital part of the community. While there were natives, many of the town's inhabitants on any given day were temporary and would return to their homes either prior to the start of the weather changing to autumn, because they'd come for the summer activities, or just after the last big snowfall, because they'd been in town for the winter activities. The permanent population was just over twenty-one thousand. That was a hamlet compared to the near seven hundred thousand of Las Vegas. She'd been a resident there for five years when she'd gone to school at UNLV with Remy. She'd been an education major and had gotten her five-year teaching certificate, while Remy had studied physical therapy and now practiced in South Lake.

For the past year, she'd spent at least a few hours each week explaining trails and pointing out the best views of the lake along with the best activities for tourists to partake in. She'd led hikes for groups every so often but stopped that part of the job when she'd tripped over an overgrown tree branch on one of the trails and broke two toes and her pinky finger from trying to catch her fall. She'd gone to the doctor too late then, too, and had to keep off her feet for an extra week because of it. That had been over a month ago. And now, fully healed from her own klutziness, she was ready to get back out there. Unfortunately, Remy and Stan, the man that ran the visitor's center as a paid employee, both wanted her to stay inside the center and not get back on the trails anytime soon.

"Hi. I'm looking for an easy hike. It's me and my wife, and she's never been hiking before." A tall man, dressed in a light jacket, a pair of worn jeans and hiking boots, approached as she reorganized the stack of Keep Tahoe Blue bumper stickers the center gave away for free.

"Sure. Let me grab a map for you." Reese slid the stickers back into their organizer before moving back behind the long counter. "Are you looking for something with a view during or at the end, or just the hike itself?"

As she asked the question, she noticed one other person enter the center and begin perusing the book section against the far wall. The woman had shoulder-length blonde hair and was wearing weather-appropriate gear. She sported some old, worn in hiking boots complete with dried mud on the heels. The woman wasn't facing her, and she wondered if the beauty of her face matched the beauty of the rest of her body. Her jeans were tight, but not overly so. They provided Reese with a nice view of the woman's ass. She thought back to the last female tourist she'd found attractive and their weekend together prior to the woman leaving Tahoe.

"A view would be nice," the man replied.

"Sorry?" she asked when she realized she hadn't been paying attention to the man standing right in front of her.

"A view. I think she'd like a reward at the end." He smiled.

Reese pulled out one of the folded maps they used for marking destinations for tourists. She circled two

11

trailheads before turning it around for him to see. As she did, she glanced over at the woman who was now moving in the direction of the stickers she'd just organized.

"These two are the easiest trails that get you up high enough to get a great view of the lake." She pointed her red pen at the two circles.

"And I just take a right out of here?" he asked.

"Left is faster. Then, turn right past the grocery store. You'll get to both of them from there. Shouldn't take more than a few hours."

"Great. Thanks." The man folded the map into his pocket and walked off toward the exit.

Reese gave him a nod with a polite smile before her glance moved to the woman who was reviewing a pamphlet. Reese turned around behind the counter to the back office to see that Stan was staring at the computer screen, likely engaged enough to not notice or care that she was about to approach this woman because she wanted to and not because the woman needed help. When she turned back around to the open room though, she could just make out the woman's back as she made her way through the exit.

CHAPTER 3

KELLAN'S FEET were killing her. It had been far too long since she'd been hiking like that. Doing ten miles on her first full day was probably too much. She'd chosen three separate intermediate trails, had lunch overlooking the Emerald Bay, and then made her way back down just in time for dinner. She had nothing in the cabin, and she was regretting that as she parked her car at the small grocery mart down the street from her cabin.

She picked out some easy to cook meals from the freezer section and a steak with fresh vegetables for one night when she'd cook something good for herself. She grabbed one and then two bottles of wine before she decided to add a bottle of white to the reds. She made her way to the frozen food section, reached for the last pint of mint chocolate chip and added it to her cart.

"Mint chip, huh? Hitting the hard stuff."

Kellan turned around to see a woman standing behind her. She looked to be around her age and was pointing to the items in Kellan's cart.

"I'm sorry?" Kellan asked.

"You've got wine, comfort food, and ice cream. All you need now is the breakup music." The woman shrugged. "Sorry, that's rude of me."

"Oh," Kellan stated, glancing at her cart cliché.

"Tourist, right?"

"I'm here for a couple of weeks. Just stocking up."

"Welcome to our little town."

"Thanks." She paused. "And it's not because of a breakup."

"Huh?"

"My choices. I didn't break up with someone, and no one broke up with me."

"Then, I feel really bad. I'm sorry. I'm kind of an asshole."

"It's okay."

"I'm cooking for my sister and I tonight. I needed to pick up some stuff. I was hoping to get her favorite ice cream, which you just grabbed a second faster than I could get to it." She pointed to the pint in Kellan's cart.

"Oh, sorry. You can have it. I just grabbed the first one I saw."

"So, not an ice cream connoisseur?"

"No, I like it all," Kellan stated with a smile. "Here." She reached down to pull out the pint and held it out for the woman to take. "Take it to your sister."

"Thanks. I appreciate it." The woman nodded and smiled wide. "And she will, too." She dropped the ice cream in the red basket she held over her left arm. "I'm Remy, by the way."

"Kellan."

"Kellan? That's an interesting name."

"I get that a lot."

"And you're here for a couple of weeks?"

"I rented a cabin down the street," she answered.

"I'd invite you to dinner with my sister and I, but it's just a sibling thing. If you're interested, a few of us get together on the weekends. This time of year, we play flag football on Saturdays on the beach. We drink while we play, so it's not exactly a real game. It's early because we're all old." She laughed at her comment. "And then, we pack it in and get home to soak our sore muscles."

Kellan thought the woman attractive to be sure, but she wasn't certain if the woman was merely being polite or if she was flirting and maybe even asking her out by inviting her to hang out with her friends.

"I don't want to intrude on your friends," she offered with a slow shake of her head.

"You wouldn't be. We invite random people all the time. It's a constantly evolving group. But if you don't want to join, it's no big deal. Just wanted to repay you for the ice cream that is now melting in my basket, so I should run." She laughed and met Kellan's eye again. "My sister will be there. She can't play, so she'll be on the sidelines. You can hang with her if you aren't the sporty type, or you can play wide receiver. Either way, turn right out of this parking lot, go about three miles, and park on the lakeside. You'll see a short trail and the beach. That's where we'll be at noon." She took a few steps backward. "Nice to meet you, Kellan."

"You too," Kellan replied, feeling like an idiot.

She gathered up her purchases and loaded them grumpily into the back of her jeep. On the very short trek home, she silently chastised herself for the fact that she might have just been flirted with and had absolutely no response to it. The woman had been attractive. Her eyes were gray, or maybe it was a light green that resembled gray in the unflattering bright lights of the market. Her blonde hair was long and had been pulled back into a ponytail. Kellan thought the blonde was a few shades too light for the woman's face, but that wasn't exactly her place to say.

She unloaded her groceries and stabbed at the plastic cover of one of the frozen dinners before shoving it into the provided microwave, setting the timer, and opening one of the bottles of wine. She grabbed a wine glass that seemed far too small for the amount she planned to consume, filled it to the top, and plopped onto the sofa. She picked up the remote and turned on the television. She gulped once at her wine before deciding she'd need water, too. As she reached for the bottle in the fridge, she heard her cell beep. She'd turned it back on earlier in the day to use the GPS and had forgotten to turn it off. She took a long pull off the water and walked to her pack, pulling out her phone to switch it off again and draw out any notifications when she noticed it was a text from Macon Greene. Greene had been one of Keira's friends and one they'd then shared, but not one she'd ever felt particularly close to.

"How are you?" Kellan read Macon's text out loud and chuckled. "How am I?" She laughed again. "My ex doesn't even consider herself my ex because we were never an official couple. She's moved on so easily with the new girl in town. They're in love. And last week, I saw you on a Facebook post with some woman named Joanna at a bar, smiling and having fun. So you seem to be doing fine in the woman department. Hillary won't admit the woman at the coffee place is totally into her. And when she does, I'm sure they'll finally fall madly in love. And then there's me..." She paused as the microwave beeped. "I have feelings for a woman I want to go away, but they won't, and that pisses me off. A beautiful woman may or may not have been flirting with me earlier. I couldn't tell because I froze like an idiot." The microwave beeped again after not being opened the first time. "I heard you," she yelled at the appliance. "So, I'm great, Greene. I'm just great."

CHAPTER 4

REESE ONLY CAME to these weekly games because it gave her an excuse to be outside. Reese loved being outside. She used to hike a lot and found herself missing the activity more and more each day. Sitting on the beach wasn't exactly a substitute, and part of her wished she'd get out there and play instead of drinking a beer and watching everyone else enjoy themselves. The other part of her knew she was terrible at football and most other sports that involved a ball and possible contact with another human being. She settled for watching her friends have fun and occasionally going for a short walk to the water's edge to dip her toes in.

"Hi."

Reese looked up to see someone slightly familiar standing next to her on the beach. She did a double take to confirm that it was indeed the woman from the visitor's center the other day. And it took even longer for her to realize the woman was saying hello to her.

"Hi," Reese replied.

"I came." The woman offered a shy wave from her hip, and Reese smiled, thinking it was cute.

"Okay." Reese nodded.

"You dyed your hair." The woman pointed to Reese's head. "And cut it."

"Oh." Reese understood now. "The woman you're looking for is over there." She stood from her beach chair and pointed in the direction of Remy, who was running near the edge of the water, attempting to catch a pass from her boyfriend.

"Oh." The woman did a quick turn of her head back to Remy and then again to Reese. "Sisters?"

"Twins." Reese shrugged. "Happens all the time. One of the reasons we have different hair. Makes it easier for people to tell us apart." She took in the tightly clasped hands at the woman's side. "I'm Reese, by the way." She held out her hand for the woman to shake.

"Kellan."

"That's an interesting name." Reese waited as the woman shook her hand and then lowered her own to her side.

"Yeah. Sorry about the confusion. Your sister invited me to watch the game."

"Because you let her have the ice cream? I remember now. You're the ice cream woman."

"I guess I am." Kellan laughed.

Reese smiled at the sound and said, "Thank you for that."

"The ice cream?"

"It's my favorite. They don't always carry it there. Sometimes, I have to go to the big grocery store. I hate going to the big grocery store."

"No problem."

"Aren't you going to ask me why I hate the big grocery store?" Reese chuckled.

"Why don't you like the big grocery store?" Kellan asked and glanced to the side as the football landed a few feet away from her, and Remy approached to pick it up.

"Hey, Kellan!" Remy took the ball from Kellan's outstretched arms. "You came?"

"I did."

"This is my sister, the ice cream-holic." She pointed with a thumb toward Reese.

"We've met." Kellan nodded in Reese's direction.

"You want to play?" Remy asked her. "Morgan can tap out for a few. She's missed the last two passes thrown her way," Remy half-yelled this, and Morgan came up behind her, jerked the ball out of her arms, and scowled.

"The pass was behind me." She looked toward Kellan.

Reese took a step toward Kellan instinctively and wondered why for a moment, before Morgan reached out her hand, tucking the ball under her other arm.

"This is Morgan Burns," Remy introduced. "She's terrible at football but brings the beer. So, we forgive her."

"Nice to meet you." Morgan and Kellan shook hands.

"Kellan Cobb," Kellan introduced herself

"So, you in?" Remy asked.

Reese glanced with a side-eye at her twin, wishing their twin powers would activate so Remy would know Reese didn't want Kellan spending any time with her ex-girlfriend. She also wanted Kellan to sit on the sidelines with her.

"I'm not much of a football player. Actually, I don't think I've ever played football." Kellan smiled in Morgan's direction.

Remy finally met Reese's eye and then she nodded. Every now and then, the fact that they were identical twins and had this power to understand one another without words paid off.

"Morgan, you're quarterbacking now. Maybe you can pass better than you can catch," Remy suggested.

"Cool, but Kellan can take my place as a wide receiver. Laurie has to leave anyway. She has to pick up the kids from the sitter."

"Lame." Remy rolled her eyes. "Fine. Kellan, you've never played before?"

"No."

"Well, you don't know how good you could be then, right? And you're dressed for it." Remy motioned to Kellan's outfit.

Kellan was wearing navy yoga capris with a black short-sleeved V-neck shirt that looked like a nice nylon-cotton blend made for outdoor activities. Her tennis shoes were well worn in without being too worn in. She'd brought a pack with her that Reese finally noticed was on the sand next to them. Kellan was no rookie. Reese smiled at the thought.

"I dressed for a short beach hike just in case." Kellan gave an exaggerated shrug of her shoulders and glanced at Remy. "Sorry, I haven't been the most social person recently. I came here to get away for a couple of weeks. I wasn't sure I'd be up for a big beach day." She pointed to the group that continued to play, despite missing a few players.

"I'll throw; you catch. It's pretty easy." Morgan took Kellan by the forearm and off they went to where the rest of the group had paused between plays.

"She came." Remy turned to stand beside Reese.

"I guess." Reese resolved herself to be unaffected by Morgan's hand on the small of this stranger's back as they made their way to join their team.

"Morgan seems interested," Remy said.

"I guess." Reese turned her face to her sister's. "Your point, Rem?"

"You seem pretty interested there too, sis." She winked. "Who exactly are you interested in though? The new arrival, who you can sleep with, she leaves, and you never see her again – which is usually your MO, or the ex-girlfriend you dumped?"

"Go play your stupid game." Reese gave her a light shove and moved to sit back down in her beach chair.

Remy only laughed as she made her way back to join the next play. Reese's eyes darted from her ex to Kellan and back to Morgan, who did look really good in her sports bra and tight shorts. Reese had missed when she'd peeled off her shirt. For a moment, she thought back to their last time together, and how Morgan's skin had been almost as sweaty from a different activity. She shook her head rapidly. Her eyes flitted back to Kellan, who was running down the beach close to the water. She was the only one wearing shoes, but that seemed to give her an advantage as she sped past her defender, caught Morgan's pass, and kept running until the entire group began yelling that she'd scored and could come back. They never bothered marking the end zones on the beach, but no one had told her that the yardstick, painted blue, that had been there for as long as any of them could remember, indicated a score for her team.

She received some high-fives and some fist bumps. Reese watched as she seemed surprised at herself and at everyone's overjoyed reaction. Kellan tossed the ball to Remy, who then tossed it to her boyfriend, Ryan. Reese continued to observe Kellan in their huddles as she nodded along with whatever Remy or Morgan was instructing her to do. She lined up and leaned forward in the ready position. Once the ball was snapped, Kellan took off at full speed, kicking up sand behind her. This time, her defender gave Kellan's shirt a playful tug to try to prevent her from blowing past her. Kellan turned as if pivoting on a basketball court and continued past her. The ball was a little behind her, but she managed another thrilling catch and scored. There were more cheers this time. Clearly, everyone was impressed but also very tired as many of them knelt in the sand. A few made their way over toward Reese to grab their water bottles.

"Nice catch, rook," Morgan said as they both made their way over to the giant bucket, filled with mostly ice, bottled water, and beer. "You're a natural."

"Thanks," Kellan replied and sat down next to her pack.

"You've got some moves for sure," Morgan continued, and Reese recognized her flirtatious tone.

"Okay, it's time for real introductions." Remy approached with a water bottle in hand and placed her arm around Kellan's shoulders. "You've met Morgan and Reese officially and the rest of our team unofficially.

Everyone, listen up. This is Kellan. Kellan is here for a couple of weeks. Kellan, this is everyone."

"Did you play soccer or something? You're pretty good." Ryan chugged half of his water.

"No, I played basketball. But it's been a long time," Kellan replied and slid off one shoe after the other before removing both socks. "Sand," she added, and Reese realized she was saying that to her.

"It's the worst." Reese cursed herself for sounding so stupid. "They usually play shoeless."

"Why aren't you playing?" Kellan shook out both shoes.

"She's lazy." Remy sat on Kellan's other side. "I'm kidding. She's too good for football."

"What's that mean?" Kellan laughed a little.

"I prefer other outdoor activities," Reese answered.

"How long are you here for, Kellan?" Morgan had joined their conversation after grabbing water for herself and standing behind and off to the side of Reese's chair.

"About another week and a half."

"You ever been to Tahoe?" Ryan asked as he sat next to his girlfriend.

"Not in a while, but yeah. I've been here a few times."

"And what brings you here now?" Morgan asked.

"Oh, everyone wants to know about me." Kellan chuckled and pulled her water bottle out of the side net pocket of her pack. "I'm not all that interesting." She shrugged and took a drink.

"I doubt that," Morgan said.

Reese turned her head in shock at the tone.

"What?" Morgan huffed out in a whisper at her.

"Nothing." Reese stood and smoothed her jeans with her palms for no reason. "I'm going for a walk."

"Use the trail," Remy reminded and pointed to the cement trail about twenty feet behind her.

"I'm fine, Rem." She set off down the sand instead.

Once she got far enough away from the rest of the group, she let out a deep sigh at her ex-girlfriend's antics before she remembered *she* had broken up with Morgan. Morgan was a free woman and could flirt with anyone she wanted. They hadn't been dating in over a year. It was unlikely Morgan had been celibate the entire time. The girl was striking with light blonde hair and bright blue eyes. When her parents had moved to Tahoe for her father's travel agency, she and Reese had become friends. Travel agencies were now a thing of the almost past. Her family opened a sporting goods store in South Lake, and Morgan led the work there with them.

"Reese?"

Reese heard the voice come from behind her and turned to see Kellan jogging barefoot to catch up. She smiled slightly and then tried to cover it up while she waited until Kellan was at her side.

"Hey. Needed a walk?" Reese asked.

"Yeah, I guess. They all seem very interested in learning more about me. It's kind of a lot." Kellan ran her hand over the back of her neck.

"You're new. They've all known each other for years."

"I'm not that interesting. That's the problem."

"I'll be the judge of that." Reese turned her head toward Kellan and gave her a wide smile. "Age?"

"That's where we're starting, huh?" Kellan laughed. "Playing dirty, aren't you?"

"Yup." She nodded playfully.

"I'm thirty-three," Kellan answered.

"Occupation?"

"No, not fair. You can't just make me throw my age out there and not share yours."

"I hardly think I *made* you do anything." Reese shoved her hands into the pockets of her jeans.

"I'm a vet," Kellan said.

"Vet, huh?"

"I live in San Francisco and work at a clinic. I have an older brother and a younger sister, Kevin and Katie."

"Your parents have a thing with Ks," Reese replied.

"My mother, Kerri Ann, and my father, Kyle, yeah, they like the letter K."

"Well, I am thirty-two." She received a smile from Kellan at revealing her age. "I'm a preschool and kindergarten teacher. I have one sister, but you know that because you met her already. And I live here."

"Parents' names start with R?" Kellan asked.

"Huh?" Reese flashed back to the last time she'd seen her parents.

"Reese and Remy?"

"Oh, that's just a twin thing. They wanted us to have the same first initial. At least they didn't make them rhyme, too." She paused. "Their names were Auburn and Steven."

"Were?" Kellan's voice softened.

"They died last year. Car accident."

"I'm sorry."

"Me too."

"Auburn. Your mom had a beautiful name."

"Auburn was my dad's name," Reese teased, and Kellan smiled back at her.

"Hey, ladies." Morgan approached soundlessly from behind them. "Kellan, can I borrow you? We have a second half to play."

"The game's not over?" Kellan asked her and checked with Reese.

"Nope. We're up by seven though, thanks to you."

Morgan squeezed Kellan's forearm and glanced at Reese. Reese wasn't sure what that glance meant, but it was almost a shy look Morgan offered her. She wasn't being cold, but Reese still didn't appreciate the interruption from the woman she used to love.

"Okay. I guess I've got to go," Kellan said and then headed back with Morgan while Reese stood watching them hustle away.

CHAPTER 5

THE GAME ENDED with Kellan's team winning by fourteen and Remy and Ryan bragging to their friends Jarod and Gary, who'd played on the other team. The trash talk had been going on for over an hour. While Kellan hadn't joined in, she also hadn't left the gathering either as the afternoon had turned into an early evening. She sat on a blanket, provided by one of the other girls, alongside Morgan and Stacy as they talked about Kellan's life and their own.

"I don't think I could do what you do." Morgan took a sip of her beer. "Do you have to put animals down sometimes?"

"Yeah, those are the bad days." Kellan nodded somberly.

"I don't know how you do it," Stacy said. "I have two cats. I have no idea what's going to happen when they die. I've already told them they're not allowed to."

Kellan offered her a smile. She glanced up at Reese, who was talking to her sister. They were laughing at something. Kellan liked Reese's smile; it seemed so genuine. Her light gray eyes were lit up by the light of the setting sun over the water. Kellan recalled wondering if Remy's eyes were green or gray in the market the other day. Now that she'd had a chance to see them in light, she could tell that both sisters had light gray eyes. She still felt like the darker hair that Reese had worked better with their lighter color. She wondered if Remy had dyed her hair or if Reese had chosen the darker shade.

"Tomorrow, I'm taking a group on a hike to Emerald Bay. It's intermediate at first, but after we take in the view, we go higher, and it turns more advanced then. You interested?" Morgan asked, and Kellan realized she only heard part of what she'd said.

"A hike?" She turned back to Morgan.

"It's ten miles in total. Parts are pretty intense, but it's a good workout. The views at the top are amazing."

"Sure," she agreed while she watched Reese and Remy approach.

Reese took a seat in her beach chair, appearing to be a little worn out, while Remy sat on the blanket next to her.

"Reese, Ryan and I are getting out of here. Ryan's pulling the car up closer," she announced.

"Reese okay?" Morgan asked with apparent concern.

"She's just tired," Remy stated.

Kellan wanted to ask why Reese was tired, or why Morgan had expressed immediate concern for Reese, but she didn't think it was her place. Instead, she took a drink from her water bottle and turned slightly to put it away. She suddenly found herself tired, too. With the ten-mile hike she'd agreed to, she needed to get some sleep.

"I'll grab my husband." Stacy stood and headed in the direction of a few guys standing off to the ice bucket.

"I should get out of here, too." Kellan slid her shoes on without her socks and put her bag over her shoulder. "I think I'm going to regret playing football tomorrow when I wake up and have to do a ten-mile hike."

"Epsom salt bath." Reese's voice came from behind her. "Add rubbing alcohol to it to make it more effective."

"I don't think I have any of that at the cabin," Kellan replied.

"They sell it at the market – aisle seven, on the bottom. They usually have a few bags, and they always have a ton of alcohol. Tourists can be klutzy." She smiled at Kellan. "You ready, Rem?"

"Yeah." She looked toward the small parking lot where Kellan could now see a red SUV with the back passenger door open and Ryan standing there, waiting for them.

"It was nice meeting you," Reese said.

"Do you hike?" Kellan asked.

"What?" Reese turned back to her.

"I'm going hiking with Morgan tomorrow. Do you hike?"

Reese glanced around her at Morgan and then back to Kellan before she said, "I don't hike as much as I used to, no."

"Do you want to join us tomorrow?"

"I'm volunteering at the visitor's center tomorrow. I'm there most of the day. Then, I have dinner with Ryan and Remy."

"Oh, sure. I guess I'll see you around then, or maybe I won't. I'm not here much longer."

"I'm sure I'll see you again, Kellan. Small town, remember?" she offered.

"Right."

"Good night." Reese smiled, but it didn't reach her eyes.

Kellan did the same. She watched as the twins made their way to the concrete path that led to the parking lot where Reese climbed into the backseat, Remy took the passenger's seat, and Ryan drove them off.

"If you give me your number, I can text you the info for tomorrow," Morgan suggested.

"I don't have my phone," Kellan replied. "I decided not to turn it on while I'm here. I kind of needed a break from that, too."

"Old school. I can do old school. One sec." She rushed off to where her bag was lying in the sand and pulled something out. When she returned, she held out a brochure for Kellan to take. "It's the Emerald Bay advanced hike on the inside. That has all the info you'll need in it. Bring lunch. We eat while we're up there."

"Okay."

"I'll see you tomorrow." Morgan offered her a smile.

***

"Hey, early bird." Morgan had just parked her car and was getting her pack out of her trunk. "That excited, huh?"

"Yeah." Kellan was excited to be hiking again and to go up a different trail than she'd taken before with experienced hikers.

"We have a group of four coming, too. Two couples from Canada. They all know each other. And they're experienced, so we shouldn't have a problem with the trickier part up top."

"Sounds good." Kellan stood upright and stretched her arms straight above her head.

"Not bad." Morgan wiggled her eyebrows and offered a flirtatious smile.

"Oh." Kellan lowered her arms when she realized Morgan was staring at her stomach where her shirt had ridden up.

"Don't stop on my account," Morgan replied with confidence.

"Sorry, are we late?" A man approached with three people in tow.

"Right on time." Morgan went immediately into tour guide mode.

Kellan had no problem with the first part of the hike

that took them up to Emerald Bay. Morgan had been at the front of the group, leading the way, while she'd taken up the rear. She didn't want to be rude, but the two couples were occupied, talking to each other and Morgan, so she'd put her headphones in at about mile two and used the music to calm her as she typically did while hiking.

"Having fun?" Morgan asked as they all sat just out of the way of the crowd of tourists at the photo spot with the perfect view of Emerald Bay.

"I love a long hike," Kellan revealed and unpacked her sandwich.

The four other members of their group had headed over to join the rest of the tourists in taking pictures of the clear water and tiny island beneath. Fannette Island was the only island in Lake Tahoe. The ruins of a small stone building called the "Tea House" could be seen. The island was accessible by boat, canoe, or kayak. Kellan had always loved the view of the island, but in the many trips she'd made to the lake, she'd never been out to it. She'd always stuck to hiking and swimming in the lake, but swimming to the island was prohibited.

"Can I ask you a question?" Morgan said.

"Sure."

"What really brought you here?"

"Oh, *that* question. I needed a break. I haven't had a vacation in a while, and I've always loved this place."

"Needed a break?" Morgan's expression led Kellan to believe she wanted to know more, but she wasn't pushing the envelope either.

"I graduated from vet school late. I only started working after school a couple of years ago. I haven't taken a real vacation since. I asked my boss if I could have a couple of weeks to recharge."

"Got it." Morgan nodded and took a drink of her water. "And you didn't bring anyone with you on this trip?"

"No, just me."

"So, no significant other, or they just couldn't get away?"

"I'm single." Kellan smiled and took a bite of her sandwich.

"Single and looking or single and recovering?" Morgan asked.

"I don't know how to answer that," Kellan replied honestly and finished off her sandwich.

"Interesting." Morgan leaned forward. "Go on."

Kellan laughed. She stuffed the empty plastic bag into her pack before opening one of her power bars and taking a bite, more as a stall technique than to address hunger. She glanced over at the two couples they'd hiked with. They appeared to be happy and in love as they took selfies and exchanged phones to take pictures for the other couple. She wanted that with someone. She'd once thought that someone would be Keira. Now, she laughed at that thought, because it was more than obvious that Keira had found her someone. Kellan was left looking, but not necessarily looking right now. She also wasn't sure how much recovering she had left to do.

"I've dated, but nothing serious since my last attempt at a serious relationship, which wasn't a relationship at all."

"How so?"

"We hooked up first, became friends after that, and then decided to date after all, but it didn't work out."

"Because?"

"You're inquisitive, aren't you?" Kellan laughed.

"I guess I am when it comes to the gorgeous stranger that showed up at my lake."

"Your lake, huh?" She laughed again and tried to ignore Morgan's *gorgeous* comment.

"Yeah, *my* lake." She smiled and slid over on the concrete toward Kellan but remained about a foot away. "What happened?"

"She just wanted to be friends. After all that, she said she thought we were better as friends." She paused and met Morgan's eyes to see if she'd noticed the female pronoun in her story. "Her name is Keira. I'm pretty sure she just met the love of her life." She ran her hand through her ponytail, which was a nervous tick she'd tried to stop.

"And you're still in love with her?"

Kellan turned to answer that question, but as she did, one of the couples approached to eat their lunch. Morgan went back into tour guide mode, explaining the history of Emerald Bay.

***

"Tomorrow, I lead a kayak trip on the lake, but we don't have anyone signed up yet. Do you maybe want a free kayak tour?" Morgan asked her once the couples had departed and they were alone in the parking lot at the trailhead.

"I'm a hiker; not much for kayaking." Kellan dropped her pack in the back of her Jeep.

"You said that about football, and you turned out to be a rock star."

"I was okay," she replied.

"I'd like to get the whole story about your ex and what brought you here. Maybe we could consider it a date or something." She was blushing. Kellan's eyes got big at the word *date*. "Or not."

"It's not—"

"No, it's fine. I'm sorry. I shouldn't have said *date*. It can just be a kayak tour."

"How about we compromise?" Kellan suggested.

"Compromise?"

"We do the kayaking tomorrow, and if that goes well, we can consider the other thing."

"The date thing?" Morgan checked.

"Yes, the date thing." Kellan laughed at Morgan's hopeful smile. "You do know I'm leaving in a little over a week, right?"

"Yes, I do."

"Is this a sex thing?" Kellan asked.

"What?" Morgan laughed.

"Well, it can't exactly go anywhere."

"You're asking if I just want to get in your pants?"

"I guess."

"No, I don't just want to get in your pants, Kellan." She paused. "And who says it can't go anywhere? San Francisco isn't that far away. People do have long-distance relationships. But I'm getting ahead of myself. Kayaking tomorrow, and then we'll see."

CHAPTER 6

"OH, HEY." Reese noticed a very sweaty looking Kellan standing at the end of aisle seven in her local market.

"Hi." Kellan seemed to be struggling to bend over to pick something up. "Is your friend Morgan a sadist?" she joked as she grabbed for a large bag of Epsom salt to load into her cart.

"What?" Reese approached with her basket and laughed at Kellan who moved to reach back down. "I'll get it." She sat her basket on the ground and grabbed a bottle of alcohol. "How many?"

"All of them," Kellan replied and stood hunched over her cart.

"What happened?"

"Advanced hike." Kellan looked up as Reese placed four bottles of alcohol into her cart. "I thought you were getting this stuff last night."

"I did. I used it. Now, I need more."

Reese laughed and picked up one more bag of Epsom salt to add to Kellan's nearly empty shopping cart.

"Rough hike?" she asked.

"I didn't think it was that bad earlier, but I started driving back, and the soreness in my back just kicked in. I should really stop pushing myself this hard."

"Seriously, you're supposed to be on vacation," Reese offered with a smile and glanced at the only other items in Kellan's cart. "Is that your dinner?" She pointed at a TV dinner.

"It might be. I have a few more at the cabin, but none of them sounded good, so I picked up this one."

"No, you're not eating this after you've hiked all day. I'm here for baking powder. I'm making cookies. Ryan's favorite is chocolate chip. It's my mom's recipe. I don't make them often. Why don't you go home to change, shower, and get ready? Come to our place around seven."

"Our place?"

"Remy and mine. We share a house. Ryan's there most nights."

"I don't want to intrude on your dinner."

"You won't," Reese insisted. "I'm sure you could use a home-cooked meal. Remy's making my dad's meatloaf, and Ryan's making the sides. It's a team effort."

"What can I make?" Kellan asked.

"Wine."

"Okay, but that might take a while. I should get some grapes and start stomping," she joked.

"Just bring it." Reese laughed. "No need to go all Lucy and Ethel on me."

"You're a Lucy fan?" Kellan asked.

"More Mary Tyler Moore."

"Me too. I have the box set at home," Kellan replied with a wide smile.

"Maybe we can watch an episode sometime."

"Sure," Kellan agreed. "I should go if I'm going to make it by seven."

"Make it 7:30 then. Take a long bath in this stuff, and then come over."

Reese made it home and immediately got started on the cookies. She wanted them baked and cooled in time for dessert. Initially, she'd promised a batch to Ryan to take home with him, but now she wanted them for their dinner tonight. Ryan could take what was left over. Once the cookies were in the oven, she showered and dressed, paying special attention to her hair. She'd loved the shorter cut since she'd chopped it off a couple of years ago. Morgan had told her it looked like Erika Linder's hair in Below Her Mouth, which they'd watched together and subsequently had the best sex of their relationship after. It was the same cut, only brown instead of Erika's blonde, but it worked for her all the same. She put a little gel in it so it still moved but stayed in place enough and made her way back out to the kitchen, where Remy was working on the meatloaf.

"Well, you look dressed up," she said when Reese made her way to the refrigerator.

"I'm dressed normally."

"No, you're not. You changed. Did you shower?" she asked.

"I'm not allowed to take a shower before dinner?" Reese asked.

"You're wearing my sweater." Remy pointed with a spatula.

"I borrowed your sweater, so what?"

"You're acting weird. Ryan, isn't Reese acting weird?" Remy asked of her boyfriend, who was sitting on the couch, trying to find something on TV.

"What?"

"Never mind. Why are you acting weird?"

"I'm not acting weird." Reese closed the refrigerator, not having pulled anything out, and noticed her cookies had been taken out of the oven. "They're done?"

"I pulled them out when your timer went off. You're welcome."

"Thanks." Reese made her way over to the stove and

inspected her cookies. "Oh, and Kellan might stop by for dinner. We should set another place."

"Aha!" She turned all the way to her sister. "Kellan's coming over."

"She might. She said she would, but I don't know. The hike took a lot out of her. She could cancel."

"That's why you got all dressed up."

"I'm not dressed up. I'm in jeans and a sweater, Rem."

"You were wearing sweatpants when you went to the market." Remy squinted at her for a moment while Reese exhaled a deep sigh. "You're interested in Kellan, aren't you?"

"I am not interested in Kellan," she defended.

"Yes, you are." Remy shoved both hands into the bowl and began mixing her meatloaf ingredients by hand. "And I think it's great."

"Why?"

"Because you haven't been interested in anyone since you broke up with Morgan. That was a while ago. Yesterday, she was obviously flirting with Kellan. I worried you might be jealous. I just didn't know whom of."

"I wasn't jealous."

"Kellan's cute, Reese."

"She's here for another week, Rem. There's nothing going on, and nothing will happen because she's leaving."

"But you'd be interested in something happening if she was staying?" Remy asked.

"This is dumb. I invited her for dinner because it looked like she could use a real meal."

"If that's what you're sticking with, I won't bother you about it anymore."

"Really?" Reese asked.

"No. Of course, I'll bother you about it." Remy laughed and finished mixing the meatloaf while Reese plated the cookies.

Right on time, the doorbell rang. Reese tried to get to

it before Remy, but Remy cut her off at the table and opened it before she could get there.

"Hey, ice cream girl," Remy greeted Kellan.

"Is that my new nickname?" Kellan asked with a light laugh.

"I think your regular name is better, and my sister is an ass." Reese approached behind Remy. "Come on in." She waved Kellan through the door. "Everything's ready. You're right on time."

"Hey, Kellan," Ryan acknowledged as he sat two large bowls on the table.

"Hi."

"Are you playing with us next Sunday?" he asked and took a seat at the table.

"I don't know. I might leave Sunday," she replied, and Reese looked at the floor.

"I thought you were here for another week and a half." Remy sat down.

"Here. Let me take those." Reese pulled the wine bottles from Kellan's hands. "You look nice, by the way." She lowered her tone to deliver that close to Kellan so her nosy sister wouldn't hear.

"I didn't have anything nice to wear," Kellan replied. "I brought outdoor stuff. I happened to have this in my car." She tugged at the hem of a tan cable-knit sweater.

"I'll open one of these." Reese held up a bottle and made her way to the kitchen.

Kellan had worn the sweater with a pair of nice jeans, from what Reese could see, and with her hiking boots as well. She likely hadn't planned on being invited for dinner anywhere and seemed fine with eating microwaved meals alone instead of going to any of the lake's quality restaurants.

"So, you're leaving on Sunday?" Remy questioned again as all four of them sat down.

"I don't know yet. I haven't decided. Technically, I have next week off too," Kellan revealed. "I just only planned on staying in Tahoe for a couple weeks. I kind of took a leave of absence. A short one, but it's got an indefinite timeframe on it."

"How'd you work that out with your boss, and can I work there?" Ryan asked as they all began making their plates.

"My boss is sort of an old friend. It's her vet practice. I've known her since I was a kid. She went to vet school before me and started her own clinic. When I graduated, I joined her. She's been great with giving me time off."

"That's pretty cool," Remy stated.

"It came in handy," Kellan agreed. "I want my own place one day, though." She paused and glanced over at Reese. "My own practice. It's just not possible for about the next two decades or so."

"It's a nice goal to have though." Ryan bit into his meatloaf.

"The vet we have here is pretty good. Dr. Sanders is like sixty. He's been here for years and sees all kinds of animals. Mainly the regular ones you'd expect, but he gets some wildlife in there occasionally," Remy explained. "They get hit by cars sometimes."

"I did an internship with an exotic pet vet in the city. It was great experience."

"How are your muscles now?" Reese changed the subject. "After your bath, I mean."

"Oh, they're okay. They'll kill me when I wake up. I'll probably just climb down to the beach tomorrow and hang out there most of the day with a book and my music."

"Sounds like a pretty relaxing day," Reese said.

"Reese is a teacher. Did she tell you?" Remy asked.

"She did, yeah." Kellan finally took a bite of her meatloaf. "Preschool and kindergarten, right?"

"It's a small school," Reese explained. "We combined the preschoolers and kindergartens last year since we didn't have enough kids for both."

"I went to a huge city school. I bet it's much better

than that."

"How huge?" Ryan asked.

"About four thousand students in my high school."

"That is huge. My school has two hundred in preschool through eighth grade," Reese informed. "I have fifteen in my room."

"You handle fifteen kids every day?" Kellan laughed a little. "How do you do that?"

"You handle animals who can't tell you where they hurt every day. How do you do that?" she tossed back with a smile.

"Sometimes I can tell. I just have to really listen."

They continued their light banter until the meal was complete and both bottles of wine were empty. Kellan had smiled and laughed throughout. Reese found she greatly enjoyed the woman's company. When she'd first seen Kellan in the visitor's center, she'd thought about flirting her way into Kellan's bed. Now that she'd gotten to know her, she knew she wouldn't be able to do that. Sex was sex, and she'd done that before when she'd needed to, but she didn't just want to have sex with Kellan Cobb. She grew sad when the cookies had been enjoyed by all, and it was presumably time for Kellan to leave.

"Thank you for this. I had fun, and the food was great," Kellan told her as they headed to the door.

"Of course." Reese turned to see Remy and Ryan sitting on the couch, watching them. "Do you maybe want to sit outside on the porch for a minute?"

"Sure," Kellan agreed.

Reese opened the door, ushered Kellan out, and promptly turned to her sister to stick her tongue out at her before closing the door behind them. The porch was old but taken care of. It had a swing that her father had fixed a few years back on the left side of it. The front of the house faced the trees and the street beyond. The view wasn't great, but it was nice to come out sometimes to read or just think.

"So, it's the beach for you tomorrow, huh?" Reese asked once they were both seated and the swing moved slowly back and forth.

"Oh, shit. I almost forgot. I'm going kayaking with Morgan tomorrow. I completely spaced it."

"Kayaking?" Her smile turned into a straight line. "With Morgan?"

"She asked me earlier today, after our hike."

"I see." Reese looked off into the trees.

"She actually asked me out. She wanted it to be a date," Kellan continued.

"I bet she did," Reese muttered more to herself than to Kellan.

"What?"

"Nothing," she deflected. "So, you're going on a date with Morgan tomorrow?"

"No." Kellan relaxed more into the swing. "I told her we could go kayaking tomorrow. If that goes well, we'll see about a date. I doubt we'll go through with it. I'm leaving soon. What's the point?"

"Right," Reese agreed. "So, you're..."

"Gay?" Kellan finished as she turned her head toward Reese. "Yeah. Morgan is too, I guess."

"She's my ex-girlfriend. We dated for over three years a while back."

"Oh." Kellan sat nearly straight up.

"No, it's okay. I'm not telling you because I want it to determine what you do or anything."

"Why are you telling me?" Kellan asked.

"I'd thought about asking you out myself." Reese shrugged and leaned back against the hardwood of the swing.

"Oh."

"Yeah. I saw you at the visitor's center the other day when I was working. I thought about it then, but by the time I got done with the tourist, you were gone." She hesitated. "My intentions on that day weren't exactly pure.

I should probably admit."

"Yeah?" Kellan lifted a leg under her body and turned more toward Reese.

"You're, well… you know." She waved her hand around for a moment, as if that would explain it. "But we talked a little yesterday, and I thought I'd ask you on a date. We'd see if it got that far. Morgan got there first, though."

"You really wanted to ask me out?" Kellan sounded surprised.

"I did."

"I haven't been out with anyone in a while," Kellan revealed.

"Why not?" Reese turned to Kellan to match her posture.

"Her name is Keira Worthy," Kellan began, and Reese listened intently as Kellan told the story of their short-term relationship and an attempt at friendship followed by Keira's new relationship. "I just needed to get away for a while."

"Still not over her, huh?"

"I don't know; that's the thing. I thought I was. It's why I left. Seeing her with Emma was hard, but… I don't know."

"Don't know what?"

"If I'm actually still in love with her or if I just thought I was because I saw her moving on and wanted that for myself."

"Been there. My first girlfriend in college broke up with me after six months. I thought I was over her. Then she got a new girlfriend. When I'd see them together, suddenly the pain was back." She paused. "I met my second college girlfriend after. And even though it was only about a month after my ex found someone else, I realized I was over her and ready for a new relationship. I'd thought I was still in love with her, but it was more loneliness than anything, I think."

"I think that's what it is, yeah. I'd been single for a long time before Keira. I'd had a girlfriend here and there, but nothing really long-term. When I met Keira, we fell into bed. She told me we should just be friends after, but I'd flirt with her and touch her a little when I could get away with it. Just on the arm, or on the back," she added when Reese's eyebrows went up at her comment. "I think she wanted to be friends all along. I might have pressured her inadvertently into more because I wanted more back then."

"Once, I told a girl in high school that I liked her. Actually, I used the phrase *like* like." She used air quotes around the last two words. "I told her, 'I *like* like you and would like us to be more than friends'. When she told me she didn't *like* like me and *only* wanted to be friends, I asked her to think about it. I asked her to reconsider. Maybe if she thought about it some more, she'd change her mind and like me how I liked her. I think it's in our nature for us to want the people we like to like us back. When they don't, we need to understand why."

"Yeah." Kellan nodded and smiled at her almost wistfully. "Did she reconsider?"

"No, *she* is Stacy. And you met her yesterday."

"Stacy with the husband and–"

"Yes." Reese laughed. "We've remained friends throughout. She told me that day that there was nothing to think about because she knew how she felt, and she had to trust it." She paused. "I think when we meet someone that isn't interested in us like that, it's best to just move along. I don't think you should have to convince the person you're meant to be with to be with you."

"You are very smart." Kellan looked off into the trees. "I should probably go. I have kayaking tomorrow morning."

"Right. Kayaking with Morgan."

"It's not a date," she reminded. "She just offered to take me to the island. I've never been there."

Reese lowered her head. The last time she'd been to the island had been by kayak with Morgan. They'd spent the entire day walking around and talking before they had to head back. She hadn't been in a kayak since. She missed it. She wished she could take Kellan for her first trip out there.

"I hope you have fun," she offered after a moment.

"You could come. Maybe I can ask her to go this weekend instead. Saturday maybe, if she's not busy. That way you could join us."

"No, I can't." Reese stood. "I should get back inside. Those two won't do dishes unless I force them."

"Why can't you—"

"Because I can't," she replied hastily. "You should go."

"Okay." Kellan stood. She pulled her keys out of the pocket of her jeans and headed down the three steps toward her car. "Can I ask what just happened?" She turned back to Reese. "We were sharing embarrassing stories. Everything was fine. And then it wasn't."

"It's a long story, Kellan. It's late."

"Tomorrow then?"

"You're kayaking with Morgan tomorrow."

"After you get off work." Kellan moved to the bottom step. "Meet me?"

"I can't."

"Can't or won't?"

"You're leaving in a week, Kellan."

"You knew I was leaving tonight when you invited me here. Why'd you do that?"

"Because—"

"Don't say it's because I needed a home-cooked meal," Kellan interrupted. "I'll be back from kayaking by two at the latest. Come over when you get done at work."

"I'm not done until three."

"Fine. Any time after that is fine."

Reese turned back to look at the door. Then, she

turned back to face Kellan before letting out another of her deep exhalations.

"Okay."

"Okay." Kellan smiled. "I'll see you then."

"Okay," Reese repeated.

"Good night."

"Good night, Kellan."

Kellan gave her a small nod and turned to head to her car, which she started and backed out of the driveway before turning onto the main street. Reese waited until she was gone before she turned and went back inside to see Remy and Ryan doing the dishes.

"How was it, Casanova?" Remy asked. "Did you get to first base on our porch swing?"

"I got to no bases," Reese replied pointedly.

"Did you even try?"

"I don't want to talk about this."

"What happened?" Remy stopped drying the plate and set it on the counter along with the rag.

"She wants me to meet her tomorrow."

"Like a date?" Remy brightened. "That's what you wanted."

"She's going to find out, Rem," she explained her position. "I'm not going. She's going to ask questions. I'm no good at lying. She'll know, and that'll be the end."

"Why? Come on, Reese. Just meet the girl. Fill her in if you want. But that doesn't mean she's going to react poorly. You just have to be careful. That's not a deal breaker."

"I don't think I'm ready for this, Rem. I thought I was, but I don't know that I am. I'm going to bed. Can you two clean up?"

"Reese..."

"It's fine." She headed in the direction of her bedroom. "Good night, Ryan."

"Night, Reese," he replied.

CHAPTER 7

"HEY," KELLAN GREETED Reese who was standing in her doorway. "Come on in."

"Hi," Reese replied nervously.

She entered the cabin. Kellan closed the door behind her, walking into the living room with Reese following behind her.

"Do you want anything to drink?"

"I'm okay." Reese stood next to the couch with her hands clasped in front of her.

"I was thinking about heading back down to the beach."

"*Back* down? Did you get back early from kayaking?" Reese asked.

"I didn't go," Kellan revealed and grabbed her pack off the small table by the back door of the cabin. "Outside?"

"Why didn't you go?" Reese asked as she followed Kellan out the back door. "Was it because of what I said? Morgan being my ex?"

"Not exactly." Kellan slung her pack over both of her shoulders and nodded for Reese to walk with her down the hill. "I was kind of ambivalent about the whole thing before I talked to you. And then after, I guess our talk just helped me make the decision."

"What did you tell Morgan?"

"That I needed to take the day off. Maybe tomorrow, too. She asked if I wanted to go tomorrow morning. But I don't know yet. I'm supposed to text her later. The beach is just down here through these trees. There's a path."

"Why can't we just drive?" Reese asked.

Kellan turned back to see that Reese was still standing near the back of the cabin. She walked back up to meet her.

"It's actually slower to drive. Are you okay?" she asked.

"Can we go back inside?"

"Reese."

"I can't hike anymore, Kellan."

"Why?"

"I'm going home. I don't want to talk about this." She turned and opened the back door.

"Wait," Kellan pled. "Just wait. Please. I'll get my Jeep. We'll drive."

"Why can't we go back inside?"

"We can. If you really want to go back inside, we can. I'll get us something to drink. We can talk. I just thought we could watch the sunset on the beach. I have a bottle of wine in here and some cheese. I thought we could – I don't know, make an evening out of it."

"Like a date?" Reese turned fully toward her.

"I don't know. Maybe. I'd be lying if I said I ditched Morgan today just because my body needed a rest. It was something you said last night, and it wasn't about her being your ex."

"What was it?"

"That it shouldn't take convincing," she revealed. "I was trying to convince myself to spend time with Morgan. That's wrong. When I got home last night, I called her because I wanted to spend more time with you."

"Oh."

"It's awkward now, isn't it? I've made it awkward."

"Pretty sure I made it awkward when I alluded to the fact that I wanted to sleep with you when I saw you at the visitor's center." Reese laughed. "We can drive."

Kellan drove them the short distance to a lower point near the shore and parked. They headed toward the beach with her pack and a blanket she always kept in the car. Reese held her pack as she laid it out on the sand, and they both sat down. The beach was quiet, with no one else around, or at least if they were there, they were behind the row of trees that came up close to the shore at this part of the beach. Kellan didn't unpack the items she'd brought. They sat in silence for several moments, not wanting to eat or drink but stare off into the distance. Both, apparently, needed some time to figure out what came next.

"I fell a while ago," Reese uttered so softly Kellan almost missed it.

"What?" She turned her head toward her.

"It was about a year ago. A little more, I guess, now. I was on one of the advanced trails and pretty high up. I took a bad spill and injured my ankle." She paused, and Kellan wondered if she was thinking about how to proceed. "I didn't realize it when it happened. I was alone. You shouldn't hike those trails alone even when you're as experienced as I am. I managed to make it back down on my own and get home but ended up in the hospital a day later, when Remy stopped by and noticed how bad it was."

"How bad was it?"

"It was a fracture. After the first day, the swelling was pretty intense. I'd iced it when I noticed, but that wasn't helping. The break was strange, I guess, because they needed to operate to make sure it repaired itself correctly. They put a pin in my ankle. Technically, I should have been good as new after a couple of months, but I developed an infection. Osteomyelitis is what it's called. Because I'd broken my ankle before, and they had to operate this time, I guess bacteria made its way to the bone. That made me sick. With a weakened immune system, they put me on a round of antibiotics. That should have fixed the problem, but I kept getting worse, and the infection reached my spinal cord." She took a deep breath. "I've spent the past six months teaching myself how to walk again."

"What?" Kellan turned her entire body toward Reese.

"It managed to make my legs not work there for a while. I thought I'd be paralyzed. Once they got me on the right combination of meds though, the feeling came back. I started physical therapy. Luckily, that went well. I was doing more and more on my own without a problem, until I tried hiking one of the beginner trails last month and fell on a tree branch. It wasn't a big deal, but I did break some fingers and toes. Ever since then, I've avoided hiking hills or around trees."

"I'm sorry, Reese. I didn't know. I wouldn't–"

"I know. I wanted to explain my inappropriate outbursts to you last night and today. I haven't kayaked since before the accident." She stared off at the water. "And you should also know that when I ended up in the hospital, Remy called our parents, who had moved to Reno. They left us their house here. That's where we live now. At the time though, Remy had her own place. Anyway, she called them when I got admitted, and they rushed down." Her head lowered as she delivered, "They got hit by a truck. They both died. So did the truck driver. I was in the hospital and then got the infection. Remy had to deal with the arrangements and everything along with giving me the news and taking care of me. When I needed help after, she moved back home. She's been there ever since."

"Were you able to go to their funeral?"

"They both wanted to be cremated. We waited until I was in the clear and held a small ceremony with close family and friends. We spread their ashes here." She motioned to the expansive lake. "They loved this place."

"How are you now?" Kellan asked after a moment.

"I'm still technically recovering, but I'm okay. I think it's more psychological than anything else. Remy worries a lot," she explained and looked off into the water. "This is all pretty heavy stuff for a non-date." She turned back to Kellan and offered her a small smile.

Kellan smiled back. Then, she turned to glance at the water herself. She wasn't sure what they were doing here. She was trying to move past Keira and had a little more than a week left in Tahoe. She shouldn't be going on a date with anyone. She'd come for a break and to try to put her heart back together. Reese didn't seem like she was in a good place to attempt anything either.

"What happened with Morgan?" she asked as a way to change the subject. "Or is that too personal?"

"I just told you I nearly died. I hardly think my ex-girlfriend is too personal." Reese laughed and bumped Kellan's shoulder with her own. "Morgan and I dated for a long time, but it's been over for a while."

"Did you end it, or did she?"

"I did."

"Got it."

"No, I'm sorry." Reese's hand landed on her own between them. "I didn't mean to make you think you can't ask about Morgan. It's just a sore subject for me."

"I understand. I have one of those myself." She shrugged but enjoyed the fact that Reese's hand still hadn't moved.

"The ex?"

"The ex," she confirmed. "Can I ask what happened with your ex if I promise to fill you in on what happened with mine?"

"Like ex-girlfriend therapy or something?" Reese chuckled and squeezed Kellan's hand before removing it.

"Sure. Let's call it that." Kellan leaned back on both hands and aimed her glance at the clear sky above them.

Reese moved to lay beside her and placed her arms over her stomach. Kellan glanced over and down at her, taking in the peacefulness of the woman who had her eyes closed and seemed completely comfortable in her own skin.

"Morgan and I are old friends. We stayed that way for a while but started dating after we'd both ended serious relationships. It was good for a long time."

"What happened?"

"Nothing." Reese's eyes opened and met Kellan's. "Nothing happened."

"So, you fell out of love with her?" Kellan laid down fully beside Reese, facing her but keeping a foot of distance between them.

"No," she answered honestly as Kellan settled next to her. "I got sick."

"And she wasn't there for you?"

"No, she was great, actually. Morgan is a great person. I loved her as a friend long before I loved her as more. She's always been there for me. She still is even though we're not together anymore." She closed her eyes again. "It's my fault. When I got sick, I pushed her away."

"Oh, did you think–" She stopped herself. "Was it that bad?"

"It wasn't that." She turned her head to Kellan. "It was, but it wasn't." She turned her whole body to Kellan to match her position. "I was close to dying, yes. There were a couple of days where I was technically in a medically induced coma, but I got better. It wasn't until after I got better that I ended things with Morgan. I was still in love with her. I planned a life with her prior to the accident and the loss of my parents. We still lived separately, but that was because we both had houses our parents had left us. We were trying to decide who moves and when at the time of the ankle thing."

"You were going to move in together?"

"That was the plan. After everything happened, I felt like a different person. It's like I woke up from that coma and suddenly couldn't do most of the things I love.

Morgan was amazing. But to me, it felt like she was almost too amazing. I didn't deserve that. Plus, the majority of our relationship was based on our shared interests in the outdoors. I couldn't do those activities anymore. I could see her growing more and more miserable with me over time. She wasn't, of course. She put on a brave face back then, but I could see the future somehow. If I never got well enough to go on those long hikes we used to take together, or go kayaking out to the island, or camping, or skiing like we used to do in the winter, things would change between us. I didn't know *what* I'd be able to do or *when* I'd be able to do it. I knew I was in love with her, and that she loved me, but the accident put things into perspective for me."

"Do you still love her?" Kellan leaned in an almost imperceptible amount.

"No," she replied with a smile. "I don't. I do love her as a friend. That will never change. When I started to improve, it felt like what she and I had was in the past and wouldn't work in this new present. We talked, and we cried. It was terrible. She didn't want to break up. I didn't think we should stay together."

"But you're friends now?"

"She's one of my closest friends. She always will be. Whoever I end up with will have to put up with our history, I guess."

"How did you do it?"

"Do what?"

"Stay friends with her?"

"Oh, that?" Reese pulled back a little. "I don't know. We were friends before; maybe that helped. But we took some time apart. Then, we started hanging out again; in groups at first, but then we were okay on our own. I have to admit that it's still weird seeing her date. I'm sure it's strange to her to watch me do the same."

"Do you?"

"Do I what? Date?"

"Yeah."

"I do, yes." Reese moved back to where she'd been a moment ago. "Not often. I've gone out with a few women. They've been mostly tourists."

"You hook up with tourists. I get it."

"It's not that." Reese moved slightly closer to her. "It's easier because that's all I've wanted since the accident. It's a small town. We've formed our own little group of friends. Some of them, like Morgan and I, are gay; but most aren't. The number of datable women that live here is pretty small."

"So, you date tourists? It makes sense."

"It wasn't really dating. I took them out first, technically. Well, some of them, at least. But some just took me to their hotels or rentals."

"How many are some?" Kellan found herself asking before thinking that it might be inappropriate to do so.

"Not that many." Reese laughed lightly and rolled onto her back. "I couldn't exactly have sex for a while after the accident. I didn't want to back then, anyway. I was still trying to get past the breakup. When I could both physically and emotionally go for it, I tried. I struck out the first few attempts." She laughed again. "I think I came on too strong."

"Did you give them a cheesy line or something?"

"Maybe." She turned back onto her side. "One woman was here with her friends. We had fun for about a week. Another one was here by herself. We had fun once, and she left. One was definitely straight or at least had no idea that she was curious about women. We had some fun for a couple of weeks, but it got to be a little much for me. I was her first woman. It was one of those eye-opening experiences. I've been there myself and wanted to be supportive, but she said she wanted to write a book about her experience."

"What?" Kellan laughed again, but louder this time. "About having sex with you? Are you that good?"

"About discovering who she was. She was a writer; self-help books mostly. She thought her words might help another woman find herself."

"When is that book coming out? I need to pre-order it." She smiled at her.

"I have no idea. I told her if she writes about me, she needs to make up a new name."

"She should call you the lesbian whisperer." She continued laughing but then stopped.

"What happened?" Reese asked.

"Nothing. I just haven't laughed like this in a while."

"Keira?"

"Yeah. It seems ridiculous now," Kellan said.

"What does?"

"I don't think I ever really loved Keira," she stated, her eyes going wide at that realization.

CHAPTER 8

"How did that happen?" Kellan asked herself as she sat all the way up and clasped her hands over her folded legs.

"How did what happen?"

"Like a week ago, I was driving here to mend my broken heart. I'd just watched the woman I love fall in love with someone else. I couldn't stand to see them in the same room. Now, I'm wondering if I ever actually loved her at all."

"You know how sometimes one day we feel a certain way about something and we never think that feeling will go away. Then another day, we wake up, and it's like the feeling is gone?"

"Yeah."

"I don't think we ever stop to acknowledge those moments." Reese positioned her hand at the small of Kellan's back but didn't touch her. "I mean, at some point we stop feeling broken-hearted over someone, or we start feeling love for a new person, but we don't stop to acknowledge that this was the moment it happened. At least, most people don't do that until later. It would be after you say 'I love you' to someone and you're talking about it that you look back and think of the moment when they did this or said that; that was when you knew."

"I don't have that with Keira," Kellan stated without turning to Reese. "I've had that before with other girlfriends, but I didn't have that with Keira."

"Then, why did you think you loved her?" she asked as her hand neared Kellan's back, but when Kellan shifted forward a little to get more comfortable, Reese dropped her hand back onto the blanket and felt a little foolish for wanting to reach out and touch her.

"I was lonely. God, I was lonely," she answered and turned her head back to Reese. "We met at a friend's wedding. I was in the bridal party. She'd planned the event. Keira owned the room." She laughed out. "Keira Worthy owns the rooms she walks into. It's what makes her so good at her job. We started talking after they cut the cake. I'd had a few glasses of wine and several shots with the bridal party. My inhibitions were definitely lower than usual. When the party ended, she invited me back to her place."

"I see." Reese toyed with the loose strings on the edge of the blanket in an attempt to distract herself from the thought of someone else having sex with Kellan.

"I guess I can understand her starting up with me and then ending things, now that I have some separation from it. She'd suffered the loss of a friend, and I think we were both lonely and sought solace in our friendship."

"But you were never in love with her?" Reese asked.

"I thought this place would help me clear through the fog. I think it did." Kellan turned and gave her a small smile. "Or maybe it was just talking to you."

"Me?" Reese sat up to join her.

"I can't talk to my other friends like this. Keira's friends kind of became my friends. I'm not that close to my siblings. They don't really like to hear about this part of my life. We've never been a family that shares this stuff. They're career minded, and single. I don't know if they're ever going to settle down. Meanwhile, I've had exactly two long-term relationships. Neither of those lasted more than nine months. I've been single the rest of the time. I'd spent so much time focusing on my own career that I hadn't dedicated any of it to try to find someone to share my life with."

"So, you didn't date anyone after Keira?"

"No. I didn't have the time to find anyone, or the interest either, I guess."

"But Morgan struck your fancy?"

Kellan didn't respond. She turned away from the water and faced Reese while leaning back on her hands again. Reese watched her move before she leaned forward a little more, but kept her hands wrapped tightly around her legs and clasped together.

"Are you worried about me liking Morgan or about Morgan liking me?" Kellan asked and shrugged at the same time.

"How direct of you." Reese laughed and scooted forward on the blanket so that she could position herself closer to Kellan but at her own side. "I don't want to be with Morgan. It is still strange, like I've said before, to see her with someone else, but I don't harbor any jealousy or want to be with her myself."

"So, it's about me liking her then?"

"Do you?" Reese lifted an eyebrow.

"She's nice," Kellan answered. "I didn't spend all that much time with her yesterday. She was technically working."

"Right." Reese looked at a tree to her left as one of the browning leaves zig-zagged its way through the air and fell to the ground.

"She seems to want to hang out with me though."

"No, she wants to *go out* with you. There's a difference."

"Do you?" Kellan asked.

Reese met her eyes and saw there was a bit of vulnerability there.

"Yes," she admitted, and Kellan smiled. "But we shouldn't," she added and watched the smile disappear.

"Because I'm leaving," Kellan stated.

"Right," she agreed. "It doesn't make sense to start something."

"Can we start a friendship?" Kellan leaned forward, and when she did, their faces were a mere few inches apart.

"Friendship?" Reese instinctively licked her lips while

at the same time staring at Kellan's perfect pair. She lifted her eyes to meet Kellan's blue ones. "Friendship," she repeated with some difficulty.

"So, we're friends?" Kellan asked and licked her own lips.

"Yeah." Reese tried to look away from the woman in front of her, but she couldn't. "No," she then said louder than she'd meant to.

"No?" Kellan pulled back to check.

"No, this is stupid. We're not fourteen." Reese shook her head. "I like you. You like me. Let's go out." She met Kellan's eyes again.

Kellan nearly toppled over in laughter but landed safely on her back next to Reese on their blanket. Reese tried not to take offense to that reaction and turned to see Kellan staring back up at her with those damn eyes and a shy smile on her face. She moved slowly, to give Kellan a chance to stop her. She placed her hand on the other side of Kellan's body, hovering over her but giving her plenty of space. When Kellan didn't stop her or push her away, she leaned down and met Kellan's nose with the tip of her own. She pressed her forehead to Kellan's, awaiting silent permission. Kellan's hand moved to her hip. Reese took that to mean that she wanted this. Then, her phone rang.

"I know it's not mine," Kellan stated.

"Shit," Reese shouted. She lifted herself up to reach into her pocket for her phone. "It's Rem. Sorry." She stood up and answered. "You have shitty timing."

"*You* have a doctor's appointment," Remy replied.

"No, I don't."

"It's the video chat with that specialist from Stanford. The doc set it up. She emailed both of us this morning."

"She did? Wait... Did I agree to chat with some specialist?"

"No. But I told the doc you'd do this for your sister who loves you," Remy replied.

"Rem, I'm busy right now. Can't she do it some other

time?"

"She's a world-renowned specialist that is doing this as a favor. She has like twenty minutes she can give us. Time starts in fifteen minutes."

"Fine, but you owe me."

"I owe *you*? This is *for* you," Remy retorted.

"I know. I know. I'm sorry. I'll be there." She lowered her head and shook it. "You know I hate dealing with this stuff."

"Maybe this specialist can help."

"Maybe," she replied doubtfully and hung up the phone. "I'm sorry. I have to go," she told Kellan.

"Is everything okay?" Kellan stood.

"I have an appointment that I didn't know about. Remy was reminding me."

"With a specialist?"

"It's a check-up thing," she lied.

"From the accident? Or infection? I don't know what to call it." Kellan smiled awkwardly and then bent over to pick up the blanket.

"I'm fine. I just have to tell them that. Listen, I meant what I said before. I do want to go out with you. But maybe it is best if we don't."

"No, you don't get to do that again." Kellan stood with the blanket under her arms and the pack she'd brought but hadn't unpacked slung over her shoulder. "You can't say you want to go out and then take it back, Reese."

"Kellan, things are complicated, and–"

"And I'll pick you up tomorrow after work," Kellan interrupted.

"What?" She laughed.

"We're going out tomorrow night. You and I are going out on a date tomorrow night." Kellan pointed between the two of them. "And if it doesn't work – it doesn't work. But at least we'll know. Now, I'll drive you back to your car," she said.

CHAPTER 9

"REM, IT'S NOT something I want to discuss."

"It's an idea, Reese. Why are you so opposed to reading what she sent?" Remy asked.

They sat in the small faculty room Reese often ate lunch in while the kids were napping. Remy joined her when she could. Today, the two shared Bucky's, which was the best burger place in town.

"I'm not opposed to reading what she sent. I am opposed to talking about it all the time, Rem. I swear, our relationship these days is all about this. Forgive me, but I'd like to spend time with my sister not talking about what's wrong with me."

"Nothing's wrong with you, Reese."

"Of course, there is. And I know you've been dealing with this just as long as I have; that it was a major focus of our lives growing up. I'm sorry for that. But I spent months trying to recover from that damn ankle. I'm starting to live my life again, Rem. I don't want every conversation you and I have to be about this. *This* won't go away, but it doesn't have to dominate my life or your life anymore. I can be careful."

"You're right. It won't go away, but it might be helped. She said there had been positive results from her study, Reese. What if you could have positive results too?"

"It's still in an experimental phase. There have been negative results, too. Did you not hear that part?"

Her phone buzzed. She smiled as she looked down to see who the text might be from.

"What's that?" Remy asked.

"Nothing," she replied with disappointment when she noticed it was a text from Stacy.

"You seemed really excited there for a second, and then not so much. Looking to hear from a certain woman?" She wiggled her eyebrows at her sister.

"What are you talking about?"

"Kellan Cobb, of course." Remy tossed a ketchup packet in Reese's direction. "You hung out with her yesterday but didn't say a word about it when you got home. That can only mean one thing. When you go on crappy dates, you tell me all about them. When you go on great ones, you say nothing, but you kind of float around like you're on literal cloud nine."

"I do not." Reese tossed the ketchup packet back.

"Oh, you do, too." Remy laughed.

"We just talked."

"And?"

"And nothing. We talked."

"And the wedding will be?"

"Right after you marry Ryan," Reese replied.

"Low blow." Remy pointed at her.

"The man obviously loves you, since he puts up with your bullshit."

"He does love me. I love him. I just don't want to get married. He keeps thinking I'll change my mind. We haven't even been together all that long."

"Is it a problem?"

"What? No, he's fine. He did ask me to move in with him, though."

"You should, Rem."

"I live with you."

"I'm fine now."

"Says the woman who tried to ignore the meeting with the specialist."

"You can still pester me about doctor's appointments when you're living with your boyfriend."

"I guess." Remy bit into her burger.

***

Reese waited outside the school building as she waved off the last of the parents picking up their children for the day. She closed her arms over her body, watching a car drive off with one of her preschoolers.

"Are you cold?" Kellan asked as she pulled up in her Jeep.

"What?" Reese looked down and uncrossed her arms. "Oh, no."

Kellan parked her car and climbed out, making her way over to where Reese was standing on the curb.

"How many times did you think about canceling on me?" she asked.

"Four," Reese replied honestly, offering an apologetic smile.

"But you didn't?"

"Didn't have your number." Reese shrugged.

"That's the only reason?" Kellan stood a few feet in front of her.

"No, not the only reason."

"So, we're still going? If you don't want to go, you can say so. I'll take the hint."

"The problem isn't that I don't want to go, Kellan," Reese started. "The problem is that I do." She reached forward and took Kellan's hand in her own, holding it between their bodies. "It's a bad idea to start something when you're leaving."

"Why don't we just see what happens today?" Kellan proposed. "Maybe we'll have a terrible time. Maybe we'll realize we'd be better off as friends."

"What if we discover we want more than just friendship?"

"One step at a time," Kellan suggested.

"Deal." Reese tried to resist the urge to go back inside, grab her car keys, and head home to put Kellan Cobb, the tourist she found herself very interested in, out of her mind.

"I planned something. It might be something that makes you mad at me, but I decided to take the risk because it's something I'd like to do with you."

"What is it?"

"I want you to take my island virginity," she offered with a wide and somewhat cocky smile.

***

"Before you freak out, let me explain." Kellan stood on the lakeshore next to a canoe.

"Kellan, I told you–"

"You told me it was more psychological than physical. I will do all the paddling," she interjected. "You can supervise." She smiled at Reese, who stared at the canoe and then looked over to her left where she spotted Fannette Island. It seemed so far away. "I brought food and some other things, too. I thought we could row over there. You could show me around."

"It's too late," she replied and glanced at her watch. "It's after four. The sun will be setting in about an hour. We shouldn't head back in the dark."

"It's not illegal though. I looked into it." She bent down and pulled out a lantern. "I came prepared. I rented this thing for the night. I included first aid supplies, jackets, and my sleeping bag in my pack just in case."

"Were you a Girl Scout?" Reese laughed at her but took a step toward the wide canoe to discover that Kellan had indeed come prepared. "Is that a box of granola bars? How long do you think we'll be gone?"

"As long as we want. But it was just easier to throw the box in than take them all out," she explained. "So, what do you say?"

"If I say no, will you hate me?"

"No, if you honestly don't want to go out there and explore with me, or you're really not physically ready for it; just say so. We can hang out here with everything I brought, or we can throw it all in the car and head to an early dinner."

Reese bit her upper lip as she glanced at the island, then back at the canoe, and lastly, at Kellan, who seemed so hopeful in that moment.

"Okay."

"Okay, what?" Kellan lifted both eyebrows.

"If the canoe can hold both of us and all that crap you brought, we can go."

"Hey, you two." Morgan approached from a trail off to their right along with six other people.

"Oh, hey," Kellan offered an awkward greeting. "What are you doing here?" She looked around as if expecting more people to magically appear.

"Hey, Mo," Reese greeted her ex. "Cascade falls?"

"Yup," Morgan replied. "Just getting back with my second group of the day. Hey, Kellan." She looked over at Kellan and pulled her water bottle out of her pack to take a drink. "What are you two doing?" She looked down at the canoe loaded with supplies.

"Just hanging out," Kellan answered.

Reese looked at her and ran a hand through her hair before glancing over to Morgan again, deciding to embrace the awkwardness instead of avoiding it.

"We're–"

"McBride Outfitters," Morgan interrupted. "Rental?" She glanced back at Reese.

Reese glanced in the direction of the canoe. On the side, there was a label with the logo of McBride Outfitters.

"I rented it, yeah," Kellan replied.

"I know. From me," Morgan stated. "That's my parents' store. Well, mine more than theirs these days, since I run the business along with the tours most days."

"Oh, I didn't know. McBride?" Kellan asked.

"Burns Outfitters would make people think of forest fires," Reese answered for Morgan. "So they named it after Morgan's mother's maiden name."

"Yup." Morgan slid her water bottle back into its pocket and turned around to see her group standing at the edge of the trail, conversing and drinking from their own bottles. "I should get going. I have to get them back."

"Morgan–"

"No, you two have fun. I'm going to go," Morgan interrupted Reese and headed back to the trail where she gathered her group and walked back to the parking lot.

"Shit," Kellan said once Morgan had the group safely in a van and was pulling out of the parking lot. "I'm sorry. I didn't see the logo. I rented this from two guys that have the shack over there." She pointed to where Reese knew there was an outpost for McBride Outfitters along the shore of the lake.

"That's Morgan's, too. They sublet it, so to speak, to a couple of our friends," she offered. "But she's not mad at you. She's mad at me."

"Because of me."

"Maybe partly because she did ask you out, but it's mostly about me." She turned back to the parking lot and then back to Kellan. "Come on. Let's get in and go. I'll tell you on the way." She wasn't exactly dressed for canoeing and hiking on the island, but she wore her hiking boots most days along with jeans and a long-sleeved shirt. "You ready?" she asked after climbing into the canoe and moving some of Kellan's things aside to accommodate herself.

"Sure." Kellan moved to push the canoe the rest of the way into the water before climbing into her position across from her. "You okay?" she asked and grabbed the oar to begin rowing.

"Morgan and I came out here a bunch of times."

"I hadn't thought about that." Kellan looked off behind her at the island.

"We'd done it as friends long before we started dating. But after I got sick and we broke up, she asked me a few times to go back out there. I said no."

"Got it." Kellan continued to row. "Should I apologize to her?"

"No, it's nothing you did wrong," Reese offered Kellan's kind eyes. "You know how you asked me how she and I did it? Became friends again?"

"Yes."

"We're friends. And we're fine. But sometimes, she'll get this look in her eyes, like I've disappointed her. It's the same look she used to get when we dated. It's horrible, and I hate it." She let out a sigh. "I just disappointed her by coming out here with you instead of her."

"We can turn around if this is something you two need to share together." Kellan stopped rowing.

"Kell, keep rowing. I'll talk to Morgan about it later. She'll understand, or she won't. But it'll be fine." Reese paused. "This is supposed to be *our* date, right?" she asked. "I don't want to talk about my ex-girlfriend anymore. And you're rowing too much on this side." She pointed to Kellan's right. "As captain of this ship, I instruct you to row more to the left so that we can drop anchor at the right port." She winked.

"Aye, aye, captain!" Kellan mock-saluted her with a smile and corrected her rowing.

They were silent for the rest of the trip. Both appeared to be enjoying their time on the water. Reese caught Kellan glancing at her more than once and smiled back each time before she'd look back at the water or around at the mountains and the beaches. She hadn't been on the water like this since before her fall and time in the hospital. She turned back to Kellan when the woman was turned to the side, taking in a bird flying low above the water. Reese smiled at Kellan's profile. She had a strong yet feminine jaw and a small nose to go with lips Reese wouldn't define as full, but full enough to go perfectly with the rest of Kellan's beautiful face. She had a slight tan, likely from her time at the lake thus far, but Reese could see a few freckles making an appearance and dotting Kellan's cheek and nose. Her eyelashes were long and light, and that somehow accentuated the lightness in her eyes. Reese's gaze moved to Kellan's arms, which were still rowing them along slowly in the water. Her muscles were taut, and there was a light sheen of sweat on them along with some of the same freckles. She had on a short-sleeved shirt, allowing Reese to see her biceps and flexor muscles. She moved her eyes back up to take in Kellan's long neck that was still turned to the side. She imagined her lips on that neck. She cleared her throat when Kellan turned back to her and caught her staring.

"Just over there." She pointed at the small patch of gravel and sand where boats would tie down. "You can take it all the way up." She motioned with her finger for Kellan to continue rowing.

When the canoe stopped at the water's edge, Kellan emerged first and slid the boat completely out of the water. She made her way over to Reese and offered her hand to help the woman up. Reese laughed at the mock-chivalry and helped Kellan remove all the items from the canoe. Kellan placed her hiking pack on her back after putting on one of the jackets she'd brought and passing the other to Reese to put on. The sun was now setting. The sky was beautiful – pink and orange. And the cool night air was apparently starting to get to Kellan, now that the rowing was done. Reese put on the jacket, per Kellan's request, and picked up the lantern and the extra bag of supplies to carry with them.

"Where to?" Kellan asked.

"This way." Reese motioned for her to follow. "It's

only about ten minutes to get to the top and see the Tea House," she instructed and then realized where they were going.

"What's wrong?" Kellan questioned when Reese stopped suddenly.

"It's all rocks." Reese pointed ahead of them. "The hike up is all rocks."

"Oh, right."

"It's not that bad. I just haven't climbed like that in a while."

"We can stay down here. We don't have to hike up," Kellan suggested.

"You came all the way here to *not* get the best view on the lake?" She turned to Kellan.

"I came here to be with you," Kellan replied earnestly. "I don't care what I see. If we sit on the shore and talk – that's fine with me, or we can go back and paddle slowly to watch the sunset over the water." She took a step toward Reese. "We can come back and hike up some other time when you're ready."

"I doubt I'll be ready in less than a week."

"Then, we won't do it this week," Kellan told her. "I'll come back. We'll do it then; make a plan for it for the summer or something."

"No, we'll do it now," Reese stated with confidence.

"Reese–"

"I don't want to wait until next summer. I'm being a coward. I want to do this now." She turned to the rocks and said, "I want to do this with you." She then turned back to Kellan.

"Okay." Kellan smiled at her. "Should I go first or follow you just in case?"

"Follow me." Reese turned back around and took steps toward the first of many large gray rocks that seemed to never end.

She lifted her leg to climb the first rock and found it to be no problem. She continued slowly while trying to be extra cautious because the rocks were often slippery. She could hear Kellan making her way behind her but didn't chance a glance back. She worried she'd be unable to continue if she saw how high up she was. Heights had never been a problem for her, and they weren't now, but she knew that if she realized she'd climbed the rocks up, she'd think about having to climb back down them and she'd stop.

She focused on her breathing. She made sure to keep it steady as she tackled the next rock and then the next one until she was at the top. She allowed herself to smile and turned around just in time to see Kellan standing in front of her.

"Hi," Kellan greeted with an equally large smile.

"Hi," she greeted back and then let out a laugh.

CHAPTER 10

"YOU OKAY?" Kellan asked as she placed her hands on Reese's waist.

Reese's response to the question was a bear hug that nearly knocked Kellan over. Luckily, Kellan held onto her and moved them both forward instead of back into the jagged rocks below. She closed her eyes and breathed in the moment. Reese's joy was more than evident. Kellan felt it in every one of her bones as the woman grasped her neck tightly for another moment before pulling back, leaving her arms draped over Kellan's shoulders.

"Sorry," Reese apologized but smiled.

"Why?" Kellan laughed. "You're great at hugging."

"Yeah?" Reese chuckled and removed her arms, causing Kellan to drop the ones around her waist.

"It's been a long time since I've been hugged like that, but it's definitely one of the best that I can remember."

"You're pretty good at hugs yourself." Reese glanced around them at the familiar yet unfamiliar view. "It's been so long."

"Do you want to take some time to yourself?" Kellan asked.

Reese met Kellan's eyes and placed a hand on her cheek.

"Keira was a dumb ass," she stated and turned around, walking off toward the Tea House.

Kellan stood dumbfounded for a moment, wondering about the comment Reese had left her with. Then, she followed the woman who had completely taken her breath away during just about every second of the strangest date Kellan had ever been on. After passing the last little hill, they came to the small room that really couldn't be called a room anymore. While the house wasn't how it once was, it was still four rock walls with three windows and a fireplace. The roof was missing, but that added to the charm of the building. Due to the late hour and the fact that it wasn't high season, they were alone. Kellan wasn't sure if they were the only two people on the island or not, but it felt like it. She watched Reese move around the small space for a moment before dropping her backpack on the floor of the structure and making her way toward one of the windows. Through it, she could see the expansive lake and the trees. She turned around to see Reese staring at her and smiled.

"Come here." Reese held out her hand.

Kellan approached and took it, allowing herself to be pulled toward the other part of the house where she stood in front of the small window with Reese.

"Wow! I've never seen it from this perspective before," Kellan said.

The sunken forest was the name for the part of the bay where several trees had fallen into the lake and remained over time. They were jutting out above the water. Kellan had often wanted to rent a kayak and move around them but hadn't ever gone through with it.

"Thank you," Reese offered.

"For what?" Kellan turned to her and caught Reese's perfect gray eyes.

"For making me do this."

"I *made* you do this?"

"You know what I mean." Reese laughed lightly and turned back to the view. "We should probably get back though. It'll be dark soon."

"We haven't even had our date yet."

"This *is* our date," Reese reminded her.

"Let's sit and eat something first," Kellan suggested and tugged both of Reese's arms toward where she'd placed her backpack. "I'll lay out the sleeping bag, and you get the food out."

"Okay, but we can't stay too much longer."

They set up their mini-meal and shared pleasant conversation while they listened to the sounds of the water, birds, and crickets as the sun moved toward the horizon. Kellan turned the lantern on. It offered them just enough light to see by as they packed up the trash and other belongings. They remained there long after they should have been gone. It was much later than Kellan had intended to stay, but they'd been enjoying their time so much, she hadn't pressed them to go. Even Reese had stopped reminding her of the approaching darkness. When they'd donned the packs again and headed out toward the rocks, Reese had stopped just before taking her first step down.

"I don't think I can," she said softly.

"Let me go first." Kellan took the lantern from her. "We can take it slow. I'm sorry. We should have left a long time ago."

"No, Kellan! I can't," Reese repeated.

"Okay. Okay." Kellan moved to stand in front of her. "What do you want to do? I have a small flashlight in my bag. Would that help? Oh, there are a few of those glow stick things inside my emergency kit. I could place them down the rocks and come back to get you." Reese was staring off into space. Kellan wasn't sure she was paying attention. She reached out her hand to touch her cheek and removed her hand immediately. "Reese, you're freezing! Why didn't you tell me?" She removed her backpack and placed it on the ground next to her, placing the lantern next to it.

"I didn't notice."

"What do you mean you didn't notice? Come here." Kellan tugged a little on her arm. "God, your hands are freezing, too." She reached into her bag and pulled out the emergency kit she always carried when going on long or advanced hikes. "Sit down, Reese."

Reese silently obeyed. She sat in the dirt and rocks in front of Kellan, who knelt and opened two of the hand warmers that came in the kit. She placed them in the pockets of the jacket Reese was wearing and took both of Reese's hands in her own. She cupped her hands around them and blew hot breath on them to try to warm them up.

"I'm fine." Reese pulled her hands back.

"You're cold, Reese. Please put your hands in your pockets. I don't think I have any gloves with me. I didn't bring a hat. Damn it! What was I thinking, bringing you out here so late?"

"I'm okay." Reese slid her hands into her pockets. "I'm just a little cold. It's no big deal."

"You're cold, and you're scared to climb down in the dark. I should have known that. I'm sorry." Kellan stared into her eyes.

"Kell, I'm scared, yes. That's not your fault. It's also not your fault that we're out here in the dark. I wanted to stay. We were having so much fun; I wasn't thinking about the climb down. I was thinking about how much I was enjoying talking to you." She stared up at the stars that were in abundance in the night sky. "Do you know how long it's been since I've just stared up at the stars after a day outside?" She looked back down at Kellan. "I don't think I can climb down without freaking out, or worse, slipping on something. I might be able to do it with your help, but I *am* scared. My heart is racing right now, thinking about what happened with my ankle and being in the hospital. I lost two days of my life to a coma and then more after that to the infection and physical therapy. I lost my parents because of it. Indirectly, I know. But I fell and ended up in the hospital. I was stupid. I didn't get proper care immediately, and my parents died. That's all I can think about when I look down there." She pointed to the rocks and their hike down to the canoe.

"Okay. Okay." Kellan comforted her by placing her hands on Reese's knees. "What do you want to do?"

"We don't have a choice. We have to go down."

"Is there an easier way?" Kellan rubbed Reese's thighs up and down.

"Not in the dark. I always came up and down this way. I'm not familiar with any other one, and our canoe is down there."

Kellan considered their options. From what she could tell, they had three. She could give Reese some time to calm down, and they could make their way slowly down their original path. Kellan could try to find another path that might be easier. They could go down that one and make their way to the canoe. The third option was both the easiest and probably the worst at the same time.

"We could stay," she suggested.

"Stay where? Here?"

"In the Tea House," Kellan clarified. "It's dry and flat. I have a sleeping bag. We can leave when the sun comes up before anyone else gets here." Kellan recalled that the kayak rental station opened at ten in the morning, and most people started lining up to get one earlier, but she doubted anyone would be there at six. "It's not a great idea, I know, but we can set up a mini-camp, and if you get more comfortable later tonight, we can try to head down and row back." She took in Reese's worried expression through the light of the lantern. "Or I can walk around and try to find an easier path. Maybe there's a trail or—"

"It's too dangerous," Reese interrupted. "For either of us to be looking in the dark when we're unfamiliar with the terrain. The whole island is basically a hill of jagged rocks that lead to water and downed trees."

"So, we're staying?" Kellan ran her hands up and

down Reese's cold legs again. "How are your hands?" she asked and slid her own into Reese's pockets. "Warming up?"

"I'm fine." Reese moved to stand.

Kellan removed her hands as Reese made it impossible for her to keep them where they were, and they both stood. They stared at one another for a moment before Reese picked up the backpack for Kellan, slid it still open over her shoulder, and picked up the lantern.

"I can get it," Kellan offered.

"I've already got it," Reese said, but her tone was softer this time. "Come on. We should get set up if we're going to be here for twelve hours."

"There's another option," Kellan revealed as they arrived back in the small room of the dilapidated Tea House.

"Yeah? What's that?" Reese asked as she set the bag down on the ground.

"Did you bring your phone?"

"Of course, I did. Didn't you?"

"Yeah, but I don't have anyone to call, unless it's the police, to come and get us. And we would absolutely get arrested." Kellan paused. "You could call your sister or Morgan. They could come get us, bring a lot of flashlights or direct us to a better path. I'm sure Morgan knows–"

"I'm not calling someone to rescue us. We're not in danger," Reese revealed. "Besides, that much light would draw attention to this place, and we'd end up arrested anyway. Morgan or Remy would just end up in jail with us. We should put that lantern out already as is. Let's just get as comfortable as we can, dim it most of the way, and we'll wake at dawn to head out."

"You're mad, aren't you?" Kellan asked.

"I'm not mad at you, Kell," Reese replied and pulled the sleeping bag out of its sleeve before rolling it flat. "I'm mad at myself."

"Why?" Kellan grabbed a sweater she'd rolled into

the pack for another hike and had forgotten it had been in there. "Here; put this on." She tossed it to Reese.

"I'm not cold," Reese asserted but placed the sweater on the ground. "It'll be a pillow." She unzipped the sleeping bag, flattened it out as they had before and sat on it.

"We're not going to talk about why you're mad at yourself?" Kellan joined her on the thin material.

"I'd rather talk about something else if that's okay," Reese replied after a moment. "Maybe we can just do favorites for a while."

"Favorites?"

"Yeah, the first date stuff. You know, favorite color, movie, book, memory, and all that stuff."

"Okay. We'll do favorites," Kellan agreed.

They exchanged their favorite things for over an hour, snacking on some of the food out of boredom more than hunger. Then, it came time to figure out the sleeping arrangements. They had their jackets, the sleeping bag, and the one sweater Kellan had brought. Reese had the two hand warmers inside her jacket at Kellan's insistence. Kellan had a few more inside the emergency kit. She was getting cold and was trying to decide if it was better for them to keep the sleeping bag between their bodies and the cold rocks or if it would be better to lie on them and have it over them when Reese rolled onto her side to face her with tired eyes.

"I was mad at myself because I knew I shouldn't be out here that late," she half-whispered. "I knew I'd get scared when we were talking and watching the sun go down, but I didn't say anything then."

"Why not?" Kellan whispered.

"Because I didn't want to ruin it."

"Ruin what?"

"Our date," Reese confessed. Kellan wondered if the alcohol was lowering her inhibitions or if she was admitting this because she actually felt comfortable enough to share it with her. "I was having so much fun with you. This has been the first real date I've been on in forever. It was going so well. I worried that if I ended it early, you'd be upset and wouldn't want to go out again."

"Well, that was dumb," Kellan stated with a chuckle and ran her hand quickly up and down Reese's back over her jacket in an attempt to keep the woman warm. "If you would have told me, we could have gone. I still would have had a good time with you."

"So, are you mad we're stuck out here?" Reese asked.

"This is one of the best dates I've ever been on."

"Really?" Reese seemed surprised.

"You don't believe me?"

"I guess I need convincing." Reese smiled at her.

"Let's start at the worst date I've ever had and work our way up, shall we?" Kellan rolled onto her back and began, "I had a third date once where we had just had sex and decided to hop in the shower afterward. It was supposed to be for round two, but we heard the bathroom door open, and her girlfriend rushed in."

"Her girlfriend?"

"Yes, her *current* girlfriend." Kellan laughed lightly. "She was just as surprised as I was. Apparently, she was supposed to be out of town. I had no idea she existed and promptly grabbed my clothes to run out of the bathroom while they argued loudly. I threw on my jeans without my underwear, and my shirt without my bra, and didn't even slide my shoes on before I headed out the door."

"Oh, my God! What happened after that?" Reese laughed wildly.

"Nothing. I was mortified. I'd just had sex with the woman for the first time and was about to do it for the second, and her girlfriend showed up." She couldn't help but laugh more at Reese's enjoyment than at her recollection of the events. "She called me like an hour later to apologize. I didn't answer. But she left a message and then a few follow-up texts."

"So, no fourth date?" Reese was still laughing.

"No fourth date," she confirmed.

Their conversation continued with each of them taking a turn at revealing their worst dates over the years. Reese had been lucky, in Kellan's opinion, and her bad dates couldn't compare to Kellan's.

"So, she left you there?" Kellan asked.

"Truckee is in North Lake. I drove all the way up there to meet her because Stacy's husband knew her from work and thought we'd hit it off. She'd gotten there before me, ran into someone she'd already been on a few dates with, and decided she'd rather spend the night with her, turned me down and left."

They'd laughed for a while after that reveal, and then they both grew quiet at the same time while they stared up at the stars. Kellan didn't want to interrupt their shared silence or break the sense of intense connection she felt with Reese in this moment. This was truly the strangest date she'd ever been on. She'd never intended it to go like this, but she didn't regret it as she heard steady, slow breathing from the woman at her side. She rolled over to face her and watched Reese sleep for a few minutes before she closed her own eyes and allowed herself to fall asleep alongside her.

***

Kellan wasn't sure how long she'd been asleep, but her eyes opened and snapped to attention when she felt an unbearable coldness. She'd placed her arm over Reese's hand. It was so cold. She lifted her own hand and placed it on Reese's cheek. She was freezing, and Kellan grew concerned. They'd both fallen asleep with the sleeping bag under them and only their jackets to keep them warm.

"Reese." Kellan ran her hand over Reese's cheek in an attempt to wake her. "Reese?"

"Huh?" Reese's eyes opened slowly.

"You're freezing."

"I am?" Reese asked softly.

"Yes, you are. Come here." Kellan first pulled Reese to her and wrapped both arms around her, running them up and down her back in an attempt to get the woman warm. "God, you're so cold. Are you okay?"

"I don't know," Reese let out; and again, her response was so soft.

"Okay. Hold on."

Kellan let go of Reese and moved to remove her own jacket. She placed it over Reese's frozen legs in the interim while she pulled the hand warmers out of Reese's pockets. They were good for six hours and still had a little heat left in them. She unzipped Reese's jacket, stuffed them inside, and zipped it back up while she moved to her pack to grab all the rest. She tore at their packages and placed one on each of Reese's legs, shoved a couple into her boots, and moved the rest to her upper body. Reese remained in place and said nothing while she worked quickly.

She had one option and unzipped the jacket Reese was wearing, pulling her arms out of it but leaving it under her body because Reese was still unmoving. She removed her own shoes, then Reese's boots, and reached for one side of the sleeping bag and then the other. Quickly, she slid her body next to Reese's and had no choice but to lie half on top of her while she worked with the zipper on the sleeping bag and drew it up as high as it would go with both of them squeezing inside.

"Kellan?"

"Hey, you're hypothermic, I think." Kellan's arms wrapped around Reese's back, and she felt the heat from the warmers on her own hands. "I need to get you warm, okay?"

"You're trying to take advantage of me." Reese let out a small laugh.

"Yes, this is exactly how I pictured our first time together."

"So, you've pictured our first time?" Reese laughed a little louder, and Kellan's worry diminished a little.

Kellan laughed and slid her hand that was now warm under Reese's shirt to provide her skin on skin contact to warm faster. She lifted her own shirt slightly and did the same with Reese's hands, pressing their bodies back together. She rested her head in the crook of Reese's neck, and a moment later, relaxed a little when Reese's arm found its way to her back and began rubbing Kellan's skin. Reese's hand was still freezing, but the fact that she was moving and talking was enough.

"Can I take your shirt all the way off if I promise I'm not trying to take advantage of you?" Kellan asked.

"Your shirt too?" Reese managed.

"Yes, you need body heat."

"I thought about taking your shirt off, you know?" Reese jested. "When you were playing football on the beach."

"Yeah?" Kellan lifted herself as much as she could and pulled her own shirt over her head, placing it under Reese's on top of the sweatshirt. "Can you lift yourself a little?"

"You looked so good in that tight shirt and those pants," she continued, and Kellan smiled and then shook herself out of it as Reese lifted herself up slightly. "I thought about peeling it off you after the game."

"Oh, yeah?" Kellan distracted Reese while pulling her shirt over her head and placing it under Reese to add to her support.

"I had this whole thing pictured. It was after a game, but not that game."

"What?" Kellan asked and moved back to lie down half on top of Reese, but Reese shifted her position. "You okay?"

"Yeah." She moved so that she could lie on top of Kellan instead. "So, it was a different game." She placed her head on Kellan's chest while Kellan moved their makeshift pillow under her own head. "You were playing with everyone, but I was playing, too." Her arm went across Kellan's now bare stomach, and Kellan suddenly felt very warm. "We were together already; I don't know. When the game ended, we went to get our stuff. I pulled your shirt over your head. You had a sports bra on. I kissed you," she finished.

"We were together?" Kellan checked and ran her hand up and down Reese's back.

"Yeah," she answered softly.

"That's nice." Kellan pressed her palm to Reese's back and was happy to feel it was beginning to warm up.

"Yeah," Reese repeated.

CHAPTER 11

Rеесе неаrd something. She couldn't register what it was while still being half asleep and also, apparently, half on top of someone. Her eyes shot open. She lifted her head quickly to look down at a very much awake Kellan Cobb, who was wearing only a sports bra. She looked down at her own shirtless chest and realized she, too, was only in a bra.

"Hi," Reese offered with tired eyes.

"Good morning. We should get going. The sun's up," Kellan explained. Reese felt Kellan's hand move up and down her back comfortingly. "We're kind of zipped in. Hold on." She laughed and moved to unzip them from their sleeping bag prison.

"God, it's hot in that thing," Reese exclaimed once free.

"That was the idea." Kellan removed her shirt and Reese's from under her head and tossed Reese hers. "You were freezing. Do you remember?" She threw her own shirt on over her head.

"I remember you waking me up and trying to take my shirt off." Reese smirked over at Kellan after donning her own shirt and pulling her cell phone out of her jeans. "How did I sleep with this thing in my pocket?"

"I don't know, but I'm pretty sure I have an iPhone-shaped indentation on my thigh," Kellan offered in reply.

"Sorry." Reese checked the time. "It's after six. We should get going." She stood and stretched her entire body while Kellan watched. "You had me pressed against you all night, and you didn't even try to get to second base?" she joked as she finished her stretch.

"I was a perfect gentlelady." Kellan stood.

"I bet you were." Reese grabbed at the jackets that had been tossed aside. "I probably wouldn't have been." She winked at her. "Thank you for taking care of me last night. Sometimes, I don't know how cold or hot I am." She tried to make out Kellan's expression.

"What's that about?" Kellan slid the backpack over her shoulders but appeared to be taking Reese's comment as an offhanded one.

"I don't know. Just happens sometimes. Thank you though," she replied.

"I was really worried about you there for a while." She moved toward Reese and placed both hands on her hips. "How are you now?"

"I'm good." Reese smiled at her.

Kellan leaned in. Reese waited for the press of Kellan's lips to her own. She considered for a moment that she hadn't brushed her teeth. Kellan's lips didn't meet Reese's though. They met Reese's forehead instead. It was a brief, chaste kiss that ended too quickly. Then, Kellan pulled back.

Reese wasn't sure what to make of that kiss. She struggled to remember everything they'd talked about before she'd fallen asleep and everything she'd said after they'd moved into the sleeping bag. She couldn't think of anything that would cause Kellan to pull away from her or miss out on the perfect opportunity to share a first kiss.

They made their way slowly down the rocks, noticing that the morning dew had created a slippery path. Reese was glad they hadn't gone down the same rocks at night. She'd been right to make the decision to err on the side of caution. She hadn't anticipated nearly freezing, though. She found herself smiling as Kellan tried to row them to shore covertly. They didn't speak as they pulled the canoe ashore together. Reese helped Kellan load everything into the car and waited for her as Kellan returned the canoe to the rental outpost.

"I promise, I'll get you home so you can do whatever you need to do. Then, I'll drive you to work since you left your car there," Kellan told her as she started the car.

"Thanks," Reese replied.

Kellan appeared to be all business now, when just a few hours ago, she'd been snuggling up next to Reese, joking about their bad dates. Now, Kellan was pulling the car into her driveway. Reese hopped out to head inside.

"Well, hey there." Remy emerged from the house with her bag in tow, dressed for work.

"Hey." Reese closed the door of the car behind her and glanced at Kellan. "Give me ten minutes?"

"No problem," Kellan said and seemed a little confused.

"Hey, Rem," Reese said as she approached her sister. "Do not say anything," she said softly once she was close enough that Kellan couldn't hear.

"About what? Your sleepover date with the hot tourist? I never do." She winked at Reese.

"You always do, and it's not like that," she returned. "I left my car at the school. She's going to drive me to work."

"Call in a substitute, take the day and continue whatever you two were doing last night."

"I can't call in a sub."

"Well, at least invite the girl in. You're just going to leave her outside while you change after you were probably all over each other?"

"We weren't–" Reese stopped herself. "Is the house all set up?" she asked more softly, and Remy met her concerned glance.

"Oh." She looked past Reese toward Kellan. "Hey, football star! I'll hang back and drop this one off at the school. I don't have a patient for another hour," she said to Kellan.

"Oh, okay," Kellan replied.

Reese turned to see Kellan staring at her. She made her way back over to the car and placed her hands on the side of the Jeep's door.

"Sorry, I didn't know she'd still be home. She can run me in."

Kellan started the car again and replied, "I should go."

"Okay." Reese was standing a few feet away from Kellan, but it felt like miles. "Can you maybe turn your phone on for me?"

"I guess. Why?" Kellan asked with a small smile.

"Because I'd like to call it."

"I think I can make that sacrifice for you," she joked.

"Put it in." Reese handed her phone to Kellan, who entered her contact information. "I'll text you later so that you have mine." She turned back to see an inquisitive sister staring at their exchange. "I have to go, or I'll be late."

"Call me?"

"I will." Reese smiled at her and turned to make her way back toward her sister. "Not a word, Rem," she said as she passed her and walked into the house.

"What do you mean not a word?" Remy followed her back inside and closed the door behind them. "Did you stay at her place last night? I'm guessing you guys hooked up, because you don't exactly look like you got much sleep; and neither did she."

"We didn't hook up. We fell asleep."

"How adorable!" Remy exclaimed in a high-pitched voice, tossing her bag onto the sofa. "So, it was a good date?"

"I nearly froze to death and didn't realize it," Reese

explained as she rushed into her room.

"You what?" Remy followed her inside. "Hey, talk to me. What happened?" Remy sat on her sister's bed while Reese tore through her drawers for something to wear.

"We went to the island. We stayed too late. I was terrified of trying to hike down in the dark. We had to sleep out there. I woke up to Kellan trying to get me warm because I was hypothermic and had no idea." She pulled out a shirt and a fresh pair of underwear. "Funny thing about it, though, is that it's the best time I've had on a date in years."

"Oh, Reese," she returned empathetically. "Are you okay?"

"She took care of me, Rem."

"She knows?"

"She knows about the fall, and the infection, and my time in the hospital. She knows I've been hesitant to get active."

"But she doesn't know everything?"

"I just met her. I never told Morgan, and we were together for three years." Reese opened the door to her bathroom and headed in. "We were friends for much longer than that. I never told *her*." She reached for her toothbrush and toothpaste and began to brush while she continued talking through it. "We had such a good time last night, Rem. Besides the obvious, I was so honest with her. I'm never that honest with women on a first date. Hell, I was honest with her *before* our first date."

"What do you mean?"

She finished her brushing and turned on the shower, dropping her clothes to the floor quickly and stepping inside before the water had even begun to get warm. It didn't matter. She needed to shower quickly and head to the school.

"I told her I liked her. I told her I wanted to go out with her. And I told her it wasn't a good idea. Then, I said I wanted to go out anyway. Normally, I'd see the complication of this whole thing, and I wouldn't bother." She ran shampoo through her hair and was grateful for its length. It would air dry on the way to school. "I conquered a few fears with her last night. I was honest with her about being scared of hiking down in the dark."

"You hate admitting you're scared of stuff," Remy said.

"She didn't make me feel bad at all; and we set up this camp out there." Reese covered her body with soap. "She's easy to talk to. She doesn't make me feel weird about the whole thing."

"She also doesn't exactly know the whole thing either, Reese."

"I can't just tell her exactly, can I?"

"Why not?" Remy argued. "I've never understood your need to keep this to yourself. You, mom and dad always wanted no one to know because they'd treat you differently. Reese, you are different. They *should* have treated you differently."

"I don't want another lecture about this from you." She finished up and turned off the water.

"I put up all that stuff around the house for you when I moved back in. You took it all down." Remy moved into the bathroom while Reese exited the shower in her towel. "It's not safe, Reese. Look at what happened last night. You didn't even know you were cold. What if you'd been out there alone?"

"I wouldn't have been out there alone. I was out there on a date. And I let you put all the stuff back up," Reese reminded her sister and ran a brush through her hair.

"You took it down when you invited Kellan over."

"Because that's a lot to explain. I let you put it back up after she left. It's up right now. It's the reason I didn't invite her inside and looked unbelievably rude to a woman I want to have a second date with." She pushed at a rubber protection barrier on the corner of the bathroom counter.

"Second date?" Remy leaned against the doorframe.

"Yes," she confirmed.

"She's leaving in a few days, Reese."

"I know that."

"Earlier, you made it seem like it was different than how it was with the other tourists."

"It is." Reese glanced at her sister in confusion.

"But it's not." Remy shrugged. "She's still leaving just like the others."

"I didn't sleep with her, Remy. I want to; but we didn't last night. The others were sex first and everything else either later or never. But Kellan's different."

"Because you didn't sleep with her on the first date?"

"Because I really, really like her."

"Baby sis, this is a recipe for disaster. You know that, right? You fall for this woman, and she leaves. Then what? Long-distance relationship?"

"I know. I know." She shoved Remy out of the bathroom. "I just don't want to be reminded about this right now. Let me have my moment."

"Okay." Remy laughed. "I'll wait in the living room."

Reese stared at herself in the mirror for a moment and thought about Kellan and their very interesting date. She wondered if the woman thought her strange or rude for not inviting her inside, or if she was worried about the same thing Reese was worried about. Maybe Kellan only wanted a vacation fling and nothing more. Maybe that was all Reese could handle anyway. She hadn't prepared herself for liking Kellan as much as it turned out she did. She hadn't thought about what it would mean if their date went as well as it had; how it would feel to have Kellan's skin pressed against her own. She'd assumed it would either be bad or, at best, an okay date. And she'd been wrong. Now, she'd have to deal with that and everything that came with it.

CHAPTER 12

KELLAN WAS both excited and bored at the same time. She hadn't been sure that was possible, but as she sat on the sofa of her cabin eating a very late lunch, she'd been proved wrong. She was bored because she had nothing to do except wait for Reese's promised call, but she was excited because she was waiting for Reese's promised call. She hoped that once school let out, Reese would call to arrange a dinner date.

Unfortunately, that time had come and gone. As Kellan grabbed her jacket to grab dinner on her own, her phone rang.

"Oh, thank God!" She grabbed it off the counter and saw Hillary's name on the screen. "Damn," she said to herself. Hillary was one of her closest friends. She'd left several messages Kellan had yet to reply to since she'd arrived. "Hey, Hill."

"You answered? Greene, she actually answered," Hillary exclaimed.

"Wait. Greene's with you?" she asked.

"Hey, Kell!" Macon Greene greeted her. "You're on speaker."

"I am?"

"What's going on, Kellan? Why haven't you been answering your phone or returning messages?" Hillary chimed in.

"I'm on vacation," she reminded. "You guys know why."

"Keira's not with us if that's what you're worried about," Greene offered. "We were worried about you and wanted to make sure you're okay. Jo's here though."

"Jo?" Kellan asked.

"Oh, I forgot you guys haven't met. Joanna's here. She's friends with Emma. We all met when we–"

"Anyway…" Hillary stopped Greene's ramble. "We're hanging out at my place. We were talking about you. How are you? We didn't think you'd actually pick up."

"Hi. I'm Joanna," a foreign but kind voice introduced.

"I'm Kellan. And I'm okay," she answered honestly. "It's been good for me, actually."

"Yeah?" Greene asked.

"Surprisingly good."

"Are you coming back this weekend?" Hillary asked her. "We have After Dark next Thursday."

The group went to the event at the museum monthly. Keira would be there. Likely, so would Emma. Kellan bit her lower lip at the thought of the two of them together. Then, she released it. For the first time, she didn't feel that pang of jealousy and hurt at the image of Keira and Emma holding hands or flirting back and forth with one another. Her mind pushed those images aside. They were replaced with one of Reese running her hand through her hair, and she smiled.

"I haven't decided yet. I probably won't go to After Dark even if I do come back, though."

"Because of Keira?" Hillary asked.

"No. I don't know. I just don't feel like doing the same things I used to do when I get back. I don't know if that makes sense."

"Are you ditching us?" Greene asked.

"No." Kellan laughed. "I love you, guys." She paused. "I might stick around here for a bit."

"Yeah?" Greene and Hillary asked at the same time.

"I feel good here. I've been hiking and canoeing. It's been fun. I feel better."

"That's great, Kell," Hillary replied. "How long can you stay?"

"I left things kind of open-ended. I'm technically on leave."

"How long will you stay if you do?" Greene asked. "Jo, you look great in that. Can we go?" she said to someone else. "Sorry. We're heading out to a movie. Joanna has tried on three sweaters already," she added to Kellan.

"Is she you're new… I don't know what you call them," she admitted to Greene in a hushed tone.

"Call what?" Greene checked.

"I think she means your hook-ups," Hillary explained in an equally hushed tone.

"What? I told you, she's Emma's friend from work. Oh, and she's straight," she answered.

"Sorry, I guess I've missed some stuff," Kellan admitted and heard a beep on her phone. She lifted it from her ear to see that Reese was calling. "Hey, guys, I've got another call."

"You're answering two calls in one day?" Greene asked.

"I'll call you guys when I decide how long I'm staying. Okay?" Kellan tried to move their goodbye along.

"Fine. Fine," Hillary agreed. "Jesus, it's like she's got a hot date on the other line or something."

"Or a hooker," Greene joked. "Is it a hooker?"

"Goodbye, Hill. Bye, Greene." Kellan clicked over without waiting for a response. "Hi." She noticed the change in her own tone instantly.

"Hey."

"How are you?" Kellan asked and fell back onto the sofa.

"I'm good. You?"

"Good. I was just talking to my friends."

"Oh, sorry. Do you want to call me back later?"

"No," Kellan nearly shouted. "No, they're good," she added more softly.

"Okay." Reese laughed. "What are you up to right now?"

"I have something I was about to do, but that shouldn't take more than about twenty minutes. Why?"

"I was thinking about asking you out to dinner."

Kellan glanced over at the sink where she'd just placed her bowl of mostly uneaten soup.

"Really?" She smiled and knew Reese could tell from her tone.

"Yes, really." Reese laughed. "But no big adventure tonight; I'm still recovering from our last one."

"You're still recovering? I still have the iPhone indentation on my thigh, remember?"

"No, I don't. Maybe you can show me to prove its existence."

"Maybe." Kellan threw back and found herself toying with the denim of her jeans with her fingers on that very thigh.

"There are a few places I can recommend. Are you a picky eater?"

"Not really."

"Okay. Would you want to go for a drive?"

"Drive where?"

"North Lake. Truckee. There's a nice place up there. Shouldn't take too long to get there since the weather's good and tourist season is over."

"Still about an hour away though, right?"

"Probably. Why? Are you starving?"

"No, it just sounds like an adventure."

"It's likely that every date with me will be an adventure. You up for it?"

"I am." Kellan smiled.

"I'll pick you up in thirty?"

"I'll be ready."

***

"You're taking me all the way to the other side of the lake? That's a long time to spend in a car with someone. You sure about this?" Kellan joked with Reese just after they hit the road.

"I'm sure." Reese laughed. "What did you do with yourself after you dropped me off this morning?"

"Just hung out near the cabin. How was work?" Kellan asked.

"The kids were extra crazy today," Reese began. "Sometimes, I think I want one or two of my own. Other times, I reconsider. Today was one of those days." Reese glanced over at her. "I got a call from Morgan earlier."

"Yeah?"

"She'd gone by the outpost and saw the canoe had been returned. The guy that works there told her you'd returned it this morning. That got her attention."

"Oh, shit." Kellan sighed. "Am I in trouble? I paid for the rental for the night. I didn't think–"

"*You're* not in trouble." She turned back to the road. "I am."

"Why?"

"Morgan's always been protective of me. She and Remy both think it's their main job in life. It is actually Remy's since *my* main job in life is to protect her, but that's a sister thing."

"I have siblings. We're not all that close, but I understand what that's like. I can only imagine it's even stronger with twins."

"She's a part of me; I'm a part of her. We'll always look out for each other. But Morgan shouldn't be *this* concerned about me, if you know what I mean."

"Is it a jealousy thing?"

"I asked her that question. She never seemed to mind

when she found out about other women I was with before. She's never been the jealous type. It's honestly one of the reasons I knew it wouldn't work between us after the accident. She'd never seemed to care when other women flirted with me. Honestly, it never bothered me all that much when they flirted with her either." She paused. "I asked her if it was because she'd asked you out and you'd turned her down."

"I didn't actually turn her down. I just…" Kellan tried to consider how to complete her sentence when Reese lifted an eyebrow at her. "Never mind."

"She told me she texted you last night."

"Oh, she did. I didn't get it until today when I turned my phone on. I haven't replied yet."

"She had your number, but I didn't, huh?" Reese asked playfully.

"She had my number because I called to cancel on her for kayaking so that you and I could go to the island together."

Reese laughed and placed a hand on her thigh. Kellan stared down at it for a moment, but then it was removed and placed back on the wheel.

"I'm teasing you, Kell."

"She asked me out again in the text," she confessed. "I checked the time it came in. It was after she saw the two of us together. I chalked it up to some kind of competition thing she has with you or something."

"How does it feel having two women compete for your attention?" Reese smirked in her direction.

"Really weird," Kellan chuckled in response. "And you're not fighting over me; you're fighting with each other."

"We are, are we?" Reese laughed and stopped them at a light. She turned to face Kellan a little more fully. "Care to tell what you think you know?" she asked playfully.

"She asked me out again via a text message, after I'd

turned her down once already. And it was after she'd seen you and me alone together, when she knows you haven't done that in a long time. She's in a weird position and doesn't know what to do about it. Maybe she likes me a little, I don't know. But I'm sure she still has some feelings for you even if they're not the same old ones she used to have."

"She admitted as much today."

"She told you she still has feelings for you?"

"Not like that." Reese turned when the light changed and drove on. "She said it was the canoe thing that got her."

"I figured."

"You did?" She glanced toward Kellan curiously.

"She's fine with you having sex with a passer-by you'll never see again because she knows that's just sex. But when she sees you doing something you haven't done since her, since your accident, it's different."

"How'd you know that?"

"Because that's how it felt with Keira." Kellan stared ahead. "She'd dated a little here and there. It was weird, but it never really bothered me until Emma."

"Because it was real?" Reese asked.

"Yes, because then it was real," she confirmed, only partially talking about Keira.

***

"Did you take care of what you needed to before I picked you up?" Reese had been particularly curious about Kellan's errand or chore since the woman had been somewhat ambiguous when they were on the phone.

They were sitting at their small dinner table in the restaurant she'd chosen based on its view of the lake at sunset. They had patio seats, which she'd been able to reserve. Kellan was sipping her red wine while staring out at the orange and pinks hues of the sunset. The sight made

Reese want to lean over and kiss her.

"I did, yes," Kellan replied and sat her glass back on the table.

"Is it a government secret?" Reese laughed and finished the last bite of their shared dessert.

"What? What I had to do?" Kellan laughed and turned more fully to Reese.

"You're being pretty vague."

"What do you think I had to do?" She smiled at her. "That I had to wrap up another hot date or something?"

"Well, Morgan did text you, so it's a possibility."

"You know I turned her down, Reese," Kellan reminded. "You really want to know what I had to do?"

"Not if you don't want to tell me," she replied. "I'm just being nosy."

"Part of me doesn't want to tell you because it might change things. The other part of me really wants to tell you *because* it might change things."

"What?" Reese chuckled.

"Can we go sit over there?" Kellan pointed to the long row of bench seats the restaurant provided to allow guests to further enjoy the view. They butted up against the rocky shore. "I kind of want to enjoy the view for a while. The sun's about to disappear."

"Sure. Let me get the check. Go on over and save us a spot," she instructed.

Kellan headed in the direction of the bench seating while Reese stood and went to find their waitress. Once she'd taken care of the check, she went back outside and joined Kellan, who was already sitting facing the water. The sun was almost entirely engulfed by the horizon. The restaurant's heaters and outdoor lighting had turned on, allowing them to still see the water fifty yards ahead. Reese sat down next to Kellan but left a few inches of space between them, as if to prepare herself for whatever Kellan might tell her. Kellan's arm went over the back of the bench. She turned herself slightly toward Reese.

"It's not a big deal. I'm not an agent for the CIA or anything." She smiled. "I just talked to my boss and the rental company and extended my stay here."

Reese's smile grew wide as she turned to face Kellan.

"You did? Wait. Why didn't you want to tell me?"

"I think part of the reason you called me today and asked me out for the next night after our first official date was because you thought I was leaving." Kellan paused. "I had no idea this would happen, Reese. I didn't plan to come here and meet someone I wanted to go out with."

"I don't know; I might have. I had a really good time last night." Reese considered Kellan's comment and wondered if she would have reached right back out to her like she'd done today if Kellan was staying for longer. "I might have waited until tomorrow, but that's because I'm exhausted from last night and work today. It doesn't have to do with wanting to delay seeing you. I like this," Reese explained. "I don't really know what *this* is, but I like it. I like you."

"I like you too," Kellan told her. "Me staying could be good because it gives us more time to figure this out."

"But it could be bad because you think I won't want to see you as often or something?"

"I don't know." Kellan chuckled and turned back toward the water.

"How long are you staying?" Reese asked.

"I'm renting the cabin week to week. I just asked for a week-long extension."

"Oh."

"I can ask for another week if that would make you feel better," Kellan offered.

"You have a life back in San Francisco, Kell. You can't keep putting that off for me."

"I want to, though," Kellan returned. "And my life is not all it's cracked up to be back there." She hesitated a moment. "I don't want you and I to slow down with whatever this is. I like the pace, okay?"

"Me too." Reese gave her a shy smile.

"But I don't know that we should speed it up either."

"Ah." Reese lifted her eyebrows. "You mean sex."

Kellan smiled at her, slid a little closer on the bench seat, and replied, "Not exclusively."

"You want to have non-exclusive sex?" Reese teased. "That either means you want to be able to have sex with other people or that you want you and I to have sex with other people together." She gave a playful wink.

"I mean neither of those things, and you know it." Kellan rolled her eyes.

"You want to wait for that part."

"That's not what I'm saying either, Reese." She leaned in. Reese's heart sped up as she met Kellan's sexy blue eyes. "I'm saying I want everything to happen naturally. I don't want us to rush anything because I'm not a full-time resident of South Lake."

"I see."

"Is that a problem?" Kellan pulled back slightly and appeared concerned.

"Kellan, just because I've had some one-night stands and a little fun doesn't mean that's what I always do or that that's what I want out of this," she began. "I don't know what's going to happen with us. But not including that time we spent on the beach just you and me, this is only our second date. It's true that, after I got sick, I played around a little. I wasn't exactly planning on stopping that. I mean, I saw you in the visitor's center and thought about doing the same thing I'd done with some of the other women I've been with. If I pretended otherwise, I'd be lying. I don't know if I'm ready for a relationship; that's the truth." She paused and placed her hand on Kellan's cheek. "I'm nervous and scared right now because I like you more than I thought I would. I'm enjoying spending time with you. But you're leaving, Kellan. Whether it's in a week or two or three, you'll go back to San Francisco. I'll be here. I don't know what happens then."

"Me neither."

"If you and I keep spending time together while you're here, will we keep doing that when you're gone? Find time to see one another?"

"I hope so," Kellan answered and leaned her cheek into Reese's palm.

"Come on. We should probably hit the road. Not all of us are on vacation. Some of us have to work tomorrow." Reese stood.

She held out her hand for Kellan to take. It seemed like a good next step for the two of them. Kellan stood with a smile on her face. She took Reese's outstretched hand and entwined their fingers. Reese stared down at their linked hands. Yeah, this was right.

CHAPTER 13

"I FEEL LIKE I hardly see you now that you've got a girlfriend," Remy teased as she helped Reese move a table into place.

"I do not have a girlfriend," Reese countered. "And you were at your boyfriend's place last night. I got home at a reasonable hour."

"Bummer." Remy unfolded the red plastic tablecloth and passed a section of it to Reese to place on top. "Is she a bad kisser or something?"

"I wouldn't know," Reese revealed.

"You haven't even kissed the girl yet?" Remy chuckled as they worked to arrange the tablecloth together. "You spent all night with her out in the cold. I seem to remember something about her taking care of you because you were freezing. And don't get me started on the fact that you nearly froze to death, Reese. You know you have to be careful. If you were going out to the island, you should have–"

"First of all, I don't even think I was that bad. Second of all, I had no idea we were going to the island. Third, I definitely didn't plan to get trapped there. And fourth, I didn't kiss her because I could barely move my lips at that point. When we got back the next morning, we rushed home so I could get ready for work. You kind of killed the mood there, Rem."

"Oh, please." Remy dismissed her with a wave. "You didn't even let the girl inside the house. I'm pretty sure that's what killed your mood. What happened last night though?"

"Nothing." Reese placed a tray of store-bought cookies on the table.

"Well, I know that." Remy moved two sleeves of red cups to the table.

"No, I mean nothing happened that made me *not* want to kiss her. Actually, I wanted to kiss her several times over the course of the drive, but that would have gotten us both killed. And then at dinner, we were out in public. I don't know her stance on public displays of affection yet."

"And when you dropped her off? Not even a goodnight kiss? When did you turn into such a prude?" Remy laughed.

"I'm not a prude." Reese glanced around the small multi-purpose room at the other people completing their varying tasks to prepare for the school's open house. "She didn't exactly kiss me either."

"You two don't have a lot of time left, Reese. She's leaving on Sunday, right?"

"She's not, actually." Reese smiled and moved a few two-liters of fruit punch onto the table next to the cups. "She's staying for at least another week; maybe longer."

"Really? What changed?"

"I guess I contributed to her decision."

"She's staying for you? That's adorable." Remy stacked napkins next to the cookies.

"I don't know if it's entirely for me, but she's staying a little longer."

"Still, Reese, another week or two isn't all that long. If you want to—"

"It's not just about sex, Rem." She moved to stand closer to her sister. "I like her."

"I know you do."

"No, I mean I really like her."

"I get it. I also understand that when you like a person how you like her, you generally move past the staring longingly into their eyes to hand holding and then to kissing. Then, sometimes, two consenting adults even get naked with one another, and–" She wiggled her eyebrows.

"I lost my virginity first, Rem. I'm pretty sure I understand how sex works."

Remy only laughed and then moved two chairs into place. Reese continued to set up the room. Parents would be arriving in a few minutes. Remy had offered her assistance along with Ryan's. Her boyfriend was currently helping with a setup of the sound system so they could play soft music in the background while parents and students milled about the room. The open house was mainly for students to decide on after-school activities, but each teacher needed to spend at least one hour in their classroom in case parents needed to stop by with questions or just to see their kid's artwork plastered over the walls.

"You should invite her to football again on Sunday. She seemed to have a good time," Remy suggested.

"Yeah, maybe." Reese considered it, but then she thought of Morgan and how that might be awkward. "I'll be right back. You good here?"

"I think I can move a few chairs out of the way, Reese."

Reese rolled her eyes at her sister and moved to the double doors, which she opened, heading out into the hallway. She walked down to her classroom. After making sure no one had arrived yet to check out the finger paintings she'd hung earlier in the day, she closed the door behind her and pulled out her phone.

"Hey," Kellan's voice greeted. "Shouldn't you be open housing?"

"I am." Reese laughed and then she remembered she had no reason to call Kellan other than the fact that she'd been thinking about her and wanted to hear her voice.

"Everything okay?"

"Yeah, Remy is here helping me set up tonight. She just mentioned something."

"Did you need help setting up? I could've come. It's not like I'm doing anything."

"No, it's fine. Ryan is helping with the sound system. He's the one we really needed. She just came along. But Remy wanted to invite you to football. It's on Sunday at the same place. Since you're not leaving, she thought you'd like to come." Reese closed her eyes and forced herself to stop pacing. "You don't have to. I know we have a date tomorrow. Maybe you want to see how that goes before we make other plans."

"I'd love to come to football if you want me there," Kellan replied. "But I assume Morgan will be there, too."

"She rarely misses a game."

"I'd like to go if that's where you'll be." Kellan hesitated then. "I don't need tomorrow to know I want to spend as much time with you as I can while I'm here, Reese. If you think it'll be awkward with Morgan there, though, maybe I should skip it."

"Hell, maybe *I* should skip it," she argued.

"Do you ever skip it?"

"Not since I was sick. I just sit there though. It's the same thing every week. I wouldn't mind missing it if I had other plans."

"Did you used to play?" Kellan asked.

"Before, yeah."

"But you don't want to anymore?"

"I don't know. I guess I do."

"Then, you should, Reese. You climbed into that canoe with me, hiked up those rocks, and spent the night outside. You can play a game of touch football."

Reese bit her upper lip in frustration; not at Kellan but at herself. She sat in the chair behind her desk and considered her options.

"Maybe."

"Maybe?"

"I'll give you a maybe."

"Then, I'll go to football on Sunday."

"Okay." Reese laughed. "I guess we'll both be there at the same time and in the same place."

"I guess so." Kellan chuckled.

"This is so lame. I feel like a teenager right now."

"So do I." Kellan's chuckle grew louder. "I stared at my phone for another ten minutes last night after we sent those goodnight texts just in case you'd send something else," she admitted.

"Oh, my God! I did the same thing. But then you didn't send anything, so I thought you went to sleep."

"I can't wait to see you tomorrow. Is saying that lame too?"

"No, it's cute, actually," Reese replied. "I can't wait to see you either." She heard a knock at the door and looked up to see one of the other teachers in the small window. "I have to go. The parents will be arriving soon. Remy's probably trying to track me down."

"I guess I'll say good night now then, since I'm sure you'll be tired after."

"I can still text you when I get home. You know, so you know I'm safe." She bit her upper lip again and smiled through it.

"I'd like that. I'll wait up for you."

The teacher knocked again. Reese met the woman's eyes. She held up one finger to indicate she needed a moment and returned her attention to Kellan.

"I really have to go now. I'm getting a glare from Mrs. Torres."

Kellan laughed. Reese enjoyed that sound so much she considered telling everyone she didn't feel well just to go hear it in person.

"I'll talk to you later. Have fun tonight," Kellan instructed.

"I will."

Mrs. Torres went back to the multi-purpose room to help complete the setup. Remy and Ryan left for dinner before everyone arrived. Reese completed her obligation to the school by shaking hands, smiling, and telling parents stories of their children in her class. When the open house ended, she helped the remaining teachers with the extra food and the trash before heading to her car to begin her drive home. She was exhausted. It was after ten, and she wanted nothing more than a full night of sleep, but there was something else she wanted more.

She pulled into the driveway, got out of her car, and tried not to run to the front door so as to retain some semblance of her dignity. She knocked too loudly and waited. When nothing happened, she knocked again and thought maybe she'd made a bad decision. She'd almost turned to go when the front door opened. Kellan stood there, wearing a pair of black shorts and a white tank top.

"Reese?"

Reese moved instantly over the threshold of the cabin and wrapped both arms around Kellan's neck. She pulled Kellan into her and pressed their bodies together before covering Kellan's lips with her own. It took Kellan only a moment to respond. When she did, her arms went around Reese's waist and pulled her even closer. Reese could feel Kellan's warmth through the thin fabric of her shirt. She balled her hands into fists to prevent them from moving down and removing it. Kellan's tongue met Reese's, and the kiss intensified for several moments before it slowed naturally. Kellan pecked her lips gently and ran her hands up and down Reese's back. Reese leaned in again and captured Kellan's lips once more, keeping it gentle too, before she removed her arms from around Kellan's neck and moved back over the threshold.

"Good night, Kellan," she said after she regained some of her composure.

"Wait. What?"

"I've wanted to do that for a while now, and I should have done that last night."

"Come inside, Reese." Kellan moved to the side and held out her hand.

"Not tonight. I really just wanted to kiss you."

"So, you kiss me like that, and then you just leave?" Kellan smirked at her.

"Yes. I'll text you when I get home though."

"You'll do better than that," Kellan insisted. "I want a phone call."

"Yes, ma'am." Reese gave a mock-salute and then realized how stupid that must have looked. "God, I swear I'm not this ridiculous."

"I like you ridiculous." Kellan smiled back at her. "You sure you don't want to come in? We can just talk."

"No, we can't." Reese took a few steps back. "Now that I know you can kiss like that, we can't be alone in your cabin and just talk." She moved back toward her car. "I will call you when I get into bed."

"I guess that will have to be enough." Kellan held her hand over her heart and offered a playful smile.

"For tonight." Reese winked at her. "It's enough for tonight, Kell."

CHAPTER 14

As KELLAN TREKKED down the hill, she turned her music off to take in the sounds of nature. She listened to the chickadees in the trees as she walked. These small, fat-looking birds were common in Tahoe and had a black top to their heads that almost looked like a hat, black bib under their chin, and a white line over their eyes. She watched one swing from the branches of the tree to her left and listened to its very distinctive three-note whistle. She sat off to the side of the trail on a large rock that had obviously acted as a resting spot for many a hiker and peeled open one of the granola bars she'd packed with her.

She wasn't starving, but she'd eaten breakfast around six and wouldn't eat lunch until Reese's arrival. She peeled the wrapper back on it, placed it on top of her pack to her side, and then reached for her water bottle to grab a quick sip when she saw a Steller's Jay scoop down from a low-hanging tree branch and land next to her granola bar on top of her bag. The pigeon-sized bird had dark blue wings, tail, and breast, along with a lighter but brighter body. She'd seen a million of them on her visits. They were one of the most common birds in the woods.

"Have to be careful around here. Those birds are fearless. I've seen them steal bread crusts from people at picnic tables," Morgan said from behind her.

Kellan turned to Morgan for a moment before glancing back at the bird that tilted its head to the side as she took the creature in and then lowered its head confidently to try to chip away at her granola bar. Kellan smiled at it and turned back to Morgan. The movement must have frightened the bird, though, because he quickly flitted away back into the trees, leaving his hard-earned reward still atop her bag. Kellan picked it up. She broke it into easy to consume bites for the birds and tossed it into the brush beside the trail before standing.

"What are you doing here?" Kellan asked once she'd donned her backpack and turned to Morgan. "Do you have a group with you?"

"It's just me today." She pointed through the heavy trees. "I live back through there. I was planning to take the kayak out this morning. This is the quickest way to get where I dock it." She motioned past Kellan down the trail, which led to the water's edge.

"I just wanted a short hike this morning," Kellan replied even though Morgan hadn't asked what had brought her to the trail.

"Well, have fun." Morgan lifted both eyebrows only for a second before lowering them.

"Morgan, can we talk for a second?" she asked just as the woman began to walk past her on the trail toward the water.

"About how you're dating my ex-girlfriend?" She stopped in front of Kellan. "Or about how I thought you and I had a good time, I asked you out, you turned me down and *then* started dating my ex-girlfriend?"

"I don't know what Reese and I are doing," she shared. "Honestly, I'm not sure."

"Have you been on more than one date?"

"Yeah, but–"

"That's called dating, Kellan."

"Hey, come on." Kellan moved back a little. "Morgan, I didn't mean for any of this to happen. I came here to spend time by myself. I had no idea I'd meet you or Reese. I planned on being here for a couple of weeks and then going home. The biggest goal I'd set for myself was to maybe start to heal a broken heart."

"Seems like that's been accomplished," Morgan said.

"It's interesting how sometimes you get some space or time away from a specific place or person and your brain clears."

"Well, I'm glad for you if you're feeling better."

"Morgan, I'm sorry if I led you on or something. That wasn't my intention." She shifted her backpack on her shoulders out of anxiousness more than anything. "I did have fun with you on the hike and when we played football before that."

"But you're not interested in me in any way beyond friendship. I get it."

"I like Reese," she confessed with a shrug.

"I can tell." Morgan hesitated, lowered her gaze, and then brought her eyes back to Kellan's. "She likes you, too."

"Do you still have feelings for her?" she asked.

There was no way Kellan would be able to compete with the decades of shared history between Reese and Morgan. They'd been friends for years and then lovers for years after that. They spent time together every week and would likely always be close. Their relationship had ended not because of Morgan, but because of Reese.

"I didn't think I did," Morgan said. "She's dated since she and I broke up. It never really bothered me until now. I could tell at football. Reese gets this look when she's into someone. I used to see it when we were just friends. Then, I realized she was looking at me that way. I still think sometimes if she wouldn't have gotten sick, we'd still be together. She started dating other women. Dating is kind of a strong word because nothing ever came of her time with anyone." She looked into the trees but appeared to be reaching her eyes out beyond them; perhaps, to her kayak and freedom from this conversation. "I saw her looking at you like that on the beach. Then, you two went for your walk, and I knew she was interested."

"So, you asked me out because…"

"Two reasons, I guess." She moved to sit on the rock Kellan had previously occupied. "One, I think you're gorgeous, and you seemed nice." She gave Kellan a shy smirk at that revelation. "And two, because I knew she was interested. Petty, I know."

"You wanted to try to get to me before she could?"

"I think there's two parts to that, too."

"What do you mean?"

"I mean, you're right. I wanted to ask you out before she could because I was jealous, but I also asked you out again after I caught you two together because I was testing *you*."

Kellan moved to sit on the rock next to her and stared at the group of birds that were now nibbling at the granola bar bits on the ground next to them while chirping softly at one another.

"You wanted to see if I'd date you too?"

"I don't know." Morgan let out a deep sigh. "Maybe. It's stupid, I know. Reese and I are exes. I loved her like crazy, but we're friends now."

"And you're very protective of her. I can understand that," Kellan replied.

"I should talk to her. I need to apologize."

"I think you two need to talk about a lot of things," Kellan suggested. Morgan turned to look at her. "I'm not trying to butt in or anything. It just seems like there's some stuff you guys need to work out."

"Probably. She's kind of upset with me right now."

"Why?"

"Because I asked you out again." Morgan turned to the birds. "I knew she liked you, that you'd gone out; and I asked you out again. It's a bad friend move. She let me hear as much when we talked."

"She did?" Kellan couldn't help but laugh a little. "Sorry," she added when Morgan's expression showed minor annoyance.

"I argued that you two had just met and weren't

exactly exclusive. Then, I may have said something about how she tended to enjoy non-exclusivity these days. She bit my head off and suggested I was calling her a slut. Then, she asked me to back off where you were concerned. I argued that that should be your decision. It was all very high school. I hate myself for the whole thing."

"She asked you to back off?" Kellan tried to stop a smile, but it made its way out through her eyes by the look Morgan was giving her.

"You really do like her, don't you?"

"I do." Kellan lowered her eyes. "She's different."

"She thinks you are, too," Morgan explained. "Just like high school; except your name isn't Cora Howard, and we're not currently sophomores." She stood.

"Cora Howard?"

"The first girl that captured Reese's heart. I hadn't yet realized I was gay, but Reese knew she was. She asked me to pass messages back and forth to Cora in chemistry class. Cora was in an experimental phase back then. I think she got off on Reese's feelings. They had a thing for like a month. It was all very secret because Cora's parents didn't allow her to date. It ended when they finally let her off her leash and she could go out with the boy she had a real crush on." Morgan got serious in that moment and made sure to meet Kellan's eyes. "I was there for her then. I held her as she cried because Cora had been her first. I held her after every breakup, after every time she declared her feelings to a woman and they weren't returned. I held her when she was sick, Kellan. I was on one side while Remy was on the other. I held her hand when she was in that coma. I cried every night, not knowing if I'd ever get her back. Then, I cried every night because she didn't want to be with me anymore. Even though that hurt like hell, we got our friendship back. I haven't had to hold her like that since. I don't want to ever have to hold her after a heartbreak again. Do you understand what I'm saying?"

There was a magnificent weight to what Morgan had just expressed. Kellan wasn't certain she could bear it. Morgan didn't want Reese's heart to ever be broken again. While Kellan knew she wanted the same thing, she wasn't sure this early on if she'd be able to prevent that from happening. The two had only exchanged one kiss, but that kiss was the best kiss Kellan had ever had. It had pushed the memories of all others away while their lips had been connected.

It had wiped Keira Worthy from her mind completely even after they'd pulled apart. They'd spoken on the phone for over two hours before Reese finally allowed sleep to claim her. Kellan had listened to her even breathing on the other end of the phone for several minutes before she'd finally hung up. She knew she liked Reese, but she had no idea if she'd cause the woman pain when she left because they'd end whatever this was between them, or if she'd cause her pain later if they continued it long-distance and it got too hard.

"I understand," she finally replied, because she did understand.

CHAPTER 15

"OH, MY GOD! What smells so good in here?" Reese asked the moment she entered the cabin.

"Don't get too excited; that's not lunch." Kellan took Reese's light jacket and hung it on the coatrack next to the front door. "I know I technically agreed to cook something for lunch, but I thought we could do sandwiches instead and that you could stay for dinner." She turned to see Reese standing in front of the sofa, smiling at her. "I made a roast."

"Are you trying to squeeze two dates into one, Kellan Cobb?" Reese asked with a smirk and a playful tone.

"I hadn't thought of it like that." Kellan made her way toward the small but open kitchen. "It's okay if you can't."

"I can stay," Reese replied.

"I got turkey, ham, and roast beef along with Swiss and Cheddar cheese. There's mayo, and mustard, and I got–"

"Kell, turn around, please."

Kellan obeyed and turned to see that Reese was right behind her. Her arms moved around Kellan's neck, and she pulled Kellan close.

"Oh, right." Kellan's arms moved to Reese's waist. "We've done this before, so we can do it whenever now," she added with a smile.

"Exactly."

Reese's lips connected with Kellan's. They shared a brief kiss before they both pulled back and smiled. Then, their lips reconnected. This time, it wasn't just a hello kiss. Kellan's hands instantly moved under Reese's shirt. Her palms spread out to take in as much of the other woman's lower back as possible. Reese's hands were playing in Kellan's hair that was down around her shoulders. The tips were still a little wet. Kellan had showered recently, Reese thought to herself while their tongues connected for the first time since last night. Kellan's hands were sliding up and down her back as Reese's own hands were moving to Kellan's neck to push her hair out of the way. Reese pulled her lips from Kellan's to move them to her neck just below her earlobe.

"Reese," Kellan whispered.

Reese explored first with her lips; then, with her tongue. She nibbled the soft skin with her teeth as she moved down Kellan's neck to her collarbone. Kellan's head was resting on Reese's shoulder, and her hands were digging into Reese's back. The woman was coiled so tightly, Reese worried she might explode there in the kitchen. She pulled her lips away and met Kellan's eyes.

"Are you okay?" she checked.

"Yeah. Why?" Kellan asked breathlessly.

"You're really tense, Kellan." She pulled back more and pressed her hands to Kellan's stomach.

Kellan let out a deep laugh and covered Reese's hands with her own before pulling them to her lips where she kissed both palms and moved them back around her own neck. She pulled Reese back into her and hugged her.

"I'm okay. You're a really good kisser. I guess I was trying to keep myself together."

"Why?" Reese laughed into Kellan's shoulder. "And did you just take a shower? You smell really good."

"I was outside this morning. I went for a hike." She squeezed Reese harder. "So, I took a shower, yes."

Reese kissed her chastely under her ear and pulled back to look into Kellan's blue eyes.

"Why are you trying to keep yourself together?" she repeated.

"Because kissing you like that makes me want more. I don't know if we're ready for more yet."

"You have to tense your entire body to keep from..." Reese lifted both eyebrows.

"I didn't realize I had to until you kissed me," she revealed. "Maybe it's just because it's been a while for me." She pulled back and released Reese from her hold. "So, sandwiches and then we can sit outside and eat?"

"Sure," Reese agreed.

Kellan turned away from her entirely then and began pulling out sandwich ingredients from the cabin's kitchen. Reese remained watching for a few moments before she moved into the living room and then to the windows, which overlooked the trees and the lake.

"I have chips, potato salad, and pasta salad. Which would you like?" Kellan asked while bent over at the fridge.

"Yes." Reese turned back to smile at her. Kellan understood the implication and removed two small containers from the fridge before grabbing a bag of chips off the top. "It's a beautiful day," Reese said after a moment. "Do you want to eat down at the beach?" She turned back to Kellan again.

"Sure. I can pack everything up, and we can drive down."

"I'd like to walk if that's okay." Reese headed back toward the kitchen and leaned over the counter.

Kellan turned to face her with a loaf of bread in her hand and asked, "Yeah?"

"I think if I can handle the island hike, I can handle the short one down to the beach."

"Really? Because I was thinking about doing something after lunch. I wasn't sure how you'd take the idea."

"Something?" Reese lifted one eyebrow at her and stood up before taking a few steps toward Kellan.

"Stop it." Kellan laughed and held out her hand to make Reese keep her distance. "Or we'll never eat lunch." She lowered her hand when Reese stopped a few feet away. "And it's a hike. I scoped it out this morning. It's beginner level stuff, with only one small hill and no rocks or tree branches over the trail that I noticed. It's only a couple of miles. We can stop whenever you want and head back. I packed a bag already. I thought we'd eat and then I can drive us to the trailhead." She placed the bread on the counter next to the cheese she'd already pulled out. "If you don't want to, we can stay here. It just seems like you miss it; and you really enjoyed yourself the other day apart from the nearly freezing to death part." She laughed out of nervousness from what Reese could tell. "I thought it might be nice to try an easy trail together."

"It does sound nice." Reese smiled at her. "I'm not exactly dressed for a hike, though." She motioned to her white button-down long-sleeved shirt and jeans. She was wearing her hiking boots, but that was the only part of her ensemble that said she was ready for a hike in the woods. "I would have gone home to change had you warned me, Kell."

"You came straight here? You didn't go home first?" Kellan asked.

"Yes, I came straight here. I wanted to see you and didn't want to wait."

Kellan took a few steps toward her to offer her a sweet kiss on the lips.

"You can borrow whatever you need from me, or I can take you home on the way and you can change if you want." She moved back to make their lunch. "Whatever you want. My bag is in the bedroom."

Reese smiled at Kellan as she turned to head into the bedroom. When she arrived in the open door, she realized this wasn't Kellan's actual bedroom. She grew disappointed because in the moment Kellan had motioned to her bedroom, Reese had grown excited at seeing Kellan's most private space. She wanted to know how she'd decorated it, what kind of bed she had, what pictures she had adorning the walls or on her bedside tables. She wanted to know if she preferred a television in her room or if she was one of the people who didn't watch TV once they'd turned in for the night. She noticed the queen-sized bed and the bedding that had obviously been used many times over by the other tourists that had rented the property. Her sadness grew.

"Maybe I will go home first and grab something."

"It's nothing like my room at home." Kellan was behind her now. Her words were soft and nearly whispered into Reese's ear. She wrapped her arms around Reese's waist. "My place is small. It's on the fourth floor but, thankfully, there are elevators. I have a one-bedroom. I'm not much of a decorator, but I've put up a few paintings. I bought a rug last year." She kissed Reese's neck. "There are a few hiking trails I go on sometimes when I need to get out of the city. I've never really had anyone that likes hiking as much as me to share the experience, but the views are great, and walking across the Golden Gate is touristy, but fun. The city on the other side is Sausalito. It's nice. You can rent bicycles, and there are great restaurants."

"Are you trying to sell me on your city, Kell?" She lowered her head as Kellan's lips met the back of her neck.

"I was hoping you'd consider visiting one day."

"That depends."

"On?" Kellan kissed her again in the same spot.

"If I'm staying with you when I'm there." She raised her head in time for Kellan to kiss the side of her neck instead. "Because I hardly know anything about you, Kellan, but I know I don't want you to leave."

"Me neither." Kellan rested her head on Reese's shoulder. "How about you find something to throw on in my bag, we take our lunch to the beach and have a picnic? Then, we'll go on our hike, and we can talk. I'll tell you anything you want to know. You do the same. We'll come back here and eat dinner, and we'll keep getting to know one another." She squeezed Reese gently. "And if you want to stay, you can."

"Stay after dinner?" Reese asked with a small smile.

"Stay the night, Reese," she replied in Reese's ear. "Just stay. Nothing has to happen. We nearly stayed up all night on the phone last night, and you could have been here. We could have done that in person."

"I have to work tomorrow," Reese replied.

"You can leave early to go home and change if you want." She pulled back a little. "If you don't want to stay though, you–"

"I do, Kell." Reese turned in Kellan's arms. "Earlier, though, you seemed to have a hard time just kissing me. How are you going to make it through the night if all we're doing is sleeping?" she teased.

***

Kellan stared down at Reese with a wide smile on her face as she ran her hands through the other woman's hair. They'd gone to the beach and finished their lunch a while ago. Reese's head was in Kellan's lap as the two alternated between bouts of light conversation and shared silences. Kellan was enjoying one of those silences as her fingers massaged Reese's scalp lightly while Reese herself smiled up at her with closed eyes.

"Tell me about your family. You've mentioned you're not really that close with them, right?" Reese asked.

"Not really," Kellan replied and rubbed Reese's stomach under her shirt with her free hand before she laid back on the blanket so they were perpendicular and both relaxed. "My parents were fine growing up. They pushed us all a little too hard sometimes, but I think that's because we had no money and they needed us to get scholarships so that we could go to school." Her fingernails scratched lightly at Reese's stomach. The muscles flexed on instinct, and Kellan smiled. "It wasn't a bad childhood or anything though."

"What did your parents do?"

"My dad worked at the port. He loaded and unloaded container ships mostly. My mom stayed at home when we were younger, but once my sister was in kindergarten, she went to work at the post office. She's still there. My dad's still working the port, too. Katie and Kevin have done really well for themselves. Kevin is an engineer. He works for the electric company. Katie just graduated from law school."

"So, all three of you turned out well. Your parents must have done something right." Reese opened her eyes. Kellan lifted herself up for a moment to remove a fallen leaf from just under Reese's neck. She took in the gray of Reese's eyes and how the sun bounced the light around them. They shifted to near green for a moment before she moved back to lie down. "Right?"

"I guess."

"But why don't you talk to them much?"

"Kevin joined the Army right after high school. He stayed in for four years and traveled a lot during that time. When he was discharged, the Army paid for school. He chose an East Coast school. He's been there ever since. He comes home to visit every now and then, but I haven't seen him in a few years. He's four years older than me, so we never spent all that much time together growing up."

"And he's still single?"

"And no plans to change that, as far as I know. He's working on his Ph. D right now when he's not at work, and that takes up the majority of his time."

"Another doctor in the family, huh?"

"My parents don't consider me a doctor," Kellan explained and opened her eyes to stare at the sky.

"What?" Reese shot up and turned to her. "You *are* a doctor. You're a vet."

"I guess being a doctor to a bunch of furry creatures doesn't count. My mom said as much once. It doesn't matter. I don't care."

Reese moved to lie beside her. She placed her hand on Kellan's stomach while she looked down at her. Kellan liked Reese there. She liked watching her eyes move slowly over her body and return to her lips and then her eyes. She liked the feel of Reese's hand on her skin under her shirt and lifted her own hand back up to Reese's hair to brush it out of her eyes for her.

"When did you know you wanted to be a vet?"

CHAPTER 16

Reese WASN'T SURE if Kellan was taking the trail this slowly for her benefit or because she was simply enjoying their time together and didn't want it to end. Reese had borrowed a pair of yoga pants and a t-shirt from Kellan. They hiked hand in hand when the trail was wide enough. Kellan took the lead when it wasn't to make sure there was nothing Reese could trip over. It had started seriously with Kellan insisting she clear the path and had evolved into somewhat of a joke with Kellan kicking away near pebbles. Reese hadn't laughed this much in a long time.

"Morgan, actually, lives up there." Reese pointed to the trees to their right.

"Yeah, I know," Kellan replied and stopped walking.

"You know?" Reese tugged on her hand. "What do you mean you know? Have you been there?"

"No." Kellan turned to her and dropped her hand. "No, I just saw her this morning when I was out here. She was heading out to kayak and mentioned she lived up there. She's leading a hike this afternoon up at Emerald Bay."

"We sort of fought the other night," Reese said.

"She told me."

"She did?"

"She said you asked her to back off."

Reese let out a sound that resembled a laugh but was more a grunt than anything else.

"That's what she said?"

Kellan took her hand again and continued walking with Reese joining her.

"I think you two should talk, Reese." She squeezed Reese's hand. "It's obvious you two have a history and that you still have things you need to address."

"Morgan and I are fine." Reese let out a sigh. "She's just being Morgan."

"She used to be your girlfriend. Now, she's watching you date someone else."

"You asked me before how we'd been able to get our friendship back. I thought we had. But now, I'm not so sure." She released Kellan's hand but wrapped her arm around Kellan's waist instead as they continued to walk. "And I don't want to talk about Morgan anymore today, okay?"

"Fine with me," Kellan agreed.

They made it back to Kellan's cabin. Reese watched as the woman plated their meal and approached her on the couch. She passed Reese her food while she sat her own plate on the coffee table and went back to the kitchen to grab an unopened bottle of wine. They sipped their wine and ate the slow-cooked meal. Kellan started a fire in the small fireplace before she returned to the couch to wrap an arm around Reese, who felt totally at home snuggling into Kellan's side.

"At home, what would you be doing right now?" Reese asked after several quiet moments.

"Right now? I don't know," Kellan replied and ran her fingers through Reese's hair, which was becoming one of Reese's favorite things. "I guess I'd be either wrapping up a shift or eating a late dinner."

"Alone?" she asked.

"You know the answer to that." Kellan's free hand met Reese's one on Reese's thigh.

"I know you're single, Kell. I meant your friends."

"Sometimes we go out. There's a bar we go to in the city. We go to After Dark once a month together."

"After Dark?" Reese lifted her head to look at her.

"The museum in the city has this thing every Thursday called After Dark. It's for adults only. My friends and I get tickets and go once a month. It's fun. There's usually dancing, drinking, and exhibits where we sometimes actually learn things. It's mainly a way to get together and unwind."

"And Keira goes too?"

"Keira is there most of the time," she replied.

"What was it about her that made you fall for her?" Reese asked as she continued to look up at Kellan.

"Where'd that come from?" Kellan pulled back slightly.

"I'm just curious. You came here to get over her."

"And I think we can safely say I've accomplished that," Kellan remarked with a smile. Reese watched Kellan move until Kellan was hovering over her on the couch. Reese wasn't sure how it had happened, but she was under Kellan now, and her hands were around Kellan's waist on her back. "I don't want to talk about Keira tonight, okay?"

"I'm sorry." She rubbed Kellan's back over her shirt.

"No, it's not that," Kellan began. "It's not that I can't talk about her because it hurts. It's that I don't want to talk about her because I'm here with you. Keira, I'm starting to believe, was meant to be my friend and nothing more. She and I made a mistake at attempting anything beyond that. I was so lonely that I took it for something it wasn't supposed to be." Reese watched the light blue of her kind eyes as flames flickered in them. "She's found Emma. I think they're supposed to be together. *I* found you."

"You did?" Reese gulped.

"You came out of nowhere," Kellan whispered as she leaned down and kissed Reese gently on the lips.

"So did you." Reese kissed her back. "Today was

amazing, Kellan. The island was amazing, and our date the other night was amazing, and today was–"

"Amazing?" Kellan smiled down at her and ran a hand up Reese's side, under her shirt. "It was."

"Can I still stay over tonight?" she asked.

"Yes." Kellan gulped.

Reese leaned up, kissed her chin and asked, "Yes?"

"Yes," Kellan replied.

Reese continued by kissing her jawbone. Her hands moved under Kellan's shirt but remained still on the woman's lower back while her lips moved to Kellan's neck. She kissed gently before allowing her tongue to flick at Kellan's earlobe, earning an unexpected gasp before her hands began moving higher under Kellan's shirt. When she arrived at the sports bra Kellan had on for their hike, she stopped, half-wishing there was a clasp there she could undo and also being glad there wasn't one because she wasn't sure she was ready to take things any further tonight. She didn't want to let Kellan down, though, and wasn't entirely sure why she was holding back.

Kellan had started kissing Reese's neck. Her hand had moved to Reese's abdomen where she ran her fingertips there lightly and then paused just below Reese's breast, as if asking for permission. Reese moved her lips to Kellan's, kissing her deeply, but Kellan's hand still didn't move. Kellan's tongue was hot as she moved her mouth away and dragged it over Reese's already heated skin. Reese's breath was rushed. Her chest was practically heaving as Kellan shifted slightly, likely to get more comfortable since she was supporting herself on one arm. Her thigh ended up between Reese's. Reese gasped loudly.

"Oh," she exclaimed.

Kellan quickly shifted back, removing her thigh. She pulled up and stared down at Reese with her hand still under Reese's shirt.

"I could use another shower after... today's activities. Can you give me ten minutes, and then we can put a movie on or something?"

"Kell, why are–" Reese lifted herself up and gripped Kellan's hips.

"Because neither of us is ready for that yet, Reese." She kissed Reese once more on the lips, stood, and grabbed their wine glasses. "Am I wrong?"

Reese stared at the woman in front of her for a moment and wondered how she'd gotten to know her so well in such a short time. Kellan could tell she wasn't ready to take things further, but Kellan also wasn't ready to take things further. She thought that this moment was a big deal for the two of them. They could give into the attraction they clearly had for one another, knowing it might be too soon for their new romance, or they could wait for the right time for both of them, knowing that it might not happen anytime soon and also understanding that Kellan was leaving Lake Tahoe soon. Her departure was quickly approaching. Reese gulped at the thought of not having this woman around. Kellan had entered her life and had changed it so completely and so effortlessly that Reese actually had hope that she could find someone and something real when, after Morgan, she'd never allowed herself that thought.

"Take your shower. I'll be here."

Kellan took the wine glasses to the kitchen, walked back into the living room, and kissed Reese simply on the lips before she ran her hand through Reese's hair again and stared down at her from her standing position. Reese merely looked up at her and tugged on Kellan's shirt for her to come back down and repeat her action. Kellan kissed her again with a smile and stood back up.

"What are your plans for tomorrow night?" she asked with her hand on Reese's neck.

"I'm going out to dinner with Remy and Ryan."

"Oh."

Reese stood, reached for her, and asked, "We'll make it a double date?" She smiled and placed her hands on

Kellan's cheeks. "Say yes, Kell." She nodded Kellan's head for her, causing Kellan to laugh.

"Yes." She pulled away from Reese's embrace. "I'll be right back."

"What you wore last night when I came here, do you wear that to sleep in every night?" Reese asked as Kellan made her way toward the bedroom door. "The white tank and those shorts?"

"Oh, sometimes," Kellan replied. "Sometimes, I sleep naked." She winked at Reese and backed into the bedroom with a laugh at what was likely a shocked expression on Reese's face.

Kellan showered and emerged with wet hair. Reese found herself enjoying the position of lying in Kellan's lap while Kellan played with her hair and ran her fingers along Reese's abdomen. They remained that way until the movie ended. Then, they moved to the bedroom. Reese slid under the blanket after Kellan and found herself instinctively moving into the woman's outstretched arm, placing her head on Kellan's chest. It felt so much better than the last time they'd done this when she'd been near freezing. Kellan had worn a black t-shirt and a pair of worn sweats to sleep in. Reese found herself trying not to laugh at how much Kellan had covered her body as opposed to last night when she hadn't been expecting Reese. Reese had borrowed another pair of soft pants and a t-shirt of Kellan's to sleep in and loved the fact that their clothes all smelled the same. It didn't take long for her to slide a hand under Kellan's shirt and rest it just above her hip. They said nothing to one another because they'd spoken so much throughout the day that words weren't necessary. Reese closed her eyes to listen to Kellan's breathing while she felt Kellan's heart beating beneath her.

CHAPTER 17

"KELLAN?"

"Hey, Keira," Kellan greeted as she sat outside on her blanket and stared up at the sun.

"How are you?" Keira asked as she was clearly surprised to be hearing from Kellan. "Are you back?"

"I'm still in Tahoe," she replied. "I'm staying a little longer than I planned."

"How much longer?"

"I don't know yet."

"So, you're not coming back anytime soon?"

"I don't know." Kellan closed her eyes tightly at the brightness. "I know you've called a couple of times. I'm sure Hill and Greene told you I talked to them. I didn't want you to think I was leaving you out."

"I did think that, but I understood. At least, I'm trying to understand."

"I'm sorry, Keira."

"Sorry for what?"

"For dumping all that on you and then leaving."

"You don't have to be sorry, Kell. I just want to know you're okay."

"I am. I think I am anyway."

"What happened? We were good. We were friends, and then–"

"I got it wrong, I think. I thought I was in love with you, Keira."

"You thought?"

"You and I met; we fell into bed. I thought I fell in love with you. But I don't know that that's what it was anymore."

"What do you think it was then?" Keira asked.

"I guess I was lonely. When I met you, I was really feeling it. A lot of the people I'd grown up with were coupling off. I was watching it happen at wedding after wedding. You were at one, and it was nice being with someone again. When I thought I'd lost you the first time to friendship, it hurt, but I thought we could work our way back. When we did, it felt good to be with you like that again. I guess I called you today to tell you that I understand now."

"You do?"

"I understand that you and I are better as friends. I think I needed time away to figure that out."

"I'm glad you went away, Kell. I do want us to be friends again. I hated that I hurt you like that, but I didn't know what else to do."

"I know." She sat up on the blanket to take in the full beauty of her surroundings. "How's Emma?"

"She's good," Keira replied. "We're good."

"Good." That was far too many *goods* for this brief conversation. "So, I met someone." She bit her bottom lip, and her hand moved to cover her mouth.

"You what? You met someone? Like a girl?"

"Yes, like a girl. Well, a woman. Her name is Reese."

"And you like this Reese?"

"I do."

"I'm glad, Kell."

"Me too." She smiled and ran her hand over the blanket.

"Emma just got here. We're heading out to lunch. Can I call you later?"

"Sure." Kellan considered for a moment. "Actually, I'll call you when I can. Is that okay?"

"Yeah, that's fine. Are you worried I'll interrupt you and your new lady friend?" Keira mocked.

"Goodbye, Keira."

"Yeah? I'm glad you called."

"Me too."

"And I'm glad you have someone you like."

"Me too."

Kellan had been dreading making that call. She'd wondered if hearing Keira's voice after so long would somehow retrigger her old feelings. Hearing Keira's voice, though, had only reassured her that those feelings she'd confused for love were gone. She stared out at the water again and wondered at its magic and its ability to help her heal. Then, she glanced down at her phone and shot a quick text over to Reese. Reese was at school and was probably busy working. But moments later, as Kellan stood and prepared to go back inside, her phone made a sound. She read the text that told her Reese missed her, too.

***

"It's nice to meet you, Kellan." Remy held out her hand to a very confused Kellan.

"Rem, you've met," Reese chastised her sister.

"Not as your sister and the woman dating you. We met as two people shopping for ice cream. It's different now."

"Yeah… no, it's not." Reese tugged on Kellan's arm and moved them both toward their table. "Sorry," she whispered into Kellan's ear once they'd sat down.

"For what?" Kellan smiled at her. "I can handle your sister, Reese."

"You can, can you? Good to know." Remy sat down at the table across from them and next to Ryan, who immediately grabbed for his menu.

"Sorry, I'm starving. I haven't eaten all day," he apologized and busied himself by looking over the menu.

"Kellan, I'm glad you could double with us tonight. Reese and I haven't had a double date in forever," Remy said.

"Am I ordering wine?" Ryan looked over at his girlfriend.

"Red, probably," Remy said.

Reese admired how the two of them fit together so well. Remy pointed to something on the wine list. Ryan wrapped his arm over the back of her chair as the waiter approached and took their drink order. Ryan added a couple of appetizers to the order. Reese noted that he'd ordered the spinach dip, which was Remy's favorite thing in the world. Remy smiled at him when he'd ordered it without her instruction.

"Kellan, how long are you staying?" Ryan asked as he placed the menu on the table.

"I don't know yet. I extended my rental through the next week."

"I thought you were considering staying for two," Reese said.

"I am. I just haven't firmed it up with the rental company."

"Oh." Reese looked away from her, but Kellan took her hand under the table, causing Reese to turn back to her. "Anyway."

"You could always stay with us," Remy offered. "If the rental is unavailable or something. We have a couch that folds out, or I'm sure Reese would volunteer her room."

"You can just take Remy's room, since I'm going to kill her later. She won't be needing it anymore." Reese glared at her twin.

Ryan and Kellan both laughed as the siblings stared on.

"I'll talk to them tomorrow. It's available. I just wasn't sure." Kellan said after their waters and wine had arrived. "But now I am." She gave Reese's hand a squeeze.

"You two are adorable," Remy teased and received another glance from Reese that was clearly telling her to knock it off. "What? It's your fault, Reese. You never bring any of your ladies around for me to get to know."

"God, Remy! We're leaving if you keep this up."

"Okay. Okay." Remy held out her hand defensively. "I'll stop." She laughed. "Sorry, Kellan."

"It's okay; I don't mind. I actually kind of like watching her squirm like this," she joked and turned to give Reese a smile. "Kidding," she added when Reese gave her a similar glare to the ones she'd been delivering to Remy.

"It's the Lee girls."

"Dr. Sanders, hello," Reese greeted. "It's nice to see you."

"You too," the old doctor replied and glanced at Remy. "How are you, dear?"

"Good." Remy nodded her head slightly in the direction of Kellan. "Dr. Sanders, this is Kellan Cobb. She's a friend of Reese's."

"Nice to meet you, Kellan."

"You too," she replied.

"So, Dr. Sanders is the premier veterinarian in South Lake Tahoe," Remy continued. "Kellan is also a vet; big coincidence." She glanced at Reese, who let go of Kellan's hand under the table and promptly kicked her sister's shin. "Ouch!"

"Remy did mention that to me earlier."

The old man had a nearly bald head, but the hair he did have was gray. He'd begun that hunch in his shoulders that most older people started to adopt unwillingly around his age. Reese had to guess he was closer to seventy than sixty these days. Their parents had known the doctor. He'd been invited to some holiday parties, so they were more than familiar with the man and his wife, Elizabeth, who was a few years younger and often volunteered at the visitor center with Reese when she was able.

"She did, did she?" Reese asked the man but stared at Remy.

"We ran into one another earlier today," Remy explained. "I was picking up my clothes from the dry cleaner, and I saw Edward there. He mentioned he comes here every week with Elizabeth. I knew we had plans to do dinner together, so I made reservations."

"And I've interrupted your meal," Dr. Sanders commented. "Elizabeth is waiting at our table for me anyway. I'll leave you kids to enjoy your dinner." He moved to walk away.

"Dr. Sanders?" It was Kellan's voice, and Reese turned to see that Kellan was leaning into her with her arm over her chair, looking in the doctor's direction. "Would it be possible for me to maybe check out your practice while I'm in town?" she asked. "I want to have my own practice one day. If it wouldn't be too much of an imposition, could I stop by and see how you run things? If not, I totally understand."

"Of course, dear," he answered with a smile. "I'd love to show you around. It's just me and my staff. I had a couple of other doctors with me up until last year, but they've both moved on."

"That's fine. I'd like to just see how it runs if that's okay, as a comparison to where I interned and where I am now."

"No problem. Remy has my number. Have her pass it along and call me on Monday. We'll set something up."

"Thank you. That's amazing."

"Of course." The doctor waved at the four of them and walked back toward his table.

"Well, that was pretty cool, huh?" Remy asked and gave Reese a wink.

"Yeah, cool," Reese replied but wanted to know

exactly what her sister was up to with her clear conspiracy.

***

"Well, that was fun," Kellan said as they drove away from the restaurant. "Remy is hilarious."

"Remy is annoying," Reese replied as she turned them onto the street. "I'm sorry. She gets a little excited sometimes."

"Stop apologizing. I really did have fun. I like your sister, and Ryan is nice." Kellan placed a hand on her thigh. "Hey, I don't know what we're going to do now, but Remy said they're staying at Ryan's place tonight. Do you want to go back to your place?" she asked.

"My place?" Reese repeated.

"Or not. You can just take me home. I'm sure you're tired. It's been a busy week."

"No, it's not that." Reese placed her hand on top of the one Kellan had pressed to her thigh. "I want to spend the night with you again, Kell. Let's just go to your place, though."

"Your place is closer, and it's a real house," she returned. "My cabin is bare essentials only."

"My place is a mess. Remy kind of spins around like a tornado and leaves stuff everywhere," she argued.

"I don't care." Kellan laughed lightly. "And it seemed fine when I was there for dinner."

"I cleaned up before you got there."

"Right…" Kellan lengthened the word and withdrew her hand. "My cabin it is then."

"Are you mad?" Reese looked over at her.

"No. I've just only been there once and thought we'd have the place to ourselves."

"I'm sorry," Reese apologized and took Kellan's hand. "Tomorrow night?"

"Yeah, sure," Kellan replied with disappointment bleeding out of her tone. "Actually, do you want to just call it a night? I am kind of tired, and I'm sure you are."

"You don't want me to stay over? It's like eight o'clock."

"I think the activities of the week are getting to me."

"Kellan, just tell me you're upset. Don't lie about being tired and not wanting me to stay over, okay? Say you're upset about me not wanting you to stay at my place tonight. Hell, yell at me if you want. But don't do the thing where you pretend you're okay when you're not and it starts a fight later on."

Kellan turned to Reese, and in that moment, she knew she was falling in love with Reese Lee. It was a very strange moment to have this realization, given that they were likely going to start an argument. Reese turned to her to gauge her reaction to her comment. Kellan had to hold back her smile because she knew it was an inappropriate response. She felt it though. She'd never had a woman call her out on this type of thing before. Most of her former flames had just gone along with her passive-aggressive tendencies. They'd let her fester until she eventually let it all out. They'd fight about whatever was causing the problem, but it always ended up snowballing into something even worse and never ended well. Reese was the first who'd just said it and made her want to stop acting like a child and tell her how she felt.

"You're right. I'm sorry," Kellan said after a long moment. "I thought tonight we could go back to your place since no one else would be there. Maybe we could talk about what comes next. Maybe that could be us being together."

"You wanted to have sex tonight?" Reese asked and removed her hand from Kellan's grasp to place it on her thigh. "I thought that was off the table for now." She ran her hand down her thigh.

"I didn't say that." Kellan leaned over toward her. "But I don't know. I had fun with you and Ryan and Remy tonight. I feel like we're spending a lot of time together.

I'm getting to know you and your family. I don't know. Tonight was just a good night."

"So, you don't want to have sex tonight?" Reese asked in a mocking tone and gave Kellan a wink.

"Oh, *wanting* is not the issue," Kellan assured and moved Reese's hand higher up her thigh. "I definitely want to have sex with you." She leaned over a little more so that her mouth was near Reese's ear. "I am looking forward to touching you, Reese. At dinner tonight, it took everything in me not to reach over and slide my hand up your thigh. You had to wear a skirt tonight? Really?"

That caused Reese to laugh. She pulled her hand off Kellan's thigh, moved it back to the steering wheel, and cleared her throat once her laughter died down.

"That's not funny. I'm driving. You can't talk to me like that. These roads can be dangerous." She let out a softer laugh. "But seriously, where did we land on the sex thing?"

It was Kellan's turn to burst into laughter.

CHAPTER 18

Reese WOKE UP Saturday morning to the sight of Kellan sprawled out in the bed next to her. The woman was occupying most of the bed, with one arm and leg over Reese and her other leg over the side of the bed. She was face down in the pillow while Reese was lying on her back. Reese laughed silently at the sight of Kellan's messy, dirty blonde hair, and realized immediately after that she needed a trip to the bathroom but didn't want to wake Kellan. She stared up at the ceiling of the cabin with its bare bones, an old ceiling fan that probably hadn't been dusted in years, and then looked around the sparsely furnished room.

She glanced at Kellan's sleeping form again and realized why the woman had wanted to go to her house so badly the night before. Reese lived in Tahoe. Her house was her home. For Kellan, this cabin was a hotel. She'd wanted to spend the night with Reese in her home. Reese hadn't been able to give that to her because she hadn't prepared her house for visitors. It had been stupid on her part. She should have gone through the normal routine, but Remy hadn't planned on staying at Ryan's that night initially. It was news to Reese at the restaurant that she'd made that decision. Reese had never brought a woman back to her house when her sister was there. She needed privacy, and having her twin sitting on the sofa while she was in her room doing explicit things to a woman wasn't something she enjoyed. She'd lost her chance last night because she'd been stupid. She'd been very, very stupid. She could have been with Kellan last night. They could have been in comfortable surroundings, alone, and with a roaring fire in the fireplace her grandfather had built himself. She could have touched Kellan and allowed Kellan to touch her. She could have woken up next to her naked this morning. They could have spent the entire day in bed together, repeating those activities and discovering more about their bodies and how they connected together.

"You're thinking hard," Kellan mumbled.

Reese watched Kellan's eyes open and close before opening again slowly. She smiled down at Kellan and ran her hand through Kellan's messy bed head.

"Good morning."

"Morning." Kellan stretched. "Something on your mind? If so, can it wait for coffee?" She held her hand out, palm up on the bed.

Reese laid flat and placed her hand on top of it, intertwining their fingers.

"Do you even have coffee in this place? We didn't have any yesterday."

"I don't," Kellan revealed. "But there's that café not too far from here. I can hop in the jeep and pick some up, or I can run to the market and get some to make here. I had some. I just ran out. I wasn't planning on staying this long."

"Well, now that you are, you should pick up enough to last a couple of weeks." Reese rolled to face her. "A couple of weeks, right?"

Kellan rolled to face her, too, and ran a hand through Reese's hair this time. She offered a smile before she leaned in and kissed her lightly.

"Yes, a couple of weeks," she replied. "I just need to run into the rental agency. Let me do that this morning so you don't have anything to worry about."

"I'm not worried," Reese replied.

"Please, you've brought it up like ten times since

yesterday, including four times at dinner and at least twice during the movie we watched. When we went down to the beach, you actually stopped making out with me to ask when I'd go to request the extension. Don't think I didn't take offense to that."

Reese rolled onto her back and stared up at the ceiling again. She let go of Kellan's hand and placed both of her own across her stomach.

"I'm sorry. I shouldn't keep bringing up the fact that you're leaving."

"Hey, I was kidding." Kellan slid over to her and placed an arm over her body. "I didn't mean to make you feel bad."

"You didn't. It's fine." Reese placed a hand on Kellan's cheek. "Let's just go to the market and rental place together. We can come back here after, eat breakfast, and then decide how we're going to spend our day."

"So, you're spending the whole day with me?" Kellan asked with a smile.

"If you'll have me."

"Oh, I'll have you," Kellan teased and leaned down to hover her lips just above Reese's. "Someday."

"Crap," Reese exclaimed just as Kellan was about to kiss her.

"Not the reaction I was hoping for." Kellan pulled back.

"I totally spaced it. I'm babysitting for Stacy today." She smacked her forehead. "She and her husband are going out of town tonight. I'm staying at their place. They're leaving around two and asked me to come by before that."

"Oh, that's okay." Kellan rolled over onto her back.

"I'd offer for you to babysit with me, but I don't know how they'd feel about that. They don't really know you, and that you and I are—"

"Not just friends?"

"I can ask. But I don't know that I'm comfortable

with you staying the night with them there. Their youngest still sometimes sleeps with them, and she might want to sleep with me tonight."

"I understand, Reese. It's okay."

"I might end up taking them to the park or something. You can join us for that."

"I'll let you do your babysitting. I've got some stuff I can do around here."

"Like what? You're on vacation." Reese giggled.

"I've got enough to keep myself occupied. I hadn't exactly planned on meeting people while I was here. I have a few trails I'd like to hit. I might kayak around the sunken forest."

"That sounds like fun." Reese smiled up at her.

"I'll try to take it easy though, since I have to play football tomorrow."

"If you need a day alone, Kell, you can tell me." She shifted until she was sitting up, causing Kellan to back up.

"I don't need a day alone," Kellan insisted. "Reese, I don't want time *away* from you. I want time *with* you. You have to babysit though. I understand that you have commitments. I'm on vacation, but you live here. This is your life. These are your friends. You can take care of them. I'll see you tomorrow at the beach."

"You sure?" she checked.

"Can we still have breakfast?"

"Of course."

"Then, I'm sure." Kellan smiled.

***

"Hey," Reese said once Kellan greeted her.

"Hey! I didn't think I'd hear from you tonight," Kellan replied.

"We didn't discuss doing the goodnight thing. I know," Reese said. "And it's only nine. I doubt you're going to sleep this early. I just wanted to ask you something before I had to put the kids to bed. What do you think about staying over tomorrow night?"

"You staying here?" Kellan asked.

"No, you stay with me, Kell," Reese replied. "At my place. Remy might be there. I don't know if she's planning to stay with Ryan or not, but I'd like you to stay over."

"Because you have time to clean up?" Kellan smiled as she climbed into her bed.

"I'll meet you at football. We can go to dinner, and you can spend the night."

"Sounds perfect."

"I have another question. Do you want to maybe take a boat out and have an early dinner while we watch the sunset?"

"It's like you're trying to woo me, Reese Lee." Kellan laid her head back on the pillow.

"I figured if I try really hard, I might be able to convince you to stay forever."

"Reese…"

Reese didn't say anything for a moment, and Kellan wondered if she should maybe say something instead.

"Babe, it was my turn to joke," Reese said, but her tone led Kellan to believe that it hadn't been a joke at all.

"Right."

"I'll see you tomorrow at football?"

"I'll be there," Kellan assured.

"Night."

"Good night," Kellan replied.

***

"She's coming over here?" Remy asked while Reese moved about the living room in a frenzy.

"Yes, tonight." Reese picked up a sweater. "Did you borrow my sweater?"

"What's the point of having a twin if I can't steal your clothes?"

"I'll just pick it up for you then." She tossed it into the hamper she'd brought out for this very purpose.

"She's staying the night, right? Do you want me to stay at Ryan's? I wasn't planning on it, since he has an early work day tomorrow."

"You don't have to," Reese replied and removed one of the stupid rubber bumpers off their square coffee table before tossing it onto the sofa.

"You don't want a night alone with your lady friend?" Remy sat on the sofa and picked up the object meant to protect toddlers.

"I don't know." Reese pulled the other three off the other corners and tossed them next to Remy. "I do, but I don't."

"Explain that to me."

"I want the house to myself, yes. I want her here, and I want us to–"

"Have mind-blowing sex?"

"God, Rem! Sometimes, you make it so hard to have an important conversation with you. You're the older one. Shouldn't you be more mature?"

"You're the one that always says I'm only four minutes older." Remy shrugged. "And should you be pulling these off now? You're still cleaning." She held up the rubber piece.

"It's fine." Reese tossed one sock into the hamper. "I want to be alone with her tonight because, yes – I want to sleep with her."

"I still can't believe you haven't yet. The way you two look at each other, it's clear you're crazy about her, and she feels the same way."

"That's why we haven't."

"I guess I get it." Remy placed the rubber barriers back on top of the table. "I waited a while with Ryan."

"I want to be with her, Remy." She flopped down next to her sister. "But not just tonight, and not just for the next week or two."

"That's great, Reese." Remy turned slightly toward her.

"How exactly? She lives like four hours away."

"It's not that far," Remy told her. "Other people have it way worse. Thomas has been dating his girlfriend for like nine months, and she lives in Orlando. They make it work."

"That's different," Reese argued.

"How?"

"Because they're so far away that it takes the pressure off."

"What?" Remy laid her head on the back of the sofa.

"We're only a drive apart once she goes home," Reese began. "Orlando and Tahoe are so far apart that they have to plan trips to see one another. It's expensive, and there's a time difference. With us, it's a drive, and it's not even a long one."

"That is a good thing, Reese."

"It is. Of course, it is," she agreed. "I want to see her as often as possible. I'm just worried that once she goes back, there will be this immediate pressure to visit one another. She has two jobs right now and works on the weekends sometimes. I have my volunteer shifts at the center."

"You two are very smart women. I'm sure you can figure out something that works."

"I guess. But what if it doesn't?" Reese laid her head back and turned it toward her twin.

"You really like this girl."

"I do."

"You see a future with her? Long-term?"

"I want to try," she said. "But I'm scared."

"Because this one matters?"

"Yes." Reese looked down. "She doesn't know about all this."

"No one does," Remy acknowledged. "Are you thinking about telling her?"

"I never told Morgan. Shouldn't I have told her if I planned on telling anyone? I just met Kellan."

"I don't think it matters how long you know someone, Reese. For whatever reason, you never felt comfortable telling Morgan. I don't get it, but it's always been your decision. I'd blame mom a little because I think she was trying to protect you but also didn't want people to treat you differently. Maybe you feel differently now that she's gone, or maybe it's just that Kellan is special. Maybe she's different."

"She'll treat me differently," Reese suggested.

"You don't know that. You never gave Morgan the chance either, as your friend or your girlfriend. Maybe you should give Kellan that chance."

"What if she runs away?"

"Why would she run away?"

"Because it's weird." Reese leaned forward.

"You are not weird, Reese. You're you. You're the best friend and the best sister in the world. You're a great girlfriend when you allow yourself to be. If that's what you and Kellan are to one another, or will be to one another, then you should tell her. Part of being in a relationship is taking care of the other person and looking out for them."

"I don't want her to go crazy, like you." She tossed the piece of rubber at Remy. "I don't know if I can stand her looking at me differently."

"Then, never tell anyone else. Never let someone in all the way, Reese. If that's what you want, do it. I'll live here with you forever. Ryan can just move in, and it'll be fine. It'll be fine," the woman repeated. "It just won't be everything, Reese. You deserve everything."

CHAPTER 19

INSTEAD OF TAKING a canoe ride on the lake after a football game that Reese played in for the first time in a long time, Reese had opted for them to walk the Baldwin Estate. It was part of the Tallac Historic Site. It was comprised of several 19th-century homes, gardens, servant quarters, a small museum, and often they had a blacksmith in action. The estate butted against the water. It was free to roam around and take in the exhibits and old homes. The gardens contained a small wooden bridge that went over a shallow pond with waterlilies and several different types of fish. There was a small gazebo and plenty of lush plants. Some had begun to hibernate for the season, but many of the plants still looked green and had lively-colored flowers. The autumn chill was beginning in full force now that it was late in the day. They walked hand in hand until the sun moved lower into the sky. Then, they made their way to the beach, where they sat a few feet away from the water without a blanket and watched the horizon carry it away.

"I could get used to this," Kellan said while staring at the beauty of the mountains, the water, and everything that made Lake Tahoe so magical to her.

"It's my favorite place," Reese said.

"Tahoe?" Kellan turned her head slightly to face her.

"This place." Reese pointed at the ground. "My parents used to take Remy and I here when we were kids. My mom worked at the visitor's center before me. That's one of the reasons I do it now. I'm trying to carry on her legacy, I guess. Anyway, most of the locals steer clear of this place, since it's a major tourist site. But we had field trips here every few years in school to learn about the history and preservation. Remy and I both hated the field trips, but we loved when mom and dad would bring us here." She inhaled. Her smile disappeared, and her lips turned straight with memories. "We'd come down here, and Reese and I would play in the water. We'd eat lunch by the garden. We'd hike around the area to find a place to camp. Even though we live minutes away from here, my dad loved camping. He'd make sure we went at least a few times each summer." She turned to Kellan. "I never told Morgan any of this. She's been here, obviously. She just doesn't know my history with the place or my love of it."

"Thank you for sharing it with me." Kellan placed her hand on the back of Reese's neck, drawing her forward to press their foreheads together.

"That's the thing, Kell. I want to share everything with you," she revealed. "But I don't want to share you."

Kellan drew back and gave her a quizzical expression. "Meaning?"

Reese moved until she was straddling Kellan's lap. She wrapped her arms around Kellan's neck once Kellan's were around her waist.

"I don't want you to date someone else when you're home," Reese said.

"Because you don't want to share me?" Kellan smirked at her and ran her hands over Reese's back on top of her jacket.

"That's right. It's early, and we have things to work out. We also still have a couple of weeks to talk about them, but I don't want to date anyone else."

"So, no more tourists for you? No more one-night deals or two weeks of not much more than sex?"

"Oh, I'll take two weeks of not much more than sex." Reese leaned in, hovering her lips an inch away from

Kellan's. "I just don't want that to be with anyone other than you."

"Tonight?" Kellan requested more than asked.

"Remy will be there." Reese pulled back to explain. "I might have asked her to stay on purpose."

Kellan pulled back entirely but left her hands on Reese's hips.

"You asked her to stay so we *wouldn't* have sex tonight?" Kellan lifted an eyebrow, demonstrating her confusion.

"I want to wait," Reese offered in explanation. "I know we're not kids. Neither of us is even close to being a virgin. But I've made mistakes in the past that I don't want to repeat with you. I know you don't want our first time to be in that less than comfortable cabin. I also know that if we're alone in the house tonight, it probably would have happened because we both want it to happen. When I kiss you, I want to kiss all of you; every part of you." She leaned back in. "But I'm nervous about what happens when you go home."

"You want to wait until after I leave?" Kellan pulled back again with that comment. "Is that what you're saying?"

"I don't know." Reese pulled back too but kept her hands on Kellan's shoulders. "I'm not explaining this right, am I?"

"Just tell me what you want, Reese. You don't have to put it into some nice, neat package. I don't want to rush this either. If you need to wait, we wait. It doesn't mean I'm going to go looking for something else or that I even want something else. I don't particularly want to share you either. And remember, I'm leaving you here with an ex-girlfriend you share decades of history with."

"You're going back to where Keira lives," she countered in jest.

"Keira is madly in love with Emma. Morgan is single."

"Morgan is my friend and won't ever be anything else again."

"But there will be more tourists, and you seem to have a fondness for them. Winter will be here soon. Those adorable little ski bunnies come with it."

"I think we should wait. I don't know if I mean that we should wait until you're back in San Francisco or if we should wait until your last night here, but as much as I want to be with you, I like the idea of waiting and making it count."

Kellan kissed her. It was slow, deliberate, and she did her best to convey that she wanted the same things. She wanted Reese to know that she wanted her, too. She was crazy about this woman. She ran her hands under Reese's jacket and under still, until she met skin and pressed her hands to Reese's abdomen. Reese's muscles tensed. Kellan stroked them gently while they kissed. Her lips moved from Reese's and made their way to her neck where she kissed her in the places she'd discovered Reese enjoyed most, earning a few gasps as she did. Kellan pulled back and met Reese's gorgeous gray eyes that had darkened, indicating her desire to go further.

She moved to roll, forcing Reese to roll with her. Then, Kellan was hovering over her and staring down at those eyes. Reese was smiling a shy smile. Kellan leaned down to kiss her once more. Her hand moved to Reese's cheek, then, to her neck, where she stilled it until she could lean down into Reese.

"If it feels this good to kiss you, I can only imagine how it will feel to touch you and to be touched by you. It's worth waiting for, Reese. You're worth waiting for."

***

"I'm crazy about her," Reese told her sister the following morning as they made coffee in their kitchen.

"I didn't hear any sounds coming from your room

last night. Should I assume she didn't enjoy it?" Remy spooned sugar into her empty mug while waiting for the coffee to disperse into it from their single-serve coffee maker.

"We're still waiting."

"She's still…" Remy motioned with her head toward Reese's room.

"Asleep. I thought I'd bring her coffee. If it's okay with you, I'll let her stay until she wants to go. I'll have her lock up when she leaves. I'm going to shower, change, and get to the school."

"She can stay forever if it means you're happy, finally." Remy stared at the coffee as it began to fill her cup. "Can I ask you something?" She left her cup to fill and turned to Reese, who was adding milk to an already full mug. "What if she just stops by and you haven't had time to prep for her arrival? Have you thought about that?"

"I have."

"You didn't use this stuff when you were with Morgan." She motioned around the house with her hands. "Mom and dad made you use this stuff when we were growing up. I took care of it in school. When I moved out, you got rid of everything. You only use it now because I put it up, and you're too lazy to take it down all the time. But, Reese, I will move out someday. Whether you stay in this house or buy another one, I'm hoping you'll have someone to share it with, who will make sure you're safe."

"Safe?" Reese asked. "I'm never technically safe, Remy. We can try to protect me from everything. I can live in a bubble, but the problem exists inside my body. The problem is that I don't realize–"

"Good morning." Kellan emerged from the bedroom.

"Hey, babe." Reese smiled immediately at her before giving Remy the glance that told her to shut down the conversation. "I was making you coffee."

Kellan approached and kissed her briefly before glancing over at Remy.

"Thank you," she replied. "Hey, Rem."

"Morning, football star." Remy grabbed her now full coffee cup. "You're up," she said to Reese and motioned to the coffee maker.

"I'm good. I need to get a move on anyway. I'll get some at school."

"You can share mine." Kellan placed an arm around her waist and rested her head on Reese's shoulder.

"Sickeningly adorable," Remy commented. "I'm going to get ready and head to work. See you two later." She headed out of the kitchen toward her bedroom.

"I woke up, and you weren't there," Kellan said from her position on Reese's shoulder.

"Sorry, I went to bring you coffee like a nice girl–" She stopped herself. "Person you spent the night with last night that you're currently dating. I have no idea what we are to one another," she blurted out all at once.

Kellan laughed as she lifted her head and turned Reese so that she was facing her.

"Call me whatever you want," she instructed. "Girlfriend, the woman you're dating, the person you like a lot; whatever works."

"Yeah? We don't need to have this big discussion about titles or how we introduce each other to people?"

"I'm with you, and you're with me. We're dating exclusively. I think, technically, that makes us girlfriends, but the title doesn't matter to me as long as we're both on the same page."

"So, you don't want to be my girlfriend? That's what I just heard." Reese winked playfully.

"Yes, I actually can't stand you and was hoping to make a clean exit this morning, but you were between me and the front door," Kellan jested.

"Liar." Reese leaned in and offered her a light kiss. "Drink your coffee. I have to get ready. You can stay as long as you want today. Just lock up when you go."

"I'll leave when you leave." Kellan pecked her lips again.

"You can hang out if you want. I know your cabin isn't exactly like home." She pulled back and slid the mug in Kellan's direction.

"I have plans today, remember?"

"You do?"

"I called Dr. Sanders after I woke up alone this morning. He said I could spend the day in his office."

"Really?"

"Yeah, he said he could actually use the help. I offered to take on some patients."

"You're going to see patients?"

"I am a licensed vet, Reese," she reminded.

"I know that. I just thought you'd hang out and watch or something." She headed toward the bedroom with Kellan on her heels.

"If he needs my help, I'm happy to offer. He told me he has someone coming in with a golden-mantled ground squirrel. I've never had a squirrel patient before, so I'll observe that. But he's got some cats and regular old dogs coming through that he said I can help with."

"You sound excited." Reese realized when she moved to her closet.

"I am. I miss it."

"The animals?" she asked as she pulled down a shirt to wear.

"Yes, but the work. I miss the work. This is the longest vacation I've ever taken. We didn't exactly have money growing up. I'm still in debt with my student loans." Reese emerged from the closet before she continued, "That's a conversation we'll have to have if we keep going, huh? My student loan debt. We'll save that until after the honeymoon period is over."

"Let's save all the hard stuff for when we're long distance and can't see one another for a while. Right now,

I wish I could lie around all day with you. I'm still in that text you every free minute phase to tell you I miss you."

"How about dinner tonight? Doctor Sanders offered to pay me for my services today. I said no. He said he'd buy me dinner, and I asked if you could come along. I can totally get you out of it if you aren't interested."

"I'm interested," she answered.

Reese genuinely liked the doctor and his wife. She also liked the idea of Kellan spending time with him, because if she liked the life here more and could see herself working in Tahoe, there was a chance she might consider moving here one day. Reese had been trying since they'd started dating, but she couldn't picture herself in San Francisco. She loved Tahoe. Her entire life was here. Her twin sister was here; all her friends were here; her students were here. Her mother and father's ashes had been spread here. She was still living in their home. Maybe if Kellan would consider moving outside of the city to somewhere a little more like Tahoe, she could be happy there. But the best solution was that Kellan liked Tahoe enough to one day consider making a move here.

"I'll call you when we're wrapping up and come by to pick you up. Are we staying here tonight or at the cabin?" Kellan asked and stood. "I just realized I assumed we're staying in the same place tonight. Should I assume that? Are we at that place where we spend every night together?"

"Considering you're leaving next Friday, I think we're at that point." Reese stood in front of her, holding the shirt she'd decided to wear. She shrugged at Kellan, who was staring up at her. "That came out wrong. Made it seem like you had no choice, huh?"

Kellan stood up and took the shirt from Reese's hand. She tossed it onto the bed and hugged her.

"The cabin isn't available after Friday, but I can stay until Sunday morning," she explained. "I can find a hotel for those two nights or another rental place."

"You said you needed to get back on Friday to have a couple days at home before going back to work." Reese pulled out of the hug but held onto Kellan's waist.

"I changed my mind. I want those two days with you." Kellan kissed her. "They're renovating the rental after me. How's that for my luck? I could've come a few weeks later and gotten a fully renovated cabin instead of this outdated one that kind of smells a little like mold now."

"Stay *here* Friday through Sunday. We'll have a couple of nights together before you have to go back." Reese pulled Kellan back in, close to herself. "I'll ask Remy to stay with Ryan. We'll have one weekend together and make sure we do all the stuff you want to do before you go."

"Reese, I'll be back," she reminded her as Reese pulled away. "And you should make a list of all the things you want to do in the city. We can tackle them one by one. Maybe when you have a school break, you can come over on a Thursday, and we can do After Dark with everyone."

"Sure. I should change." She picked up the shirt. "I'll be right back. Drink your coffee." She moved into the bathroom and closed the door behind her.

***

Kellan sat on the edge of Reese's bed for another minute while she listened to the shower run. She grabbed her bag and changed into the clothes she'd brought. She hadn't prepared to work in a vet's office on her vacation. She'd go in with jeans and apologize to the doctor for not dressing professionally. She took a sip from her coffee and realized she was standing right next to a closet full of clothing that would likely fit her. Reese was slightly shorter; Kellan wouldn't borrow pants. But she could borrow one of her button-downs and at least make herself look slightly more professional.

151

She went into the small closet and searched for something that would work for her and quickly found a nice, navy shirt. She pulled off the shirt she'd just put on, slid Reese's shirt over her shoulders and buttoned it. When she looked down, she noticed a box that was just open enough for her to see some strange objects inside. She didn't want to be nosy, but it had caught her attention. She bent down to see small, white-looking objects that appeared to be either plastic or rubber. Some of them looked like corner protectors she'd normally seen made out of cardboard to protect paintings; others were of different shapes and sizes. It was odd, she thought, but Reese was a preschool teacher. These were likely for the students' protection. She picked up her bag from the bedroom and sipped at her coffee before knocking on the bathroom door and opening it just slightly.

"Reese?"

"Yeah?" she said through the shower.

"I've got to go. I told the doctor I'd be in by the time they opened."

"Oh, okay. I'll see you tonight."

"I'll call you," Kellan replied.

"Okay. Bye?" Reese asked that more than stated it.

Kellan thought this was one of the strangest moments in any relationship she'd had. She'd never gone this long without sleeping with a woman, which meant she'd seen them naked by now and didn't need to hide behind a door when her date was in the shower. It was strange now to not be in there with Reese. She wanted to watch the water run down her skin. She wanted to lick it off Reese's neck and then kiss her after, until she had her against the back wall of the shower and her thigh was between Reese's legs.

"Bye," she said quickly.

She closed the door and shook her head back and forth to try to wipe the images out of her mind. They'd agreed to wait. She would need to muster some self-control to make it through. Just falling asleep next to Reese was hard. She'd wanted to reach under Reese's shirt and touch her breasts or slide her hand down between Reese's legs to see if she was wet. Last night, Reese was on top of her. As they kissed, Reese's hips moved at the same pace as her lips. Kellan had asked for a water break because she was about to come. That was not how she wanted to come the first time with Reese.

"Damn it," she muttered to herself. "Knock it off, Cobb." She walked out toward the living room.

"Hey, you heading out?" Remy asked just as she got to the front door.

"Yeah. Reese is still in the shower."

"You didn't join her?" She lifted an eyebrow and opened the door for Kellan to walk out.

"No, I didn't join her." Kellan chuckled as she walked outside.

"Hey, can I ask you something since I've got you alone?"

"That sounds ominous." Kellan tossed her bag into the car.

"Are you in love with my sister?" Remy asked while standing in front of Kellan.

"What?"

"Are you in love with my sister? It's a simple question," she repeated and emphasized.

"I think whether or not I feel a certain way about Reese should be shared with Reese first."

Remy squinted at her as she considered Kellan's answer. Kellan worried that if she didn't pass the twin test, she might not have any chance with Reese after all.

"Fair enough." Remy glared. "My sister is the most important thing in the world to me."

"I know."

"It's different for twins, though. It's not just a sibling thing."

"I understand. I mean, I don't, actually, because I'm

not a twin myself, but I get what you're saying." Kellan leaned against the side of the jeep.

"She's not perfect. She's got stuff she's still working through, but she's my most favorite person in the world, and she deserves the best."

"No one will ever be good enough," Kellan said.

"No, they won't," Remy agreed.

"I'll never meet your standard for your sister because that's impossible, just like I'm sure it's impossible for anyone to deserve you from her perspective. No offense to Ryan." Kellan shrugged.

"None taken on his behalf." Remy smiled at her. "And you're right. She needs someone who understands how special she is and makes her their number one priority. She's never had that before."

"What about Morgan?" Kellan stood up straight.

"Morgan and Reese were good together; don't get me wrong. They did love each other. I have nothing against Morgan. She's not the one for Reese though. When they were together, Morgan was in the process of taking over the family business. It was a lot of work. Reese can tell you about it if she wants. But from my side, Morgan seemed distracted a lot of the time. Reese was very understanding even when she'd forget dates or anniversaries. Like I said, she can tell you more if she thinks it's important. She's never had a girlfriend that was as dedicated to all the relationship things like she is. I think everyone deserves to have someone make them their number one priority at least once in their life."

"Me too," Kellan said softly.

"You okay there?" Remy asked.

"I think I just realized that I've never had that either."

"Yeah?" she double-checked, and Kellan only shook her head. "Maybe you can be that for one another."

CHAPTER 20

"DR. COBB WAS A GREAT help today,"
Edward Sanders stated as they all sat down to dinner at a
local pizza parlor. "I'm afraid I can't keep up these days."

"I didn't do much," Kellan replied as she placed an
arm over Reese's chair.

"You took care of three patients on your own and
assisted with several others."

"You did?" Reese asked her as she smiled at Kellan.

"Someone hit a deer this morning and brought it in,"
Kellan began. "It was my first deer patient."

"Broken legs, but she'll be fine," Edward told Reese.
"Dr. Cobb handled it perfectly."

"I've told you to call me Kellan."

"Fine. I'll call you Kellan out of the office," Edward
agreed.

"Thank you." Kellan laughed and turned back to
Reese. "I'm going to work at the office the rest of the
week."

"You're on vacation," she reminded her.

"I know. I had a good time today, and it's nice getting
back into things. Plus, Edward knows much more than I
do. His experience alone..." She paused. "Plus, he has
more experience with wildlife than I do."

Reese sat and listened to Edward and Kellan talk
about their day and the patients they saw along with the
interesting ones that would be coming in the next day. She

looked at Kellan, who was exchanging advice with Edward on how to handle something Reese didn't even pretend to understand. She marveled at how well Kellan fit into her life here.

Kellan had made friends with many of Reese's friends during football. Remy liked her and had given her the sibling pass. Kellan loved Tahoe. She seemed to thrive in the environment. Now, she was talking to the town veterinarian, who happened to be a family friend. She was smiling and laughing. Her hand had moved to Reese's thigh after they'd finished their pizza. She always leaned into Reese to welcome her into the conversation. With Kellan by her side, she'd already done so much. She'd done many things she'd worried she'd never be able to do again either for lack of courage or for physical limitations. She listened to Kellan laugh at something Dr. Sanders said, and she knew then that she was absolutely in love with Kellan Cobb.

***

"Hey." Reese ran a nervous hand through her hair as she approached Morgan. "Do you have a few minutes? Lunch maybe?" she asked.

"Did I know you were coming?" Morgan asked as she stocked ski poles.

"I just showed up. I have an hour. I was hoping you could take a break and we could talk." She stood with her hands in her pockets.

"I can take a break, but I can't do lunch. It's just dad and I here today." Morgan turned to her. "Let me grab my jacket."

She hadn't spoken to Morgan since Sunday before football. Even then, it had been in passing and with everyone around. Reese wanted to fix that and had been trying to find the right time and place to ask her to talk. She'd spent nearly every night with Kellan at either the cabin or her house. They'd had an amazing week together. Kellan had spent every day at Dr. Sanders' office and had enjoyed working alongside him. They'd spent time with Remy and Ryan. They'd even gone out for drinks with Stacy on Tuesday night. While the nights together had been wonderful, each one that passed with the sunrise meant they had one fewer together.

Now, she watched Morgan exit the office, zipping up her windbreaker and sliding her hands into her pockets. She was obviously guarded and seemed to be aware that this conversation she was about to have would be an important one. Reese stood in place until Morgan approached. Morgan nodded to the door without words. Reese held open the door, and they moved to the sidewalk.

"So, am I invited to the wedding?" Morgan asked once they'd walked a few steps in no particular direction.

"What?"

"You and Kellan?"

"Morgan, no," she replied.

"Then, what's this little conversation about?" She crossed her arms over her chest.

"We haven't talked in a while."

"You've been busy. I get it. I'm not mad or anything. If you think I'm upset, I'm not."

"What are you then?" Reese asked and crossed her own arms.

"Are you asking how I feel about you dating Kellan? You told me to back off. I backed off. I thought she was nice. And she's obviously gorgeous. I asked her out. She said no."

"And then you asked her again."

"That was me being petty. I *am* sorry about that."

"How are you other than the Kellan thing?"

"What's that mean?"

"Come on, Morgan. Don't be like this. Don't make me pull it out of you."

"What's wrong, Reese? You seem to think

something's up. I don't know that there is. You're dating Kellan. We're just friends. It's fine."

"I don't want fine with you, Mo. I want my best friend back."

"Your best friend is also your ex-girlfriend."

"I know. But we seemed okay until I started dating Kellan. I thought okay was enough; but I don't think it is."

"What if it's the best I can do?" Morgan asked. "We broke up, Reese. It was so unexpected and so out of nowhere to me that I sometimes still can't believe it happened. Sometimes, I look over at you and think I should be holding your hand or have my arm around you. I should be heading to your place for dinner or asking you if *we* have plans. We were together for three years. That stuff doesn't just disappear overnight."

"I know. It's one of the things I wanted to talk to you about."

"The end of our relationship?"

"I need to apologize to you. You were there for me during the whole thing. You were at the hospital. You held my hand. You were there for me when we spread the ashes. You've always been there for me."

"And that won't change no matter who you date, Reese. You know that, right?" She placed her hand on Reese's forearm stopping their progress.

"I know. I want to say some things to you that might explain what happened then, but they also might hurt you, which is why I haven't said them before. I wasn't going to, but I realized that being on the other side and not knowing might be worse than knowing and being hurt."

"Because Kellan had that thing with Keira?"

"Yes," she shared.

"So, are you giving me the choice? To know or not to know?"

They stepped aside to allow people to pass them on the sidewalk.

"I guess."

"How early on did you know?" Morgan asked. "That it wasn't going to work; that you wanted to end things."

"Morgan, I–"

"I want to know, Reese. I'm asking."

"I don't know when I knew it," Reese started. "I just remember feeling like it would end."

"We would end?" Morgan clarified.

"Yes." Reese leaned against the brick wall of a closed ice cream parlor behind her. "I always loved you. It wasn't that. I just started to see our relationship changing. I realized it wasn't what I wanted or needed. When I started picturing the future, you and I weren't lying in bed together or walking down the street hand in hand. It was different."

"We were friends."

"We'll always be friends, Mo. When we first started dating, things were hot and heavy. I was already in love with you. I was in love with you before we started dating. It was great for a while."

"And then it was just good." Morgan's lips went into a straight line. "I know I caused a lot of the problems."

"I wasn't exactly helpful. I kind of let you cause the problems and then kept how I felt about that inside."

"The store needed so much work to bring it to the modern era. My parents still used paper to keep the books."

"I remember. I don't blame you for needing to focus on them and the store."

"But you did for the dinners I missed and the things I forgot about because of it."

"It wasn't fun," Reese admitted. "Sitting at a restaurant, waiting for you for over an hour; and you didn't even text me."

"I got lost there for a while. I wanted to be with you. But there's this family obligation thing that comes with taking over the business; and it was happening at the same time."

"Morgan, you already apologized for this stuff. I'm not still upset about it. And it wasn't the sole reason things ended."

"You got sick." Morgan's lips formed a frown now. "It was horrible."

"And you never left my side. You were there when it counted, Mo." Reese slid her hand into Morgan's. "I will always be grateful to you for that. Remy had to handle so much, with me in the hospital and losing our parents at the same time. I know how much you did for her and for me. I will never forget it."

"But that doesn't make a relationship, does it? Just being grateful to someone for being there for you?"

"No, it doesn't. The timing was wrong. And for that I am sorry." She squeezed Morgan's hand. "But when I got out of the hospital, and we said goodbye to my parents, I guess I was a cliché. I saw how fast it all goes by."

"And you didn't see me at your side anymore?"

"I did, but not in that way. I saw us as friends. I could see these figures with us; they weren't fully formed people... I mean, I didn't know Kellan yet. I couldn't see *her* or anything, but I saw..." She faded when Morgan smirked at her. "What?"

"You hadn't met Kellan *yet*?"

"Yeah, so?"

"Reese, you basically just said you hadn't met the woman, but that you now see her as the woman that will stand beside you."

"That's not what I said," she countered and then thought about it. "Oh, I guess I did." She looked down at the ground. "Things are still new between us. I don't know what's going to happen."

"But you know what you *want* to happen."

"I just met her."

"Reese, are you in love with her?" Morgan asked. "Be honest."

"She makes me feel different, I think."

"She makes you happy, *I* think." Morgan paused. "That's a good thing."

"I know." Reese smiled. "Are we okay?" She pointed between them.

"We're good." The woman nodded. "We'll probably need to talk more. I think there's still stuff to be said, but I miss having you as my best friend in the way that it used to be between us two."

"We can work on it." Reese nodded, too.

"Let's hang out after Kellan leaves. I know she's only here for another week. I don't want to interfere with your time."

"I appreciate it. We'll be at football again on Sunday."

"Last one of the year. It's getting too cold." Morgan crossed her arms over her chest again. "Can we head back now? I've got to do payroll."

Reese slid her arm through Morgan's, and they walked back to the store, with Reese feeling much better about their chances of getting their friendship back.

CHAPTER 21

KⲉLLAN WRAPPED UP her Friday shift at the office and couldn't stop smiling. She had worked a full week while she was on vacation, but she had no regrets and had even offered to work the following week as well. Reese had to work, so they wouldn't be able to spend that time together anyway. They had a full day on Saturday where they'd hike some trails neither of them had tackled, and they'd play football on Sunday again. Tonight though, they'd have a relaxing night together. Reese had planned a fun Friday night for them. Kellan climbed into her car and drove straight to the market where she picked up several bottles of wine and snacks. After, she drove the short distance to Reese's house and unloaded. The front door was unlocked. She went right in to see Remy and Ryan in the kitchen, working on something on the stove.

"Hey, I got all the stuff," she told them and sat two paper bags on the counter. "Where's Reese?"

"In her room," Remy replied.

"Rem, that's too much cheese." Ryan pointed at whatever dip Remy was creating.

"There's no such thing." Remy kissed his cheek.

Kellan found herself quite at home in Remy and Reese's place. They'd developed this routine in the past week or so. Neither Remy nor Ryan seemed to have any issues with her spending more and more time there. She removed something from the bag and moved into the kitchen where she opened up a drawer and pulled out a spoon before she headed into Reese's room.

"Babe, I'm here," she greeted as she opened the door. "Oh!" She quickly turned her head away.

"Hey there," Reese returned the greeting and quickly threw on her tank top. "Kellan, you act like you've never seen me in my bra before." She laughed.

"That was different. You were freezing. You needed the body heat."

"Get in here!" Reese tugged on Kellan's hand and pulled her into the bedroom. "I just got home and wanted to change. Someone forgot to knock." She moved into Kellan's arms and placed her own around Kellan's neck. "This is getting ridiculous, isn't it?" She kissed Kellan on the lips.

"What?"

"This waiting thing. It's like we both put it out there and agreed to it. Now, neither of us will take anything further. We make out like two teenagers in the basement game room, but the moment one of us goes to grab a boob, we stop because my parents might come downstairs and find us." She laughed again.

"So, you want me to grab your boobs? That's what I took from that." Kellan backed her up until Reese's legs were against the end of the bed.

"Well, not right now. Everyone's about to come over." Reese laughed as Kellan shoved at her shoulders until she fell back against the mattress. "Kellan!" She laughed out as Kellan climbed on top of her.

"Tonight, all your friends are coming over. We've both had exhausting days. Tomorrow, we're camping. I'm not sure I want our first time to be in a tent. But maybe Sunday? What do you think?"

"Sunday? After football? I kind of told Morgan we'd help her out."

"With what exactly?" Kellan leaned down and placed

a kiss to Reese's neck.

"There's this woman she's seen at a bar. She hasn't actually talked to her yet, but she wants to try. I told her we'd go and be her wing women."

"Morgan wants you and I to help her get a date?"

"She'd settle for a conversation, but we thought it might be a good place for us to start. She wants to spend more time with you. I thought we could all go for a drink, maybe we help her meet the girl, and they fall madly in love. Now that you're suggesting we have sex on Sunday, I think I'll tell her no when she gets here."

Kellan chuckled against Reese's skin and pulled back up to look down at her.

"Don't do that. It's important that Morgan likes me."

"I'm pretty sure that was one of our original problems there, dear. Morgan does like you." She held Kellan's face in her hands.

"You know what I mean," Kellan argued. "I want to be friends with her. I want to be friends with all your friends."

"What about *your* friends?" Reese let go of Kellan's face.

"They already like me. We're friends," she teased and moved to slide off Reese.

"When can I meet them?"

"Your first visit to the city, if you want."

"We should talk about that," Reese said.

"Hey, are you guys naked?" Ryan asked from the other side of the door.

"No, Ryan." Reese stood up in front of Kellan and placed her hand over Kellan's stomach. "You look really good in professional, doctor's clothes." She kissed Kellan again.

"This is your shirt."

"And it looks good on you, but take it off. Game night rule number one is no professional attire."

"That's really a rule?"

"Remy said you have to get the games out," Ryan instructed as he opened the door slightly. "They're in your closet."

"I'll grab them," Reese offered and walked toward the closet.

"Want some help?" Kellan asked as she unbuttoned the shirt and walked behind her.

Reese turned around as she opened the closet door. Her eyes drifted down to the new view provided by the open shirt. Kellan's bra was black. It matched the shirt she'd borrowed. Reese gulped silently and turned back around.

"I've got it," she told her.

"Problem?" Kellan wrapped her arms around Reese's waist from behind.

"You're a cruel woman, Kellan Cobb," she replied.

***

"You are bankrupt!" Stacy laughed at her husband, who had gone bankrupt in their game of Monopoly that had been never-ending.

"Thank God," Reese announced and quickly reached for the piles of fake money to put the game away. "That took forever."

"Not a Monopoly fan?" Kellan asked from her seat on the floor next to Reese.

"She hates it," Ryan offered.

"Because she sucks at it," Remy added. "She's not ruthless enough."

"She's plenty ruthless," Morgan said. "I think she's just strategic with it. She knows Risk is later."

"So, reel them in with Monopoly so you can steal all their shit with Risk?" Kinsley, their friend who had spent the past several weeks away from Tahoe, suggested.

"I like it." Kellan ran her hand up and down Reese's back. "I've never played Risk."

"What?" Reese stopped stacking money and turned to her in surprise.

"Oh, shit just got real," Ryan stated and stood. "I'm getting another beer."

"She's Risk master." Remy took a drink from her own beer before handing the empty bottle to Ryan. "No one here has ever beaten her."

"Really?" Kellan said to Reese and then leaned in to whisper, "That's kind of hot."

"Remy and I started playing with our dad when we were young. It's how I met Kinsley, actually." She nodded in the woman's direction.

"Risk tournament when we were in college," Kinsley explained. "Yeah, we were nerds."

"Still are," Morgan argued and poked Kinsley in the arm.

"Shut up, Burns." Kinsley laughed at her.

"We're playing Risk now?" Kellan asked Reese.

"No, charades come first. Then, Risk," Remy explained as Ryan brought her another beer. "We haven't played couples charades in a while."

"Because we aren't all couples," Kinsley reminded.

"You and Morgan have known each other long enough. You can be a couple tonight."

"Fine. But Kinsley is clearly a top, and so am I. I don't see this coupling lasting past tonight," Morgan said, and Kinsley shoved her, nearly topping her over.

"Hey! I am not a top," she disagreed. "I have no problem being a pillow princess every now and then." She laughed as Morgan recovered.

Reese smiled over at Kellan, as Kellan watched on and laughed with her friends. Kellan's hand was on the small of her back under her shirt. The touch of the warm palm on her skin was enough to ignite that fire that having Kellan's arms around her earlier had created. Kellan's blue eyes met her gray ones, which only intensified that fire.

"Are you having fun?" Reese asked softly.

"I am having a lot of fun," Kellan confirmed and leaned in, offering a sweet kiss to her cheek.

They played several rounds of charades. Reese wondered if Kellan would get scared off by how competitive all her friends were. Morgan could not get Kinsley's interpretation of Ocean's 11. Stacy couldn't believe her husband had acted as Donald Trump so poorly. Remy and Ryan had done well and took the lead early on. Surprisingly, Reese and Kellan had held their own. Second place wasn't terrible for the pair that had known one another the least amount of time.

They took a break after that. Stacy called the sitter to check on the kids. Remy got more of her famous seven-layer dip. Morgan popped some popcorn, telling Kellan that she didn't play Risk with Reese anymore because she almost lost a tooth once. Reese explained that Morgan had nearly lost that tooth because she shoved Reese first and Reese shoved her back. Kellan laughed and sat on the floor on the other side of the coffee table while Reese set up the board.

"The object of the game is to conquer the world by controlling every territory on the board," Reese began. "You have to defend your lands while trying to take others."

"Sounds extreme. What if I just like my little slice of the world and don't want any more?" Kellan asked.

Morgan and Kinsley both cackled. Kellan couldn't help but laugh as well because Reese's face must have shown them all that *that* was not an option.

"That's not how the game works," Reese replied.

"Should I be nervous? Are you like a despot in training?" Kellan asked playfully.

"Yes!" Remy yelled and sat between Kellan and Reese. "She totally is."

"Back to the rules," Reese ordered with a slight smile.

She continued to explain, mainly to Kellan, how the game worked while the rest of the players situated themselves around the table. Those who were merely watching sat on the sofa and shared Morgan's popcorn.

"So, the goal of this is to lose all the territories, right?" Kellan jested with Remy silently laughing next to her.

"What? No!" Reese replied, causing everyone to laugh.

"Babe, you're hilarious," Kellan told her and placed a hand on her thigh.

"Um, no." Reese removed her hand. "We're at war." She met Kellan's eyes. Kellan couldn't help but smile at how serious Reese was taking this game. "I rolled the highest number. I choose an open territory and place one soldier there. Now, Kellan goes."

"I choose the ocean. I fight for Atlantis." She placed a player on the board in the middle of the water.

Everyone burst out laughing save Reese, who Kellan could tell was trying not to laugh but really wanted to let it out.

"You can't fight for Atlantis. That's not how the game works," she instructed.

"The rookie is so not getting laid tonight," Kinsley said from her position on the sofa.

"The rookie is likely sleeping outside tonight," Morgan added. "Like, outside on the porch swing. Because Reese isn't letting her in the house after this."

The game began. Kellan found the rules were simple enough, but that the game was ultimately about strategy. Early on, she attacked at every opportunity and dominated Stacy until she was out of the game. Dave was close behind. Then, it was Ryan and Remy left, along with Reese, who was dominating. She knew she had to do something if she was going to beat her. She leaned over to Remy when Reese was paying particular attention to her armies on the board. They shared a whisper. Remy leaned over to share the plan with Ryan. Reese took her turn. Kellan went next. She gained one of Remy's territories.

Then, Remy attacked Reese in Europe, causing her to lose several armies. Ryan repeated the attack on Reese. Reese, herself, looked confused for a moment before she glanced at each of them in turn and it dawned on her.

"Oh, I see how it is. I thought we had a no alliance rule in this house, but I guess I was wrong," she said.

Everyone laughed as Reese took her turn. The dice didn't roll as she wished. She ended up losing some troops. It appeared, the entire group was watching her and silently laughing as she began to fall behind. It didn't take long after that for Remy to lose. Ryan, despite his alliance with Kellan, took his leave, too. That left Reese, Kellan, and the board. Kellan had to admit to herself, and would likely tell Reese later, that she was unbelievably turned on.

Reese's game face was serious. With her jaw slightly clenched and her tongue emerging every so often to lick her lips, Kellan had to shift her body to try to get more comfortable due to the wetness growing between her clenched legs. She wasn't sure how much longer she'd be able to wait. She wanted Reese so badly it hurt sometimes. Reese ran a hand through her hair for the thousandth time that night. Each time she did it, Kellan wanted Reese hovering over her. She wanted to watch Reese do that from above while the woman rocked her hips into her and drove her fingers further into Kellan's body.

"Kell?"

"Huh?"

"It's your turn, babe," Reese said with a quizzical expression. "Or are you giving up?"

"Never," Kellan replied.

A few minutes later, there was a ridiculous number of yells and loud laughter in the small house as Kellan defeated Reese, the former Risk champion of South Lake Tahoe. Everyone was on their feet. Remy was bowing down to Kellan, who still sat next to Reese on the floor.

"Should she pack her things and go?" Stacy teased Reese. "I have a pull-out sofa if you need it, Kellan."

"You can crash in my guest room," Kinsley offered.

"Guys, she still has that rental cabin. Not that she's been there recently... Do you even remember what it looks like, Kellan?" Remy teased. "Or how to get back to it? You might need to sleep there."

Reese just kept staring at her, until finally, her smile emerged, and it extended wide across her face.

"I think I'm okay," Kellan replied.

"She's more than okay," Reese announced, leaned in and kissed her deeply.

It didn't take long for Kellan to end up on her back, with Reese on top of her. Reese's tongue was in Kellan's mouth. Kellan's hands were on Reese's back.

"Well, damn!" Dave remarked.

"Hey!" Stacy smacked him on the arm. "That's our cue."

"Is this weird for you?" Kellan heard Remy ask Morgan.

"It should be weirder for you," Morgan told her. "You're basically watching yourself make out with Kellan."

"Gross," Remy countered. "No offense, Kellan."

Kellan didn't reply. Reese had slowed their kiss, but their lips continued to find one another time and time again, until she apparently snapped out of it and pulled back, realizing they were lying on her living room floor, making out in front of everyone.

"Sorry." Reese sat up and straddled her.

"Why?" Kellan laughed as Reese climbed off and stood, holding out her hands for Kellan to use them to get up. "*I* didn't exactly mind."

"Neither did the guys." Remy pointed at Ryan and Dave.

"Hey, I didn't say a word," Ryan argued.

"And *we're* leaving." Dave grabbed Stacy's jacket and passed it to her. "That way, I can't get into any more trouble." He slid his own jacket over his shoulders. "See you guys on Sunday."

"Good night," Reese said, wrapping an arm around Kellan's waist.

"Night," Stacy replied.

"I think I'm going to call it a night too," Kinsley shared. "Morgan and I are headed up to North Lake tomorrow. We're getting an early start."

"We're going to check out some possible locations for another store," Morgan informed, sliding on her own coat. "My parents don't exactly know of my plan yet, but I'm hoping to expand to a second store instead of just the outposts. Full brick and mortar location, if we're lucky."

"That's great, Mo," Reese told her.

She pulled away from Kellan to give both Morgan and Kinsley a hug. They all waved as their four guests left the house, leaving the two couples alone in the living room.

"I vote we do the cleanup tomorrow," Remy suggested.

"I agree." Ryan raised his hand in support. "It's late."

"Or early," Kellan said, noting the hour. It was well past one in the morning. "And we have a long day tomorrow."

"Ah, camping. Sounds like no fun at all and a lot of hard work." Remy grabbed a few beer bottles and carried them to the kitchen. "Do you guys have everything?"

"We haven't fully packed yet, but we have what we need," Kellan stated.

"Reese?" Remy asked when she returned. Kellan noted that something was happening between them. "Are you good?"

"I'm good," Reese let out in annoyance.

"Are you bringing extra–"

"Remy, we know what we're doing," she insisted. "We're leaving early. We might not see you before we go. Have a good weekend." She grabbed Kellan's hand and rushed them into the bedroom.

"Is she still worried because of the whole accident

thing? You've gone hiking with me since, and you're putting yourself back out there," Kellan said the moment the door was closed.

"She's a protective older sister."

"By four minutes," Kellan reminded and sat on the bed while Reese moved into her closet.

"Damn it," Reese whisper-yelled, and Kellan moved to the closet.

"What happened?"

"I ran into this stupid box," she remarked and then stood to promptly kick the box with the same foot. "Damn it!"

"Hey, what's wrong? Are you hurt?" Kellan went to her and reached for her hips.

"I'm fine. Nothing's wrong. It's late, and I'm tired. I just want to go to bed."

Kellan took a few steps back and leaned against the doorframe of the closet with her arms across her chest.

"Are you sure?"

"Kell, can you go into the bedroom or something? I have to change."

"You didn't seem to have a problem earlier, with me watching you change."

"Kellan, please," she requested softly.

"Okay." Kellan left the closet, grabbed her bag to pull out her sleepwear, and went into the bathroom to change for the night.

CHAPTER 22

"KELL, CAN YOU grab the pole?" Reese asked as she pulled out all the parts to their tent and placed them in an orderly fashion in front of her.

"We don't have to stay out here, Reese. We can just go back to the house or to the cabin," Kellan replied but passed Reese one of the poles.

"Why do you say that?"

"Because you haven't seemed all that interested in anything we've done today." Kellan grabbed her water bottle and took a long drink.

They'd been hiking all day, finally arriving at their campsite only about half an hour ago. They'd gone slow because Kellan had insisted they take their time. This was the longest hike Reese had been on since her fall. And she hated that Kellan felt they needed to go slow. It was true that she'd been a bear most of the day. She didn't mean to take things out on Kellan. None of this was Kellan's fault. Remy's comments the previous night had pissed her off. She knew Remy was seconds away from slipping up and revealing her true concern for Reese going on this overnight trip. She'd said as much once it was planned and they'd had a few moments alone while Kellan was showering in Reese's shower. Reese had fought with her sister then as well.

"I'm sorry. I guess I'm in a bad mood." Reese began setting up the tent. "It's not about you."

"Really? Because it kind of seems like it is." Kellan set aside her water bottle and kneeled to help. "Did I do something?"

"No, Kell. You haven't done anything. Honestly, I probably should have just canceled today. I've been in a mood since last night."

"I know. I was there."

"Can we get this thing put up and get settled in first?" she asked. "Then, we can talk about it."

"I'm not sure what we're talking about, but okay. If that's what you want, it's fine." Kellan stood.

They worked silently for the next few minutes until they had their tent set up and had moved their things inside. It was already chilly, with the sun setting. They rolled out their sleeping bags, which would protect them from the elements tonight. While Reese continued to set up inside the tent, Kellan moved outside to get a small fire going. When Reese was done, she went outside to the bear container to unlock it. She removed what they'd need for dinner and locked it back up so bears wouldn't get to it. She handed the cooking gear to Kellan and opened the can of chili they'd brought while Kellan got the stove set up. They worked together again, in silence, to prepare their dinner. Once complete, they ate it in similar silence while listening to nature around them.

It had been an awkward day, at most, because of Reese's inability to shake her bad mood off. Kellan had been there to take it and deal with her as she'd walked for miles in silence and then complained about one of the trails being overgrown before she went on a ten-minute tirade about Remy not cleaning up the kitchen from her seven-layer dip. Kellan had listened and offered agreement when necessary. She'd swept brush back on the trail so Reese wouldn't have to deal with it, and she'd allowed Reese the space she needed to deal with whatever was going on with her.

After finishing their dinner, using the facilities, and

locking up everything back in the container, Kellan had put out the fire. They both climbed into their sleeping bags. It was early. Reese knew Kellan had planned this day and night for them to be special. She'd managed to ruin it. She also knew Kellan was waiting for her to talk to her about something. But Reese wasn't ready to talk. She was more than exhausted from the day and the fact that she'd gotten only a couple of hours of sleep the night before. She wasn't sure she was up to an important chat with Kellan.

"Hey, I'm pretty tired. Is it okay if we turn in early?" she asked.

"Oh. Yeah, okay," Kellan replied.

Reese sat up and pulled off the long-sleeved shirt she'd had on, leaving her in her tank top and sports bra.

"Thanks," she returned.

"Reese, when did you get that?" Kellan slid closer to her and put her hand on her upper forearm.

"When did I get what?"

"That gash." Kellan reached for the lantern they'd brought. She pulled it closer to Reese's upper arm and held it close. "You have a cut here."

"I guess I didn't notice."

"Reese, it's been bleeding." Kellan placed the lantern down and reached for the shirt Reese had taken off. "There's blood on this. You didn't feel it?"

"Must be the cold or something, but no."

"Babe, stay here. I'll be right back." Kellan slid out of her sleeping bag, unzipped the tent, and was gone for several minutes.

"It's not that big of a deal, Kell. It's already starting to dry up," Reese said when Kellan reappeared with a small first aid kit.

"It still needs to be disinfected." Kellan knelt in front of her and began the process of cleaning the two-inch-long cut carefully and gently before she applied an antiseptic gel and covered it with a bandage. "I'll change this in the morning. It's starting to close. I don't think you'll need stitches. So, that's good news."

"It's fine," Reese told her as Kellan finished packing up the trash and the kit.

"I'll be right back."

She left again and returned moments later sans the kit and the trash.

"You ready for bed?" Reese asked the moment Kellan had zipped up the sleeping bag.

"Was today too much?" Kellan asked as she peeled off her own layers and left herself in a tank top. "Did I make you do something you weren't ready for?"

"Kellan, I told you. You haven't done anything."

"But you're not going to tell me what's wrong with you?" She slid into her sleeping bag. "I was kind of hoping we'd share one of these tonight, but I take it you'll be using your own." She pointed to Reese's sleeping bag.

"I'll be fine tomorrow. I'm just having an off day. I need some sleep more than anything."

"Okay. Get some sleep. I don't know that I can just yet, so I'll put in my headphones and listen to music or something." She reached inside her bag and pulled out her phone.

Reese watched as she unfurled her headphones and put them in her ears before lying back to zip her sleeping bag up to her shoulders. Reese made herself comfortable in her own bag. Then, she stared up at the tent ceiling. Kellan dimmed the lantern but left enough light for them to see by. Reese watched the light flicker around them. Of all the things she could be thinking about, she found her mind going back to that damn box in her closet.

It was true that Remy's comment had upset her, but it was running into that box that really put her over the edge. Actually, that wasn't right. It was the phone call from her doctor on Friday after her talk with Morgan that had started her mood. She'd been able to hold it back for most of the day and during the game night. Remy's comment had brought it back to the forefront of her thoughts. Seeing that box in her closet only made it worse.

She turned her head to the side to see Kellan staring at the same flickering light while listening to headphones. Based on the tension in her jaw and the straight line of her lips, Reese knew she'd dug herself a massive hole she needed to find a way out of. She turned on her side to face Kellan, which caused Kellan to turn her head.

"Reese, don't lie on your shoulder like that. You'll open up the cut," she instructed and removed her headphones.

"Oh, right." Reese closed her eyes for a moment before opening them again. "Can we talk?"

"I thought you wanted to sleep." Kellan stopped the music and put her phone aside.

"I want to explain something to you. It's something I've never told anyone," Reese replied.

"Okay." Kellan rolled on her side to face her. "Can I ask what made you change your mind? A few minutes ago, you didn't want to tell me anything."

"Actually, I want to tell you everything. That's what scares me."

"What do you mean?"

"Remy is the only person in the world that knows everything about me, and that's because she's my sister," she began. "My parents knew, but they're not around anymore. I've never told any of my friends. I've never told any girlfriend either."

"Morgan?"

"No," Reese answered. "That's why I'm scared. I've known Morgan most of my life. We were together for three years." She hesitated. "There were moments I thought about telling her out of necessity, but that's not how I wanted to tell her. There were moments where I really wanted her to know because I thought it might help her understand a whole other part of me. But I'd think about how it might make things change between us or that

177

she might treat me differently, and I wouldn't say anything."

"Reese, you're kind of scaring me here." Kellan did look worried, and Reese placed a hand on her cheek. "You're freezing. Put your hands inside your sleeping bag, babe," Kellan insisted after placing her own hand on top of Reese's.

"That's what I need to talk to you about, Kell." She removed her hand and did as Kellan asked. "But first, I want you to know *why* I'm telling you *before* I tell you."

"If you're trying to make me less worried, you're not."

"I know. I'm sorry," she replied. "I don't exactly know how to do this because I've never done this before."

"Reese, are you sick?" Kellan's eyes welled up with tears. "Do you have something–" She stopped herself. "Is that why you wanted to wait?"

"Oh, Kellan, no," Reese answered a little louder than she'd planned. "I don't have anything like that."

"But you do have something?"

"I want you to know, Kellan. I want you to know because I want us to be together. I can see it. I can see you and me going on trips like this when we're forty or fifty. I can see us waking up together and me making you coffee, you coming home from work, and us talking about our days. I've never had that before. You're the first person I've been able to see it with. That's scary because you leave in a week. We still have to figure out what we'll do after that. It's extra scary because if you're that person for me, Kellan, you need to know." Reese hesitated. "And before you say anything to me – whether it be that I'm that person for you, or that you don't know what we are to one another, or you still need time to see if I can be that person – I want you to know because I'm in love with you." She let out a deep breath. "I'm in love with you, and I want you to know every part of me."

"Reese–"

"I have congenital analgesia, Kellan," she interrupted Kellan before she could say anything else.

She didn't want Kellan to tell her she wasn't in love with her yet, but that she cared about her, liked her a lot, or one of those other cliché phrases people used when they were trying to make someone feel better about not being on the same page when it came to those three words. She loved Kellan Cobb. If Kellan wasn't there yet, that was okay, but Reese needed to let her know what she'd be signing up for if this relationship got to the point where they were both saying those words to one another and taking the rest of those all-important relationship steps.

"I don't know what that is," Kellan stated in a concerned tone with matching expression.

"It means I don't feel pain," Reese explained. "It's also called congenital insensitivity to pain. It means I don't have the ability to perceive physical pain. I can feel the difference between hot and cold or sharp versus dull, but I can't tell when I'm freezing."

"Like that night," Kellan realized. "And your shoulder tonight."

"Yes. It can cause a lot of problems because when I get hurt, I don't feel it. I don't take the steps needed to heal properly. Like with my fall on that hike; I didn't know my ankle was that bad. I ran into a desk at school around the time you got here, actually, and I didn't feel it. Remy was the one that noticed the bruise when it had formed and made me go to the doctor."

"Are you okay?"

"It was just a bruise, but it could have been worse. Wounds, bruises, broken bones, and other things have gone undetected before. I ended up in the hospital a few times because I didn't know there was something wrong and it got worse." She paused. "Remy doesn't have it. It's just me. When my parents were around, they'd call me every day just to make sure I was okay. My mom would make me do a body check." She laughed. "I'd have to stand in front of a mirror, growing up, before I got into the shower, just to make sure I hadn't done something to myself. Remy puts these little rubber bumper things they make for kids on all the sharp, pointy things in the house. If she could, she'd have me in a bubble."

"I saw that box in your closet. Why are they all in there if they should be around the house?"

"Because I remove them whenever we expect company," Reese answered. "I haven't always had them around. When I lived there by myself, I didn't. Remy has used them since she moved back in. I mostly tolerate them."

"But they're there to make you safe?" Kellan asked.

"They are, yes. But they're also really hard to explain to people since there are currently no toddlers living at our house. None of our friends know, Kell; only a few doctors, Remy, and myself. My parents never told my teachers because they didn't want them to treat me differently. They were doing enough of that themselves at home. They told them I was accident prone and they should keep an eye on me. It didn't hurt that I actually *was* accident prone as a kid because I loved sports and the outdoors."

"What does it mean for you? Beyond that you have to be careful and check to see if you have injuries?"

"It *can* mean a shorter life expectancy, but that's nothing I worry about."

"Wait. What?" Kellan sat up, and her bag unzipped itself as she did.

"Kell, it's okay. I'm fine. It's because people don't know there's something wrong, so it's more likely things get serious instead of healing."

"Like with your ankle?"

"That was my fault. I should have known better. I was being stubborn." She sat up and faced Kellan, allowing her own sleeping bag to unzip and fall to her waist. "I sometimes fight with the thing."

"Thing?"

"I hate calling it a disease because it's not. It's a condition, but that sounds weird. I'm fine, and I feel fine. So, sometimes, when I do hurt myself, I get angry and try to fight it, which is stupid, and I shouldn't do it. I've stopped, by the way. The infection was the incident that made me realize how dumb I was being." She paused. "I lost my parents because of it."

"Reese, I'm sorry." Kellan ran her hand up Reese's arm and covered the gash with it. "So, you don't feel this at all?"

"No."

"And when you were so cold on the island, you didn't feel it either?"

"I felt cold, but I didn't know I was *that* cold. It's kind of hard to explain. Right now, I feel the cold, but I also know it's supposed to be cold because we're outside at night in the mountains, and it's autumn. I use things like that to help."

"Like cues?"

"Yes. Once, Remy and I were working in the backyard with mom, pruning her rose bushes. Earlier that day, Remy had cut herself on a thorn. I knew it was likely it would happen to me too. I kept checking my hands. I ended up with several cuts. My mom never let me help again. One winter, the heat went out in the house. It was the middle of the night, and everyone was asleep. I woke up in the middle of the night to get some water. I knew it was cold, but not that it was freezing. Remy and I shared a room back then. When I went back to bed, she was completely covered from head to toe with her comforter. Remy usually slept with the blanket half off the bed, so it was weird. I don't know if I was ever in danger of freezing that night, but when I slid back into bed, I did the same thing Remy did just in case."

"And when you hike, you have to pay extra attention." Kellan lowered her hand from Reese's arm.

181

"Yes," she said. "Kellan, I swear, I am careful, and it doesn't interfere with my life too often. I visit my regular doctor every month, and I do pay attention to my body. I check it before or after the shower and make sure I didn't miss anything. Remy is there to help, too. Technically, Ryan kind of knows, but I've never told him officially. Remy just told him I'm terribly klutzy. Honestly, he might just think it's a weird joke between twins; I don't know."

"Why didn't you ever tell Morgan?"

"When Morgan and I were friends, I had my parents and Remy keeping tabs on me all the time. I hadn't told any of my friends. It didn't seem like a big deal. When we started dating, I was rebelling against it. I'd gotten so tired of everyone always asking me how I was or my mom staring at me when we'd be watching a movie just to make sure I didn't have a cut or a bruise I didn't know about. My mom never let me cook, growing up, because she was afraid I'd put my hand on a burner and wouldn't notice. Remy doesn't like me to cook too often either for the same reason. I've only burned myself twice, by the way, which is good for someone my age who has what I have."

"And there's no treatment?"

"There are some experimental things that won't cure it but can make it easier to sense pain. That's why I was talking to that specialist the other day. Remy and my regular doctor set it up. There's this drug called Naloxone that they've done some trials with. It works for some people. Remy wants me to try it, and the specialist said I might be a good fit, but there are tests to run first. There's this hand-held injector thing that can be used outside a hospital. I'd inject myself with it in regular intervals for however long, and they'd check to see if there was any progress. Oh, and if I don't want to inject myself repeatedly, I can always shoot the stuff up my nose with a nasal spray every few hours. Remy wants me to try it. I'm convinced it's because she wants to move out of the house and in with Ryan, but she feels guilty about leaving me there alone. She talks a big game about loving him but not wanting certain things. I think she's lying though. The specialist wants another guinea pig, and my own doctor sees this as an opportunity to learn more about the condition, I think. It's rare. It's a chance for them all to test their theories."

"You?" Kellan placed her hand on top of Reese's.

Reese wondered for a second if Kellan was attempting to gauge how cold she was, given the topic of their conversation and their location, but then Kellan's eyes softened. Reese realized she was touching her because she wanted to be touching her.

"What about me?"

"What do *you* want, Reese? Do you want to participate in some trial?" she asked and linked their fingers. "Or do you want to keep doing what you're doing now? Being careful, being smart, and having people who care about you check in every so often?" She smiled shyly.

"Care about me?"

Reese didn't regret telling Kellan how she felt, but she gulped in preparation of Kellan's response to her many revelations tonight. It was possible Kellan had strong feelings for her but didn't want to take on a complicated situation like Reese's.

"I'm in love with you, Reese." Kellan's smile widened. "When I first came to Tahoe, it was to heal from a broken heart. I never thought I'd find anyone again because that's what you always think when a relationship ends. But I've found this amazing community here, and you're a part of it. I love that I can share my fondness for the outdoors with you, that you make me laugh and you challenge me. I love how it feels to hold you. I love how you've let me in just now and told me something no one else knows. I don't know why you've kept it a secret, but that's your choice. I support that in the same way I'd support your choice to join some trial or not." She unzipped her sleeping bag the rest of the way so she could kneel in front of Reese and place her hands on her cheeks. "I want you, Reese. I want us. I love you." She let out a deep exhale, and Reese wondered how long she'd been holding those words in.

"I love you, too." She smiled into Kellan's kiss, which had been unexpected, but more than welcomed.

Kellan's lips were insistent. Her tongue dove immediately into Reese's mouth. Reese accepted it and allowed their tongues to mingle. She'd thought that if she ever told Kellan about her condition, Kellan would treat her differently or more carefully, but she'd been wrong. Kellan's hands were around her neck. She was pulling Reese closer. Then, her lips were on Reese's neck. Reese moved to lie back, bringing Kellan with her. Kellan paused their kiss to stare down at her, and the desire in her eyes was more than evident.

"You do feel pleasure though, right?" she asked.

"Yes, Kellan." Reese smiled up at her. "Every time you kiss me," she added. "I want you." She gulped.

"Yeah?" Kellan's her eyes flitted to Reese's lips before meeting her eyes again.

"If you're not ready, we can wait," Reese offered to Kellan's seemingly vulnerable stare.

Kellan didn't respond with words. She shifted her weight to hover over Reese. Their lips met again, and within moments, Reese knew this was not going to be one of those slow, romantic nights of making love where R & B music played in the background and candles were the only light in the room. There were no rose petals in their tent tonight. Kellan's skin was soft, but her hand was firm as it slid under Reese's shirt and grasped her breast over her less than sexy sports bra. Their kiss grew even more heated after Reese moaned at the touch.

Reese's hands moved to Kellan's hem and lifted her tank top to her shoulders before Kellan disconnected their lips so that Reese could remove it. Kellan lifted herself up, straddling Reese. She didn't wait to begin rocking her hips into the woman beneath her. Reese's hands were on Kellan's hips, encouraging her to continue, while Kellan shoved at the fabric of their sleeping bags to push everything out of the way. Reese wanted everything out of the way, too. She'd gone without being with someone for too long. Kellan's movements were creating perfect friction, but it wasn't enough. Kellan, apparently, felt the same way because she reached for her own sports bra and pulled it over her head, tossing it into the side of the tent and causing it to shake slightly.

Reese sat up and immediately found Kellan's right nipple with her mouth. It was hard and ready for her. She sucked on it just as hard while one hand held Kellan's waist in place as she continued to rock and her other hand twisted Kellan's nipple lightly. A delighted gasp escaped Kellan's mouth while both of her hands went to the back of Reese's head, pushing the woman into her breast even further. Reese twisted harder as she bit lightly. Kellan gasped louder. Reese moved her lips to the other nipple and repeated her actions. Kellan's hips hadn't stopped, causing Reese to wonder if she was close to coming without Reese even touching her.

Kellan reached behind her and tried to tug at Reese's sports bra. Reese resisted the urge to laugh and reached for it herself, pulling it over her head and returning her attention to Kellan's firm and perfect breasts. She'd watched them bounce while they'd played football. She'd felt them pressed against her. She never imagined they'd be this perfect and fit in her hands and, more importantly, her mouth this well.

Kellan let her play for a few more moments before she slammed Reese to the ground. Reese laughed until Kellan covered her mouth with her own and their breasts pressed together for the first time. Kellan bit lightly at her lower lip before sliding her lips to Reese's neck, which she worshipped for what felt like forever, before she moved them down to her collarbone. Kellan's lips moved to her breast, but she hovered there for a moment. Reese's eyes opened. She watched Kellan looking up at her, with Kellan's lips a mere inch from her erect nipple. She lifted her body up to meet those lips. Kellan smiled around the nipple before she sucked it into her mouth.

Kellan moaned as Reese moaned. Reese hoped one of Kellan's hands would end up on her other breast because it craved the touch, but she was disappointed as Kellan's hand made its way to her hip instead. The disappointment only lasted a moment because Kellan's hand slid inside the sweatpants she'd donned earlier and covered her center over the boxer briefs she usually wore when camping.

"Oh." Kellan lifted up enough to say. Reese knew she was commenting on the wetness that had pooled between her legs. "For me?" Kellan asked.

The expression on her face at the realization would have been adorable in any other moment but was now just sexy as hell.

"Yes," Reese answered.

Kellan's hand slid up to the waistband of Reese's underwear and then back down inside them to feel her fully. Reese's hips lifted on their own to welcome the touch. Kellan kept her hand still for a moment while she continued to meet Reese's eyes with her own. A second later, she slid her fingers into the wetness, coated them, and thrust them inside her.

Kellan's fingers were inside her. She was thrusting her hips along with them. Reese was holding onto Kellan's shoulders, sliding her hands down her back and resting them there. She pressed hard with her palms to encourage Kellan to go deeper. Kellan did. Reese's hands slid inside her pants to feel Kellan's ass. Kellan had decided to go without underwear tonight, apparently, and Reese was clenching her cheeks to get her to go faster.

"Yeah?" Kellan huffed out before she latched her lips around Reese's nipple.

"Yes," Reese encouraged.

Kellan thrust harder and faster. Reese's hips were moving in time with Kellan's. Kellan's mouth moved to Reese's, and their kiss was sloppy and hard. Reese's hand slid around Kellan and found her hard and wet. Kellan nearly growled as Reese squeezed her clit between two fingers before she started sliding them up and down over it. She wanted Kellan to come with her. But she was already so close, she wasn't sure Kellan would be able to catch up. Then, the woman moved her lips to her neck before sucking Reese's earlobe into her mouth. She let out several small sounds before she released Reese's ear and her hips more twitched than rocked into Reese's hand. The fingers inside Reese continued to thrust. Reese nearly gushed as she came.

"Oh, my God," Kellan whispered into Reese's ear as she came on Reese's hand.

Reese's fingers continued to slide around while they both rode out their orgasms. Kellan collapsed on top of her, leaving her fingers still inside Reese, with Reese's hand still covering her wet center. Their breathing was fast and heavy. Neither of them said anything while they both attempted to come down.

CHAPTER 23

KELLAN REALIZED Reese was tight around her fingers and smiled. She wanted to keep them there forever. She wanted to always be inside this woman; to feel her skin warm and slick with sweat pressed against her own. She slid off Reese without removing her fingers and laid at her side. She stared down at Reese and watched her breathing begin to return to normal before she regretfully slid out of her, earning another of her now favorite gasps. Reese's eyes opened and stared into Kellan's.

Kellan slid her fingers through Reese's wetness and slowly dragged them around her clit. Reese was swollen and in need of release. Kellan's gaze went to her own arm as she watched it slide up and down under Reese's clothing. There was something so sexy about touching Reese like this without actually being able to see what she was doing. Reese's arms went around Kellan's neck, and she tried to pull her down, but Kellan resisted. She stared into Reese's eyes until Reese understood.

"Keep them open," Kellan requested.

Reese gave a small nod. Kellan placed Reese's thigh between her own legs. She rocked into her while her fingers met the rhythm. She watched as Reese's mouth opened and hung in that position while Kellan stroked her slowly.

"Kell–" Reese tried, but didn't follow it with anything.

Kellan stoked her harder and faster while her hips met the pace. She could feel her own body begin to climb again, which surprised her because the orgasm she'd only just come down from had been one of the best she'd ever experienced. It had torn through her entire body in the most intense and wonderful way. Reese coming with her had only made it even stronger. Kellan wanted her to come again, and she didn't want to wait any longer. She wanted to hear her. She wanted to feel her come against her hand. Reese's eyes were still open, but Kellan could tell she was struggling to keep them that way as she grew closer to climax. Kellan watched as they closed for a few seconds and opened again wide. Reese's hips twitched. Her hands tightened around Kellan's neck.

"You're so gorgeous," Kellan gasped out.

"Yes! Kell, there!" Reese's eyes closed.

They opened again. Kellan dove into their depths as Reese came beneath her. The gray of Reese's eyes darkened as she climaxed. Kellan was sure her own bright blues were a darker shade as well. Her own hips were still moving, but they'd slowed with Reese's release. And while Kellan's body wanted to come, it seemed less important now.

"I love you," she said to those eyes.

"I love you too," Reese replied and finally raised her head so their lips could meet.

**

Kellan's body was pleasantly tingling down to the tips of her toes as she rolled onto her side. She couldn't help the smile that appeared on her face. She knew it looked ridiculous to be smiling that widely after sex, but she couldn't stop it.

"That's why you didn't invite me in that morning when I dropped you off, isn't it? You were worried I'd see those things," Kellan asked.

"Yes." Reese laughed. "I didn't exactly expect us to get trapped on an island and require an escort home the next morning."

"I thought about that the whole day." Kellan laughed softly and rolled to face her. "I wondered what the hell I'd done wrong because we'd had such a good time – except for the near freezing part – and then you asked me to wait but didn't invite me inside."

"I'm sorry. I didn't know what to do. Then, Remy showed up."

"I have no idea why I just thought about that right now."

"Can I change the subject?" Reese asked.

"Yes." Kellan's laughter died down.

"No underwear? Really?" Reese snapped the waistband of Kellan's sweats, causing Kellan to laugh again.

"It's actually a funny story. Wanna hear it?"

"Of course."

"So, I forgot to put them on in the bathroom."

"That's your funny story?" Reese laughed.

"You're laughing, aren't you?" She wrapped an arm around Reese's waist, pulling her closer. "We were in the bathroom. Things were weird. I put my sweats on and didn't realize until we walked back that I'd forgotten a step."

"Oh, I'm not complaining." Reese smirked.

"No, but you *are* cold." Kellan rubbed Reese's back up and down.

"Kellan, please don't–"

"I know what you're going to say," Kellan interrupted. "I'm not checking on you. This isn't about that. I just noticed you're cold, Reese, and I don't want you to be cold. Plus, I'm cold."

Reese smiled at her as she drew her own body closer to Kellan's and pressed their breasts together. She hugged Kellan tightly and smiled into the embrace. Kellan had surprised her completely in her reaction to the news of her condition, but also in how she'd known how Reese would respond with her cold comment. Reese didn't want Kellan to be worried about her all the time. She also didn't want another watchdog. She wanted a girlfriend. She wanted everything to be as it was prior to her revelation. Well, except for the sex part. She didn't want to go back to a time where they hadn't had sex.

Kellan had said before that they wouldn't share their first time on the ground in a tent. Reese had also expected it to be slow, paced, and romantic. She'd pictured Kellan asking if she was sure at least three times since they'd waited so long. She thought they'd spend an hour sharing kisses and touches everywhere but where it counted in a delightful yet lengthy round of foreplay. While that would have been amazing, and they would do that soon, she loved their first time together. It was hot, fast, and a little rougher than she'd expected; in the best way. She didn't want to be treated like a paper doll because Kellan worried. She wanted Kellan to take her and claim her, and that was what Kellan had done.

"I know a way we can warm up," she suggested as her nipples hardened against Kellan's at her thoughts. "And I want to see all of you this time." She slid her hand under Kellan's pants to start sliding them off.

She kissed Kellan and rolled on top of her without disconnecting their lips. She wanted to taste her. She wanted her head between Kellan's legs. She wanted Kellan's thighs to grip her so tightly, she couldn't move her head due to the intensity of the orgasm she provided her partner. Unfortunately, in a tent this small, there wasn't room for her to do that properly, and she wanted to do it properly. She leaned up and separated their mouths while she slid off her own pants and underwear. She tossed them and hadn't paid attention to where, until the light in the tent became almost non-existent.

"Babe!" Kellan laughed.

Reese's underwear had covered the lantern. Reese leaned over Kellan and slid off the woman's pants without a word. She tossed them aside, too, and knelt in front of Kellan. She could just make out Kellan's form as light and shadow chose the perfect locations to accentuate her beauty. The little flickering of the lantern shone in Kellan's bright blue eyes while the shadow under her neck only made her strong jawline appear even stronger, balancing with the beauty of her perfectly sized nose and beautiful lips. Her breasts were just large enough without being overly large. Reese had always preferred small breasts on women, and Kellan's were perfect. Her nipples were rosy and erect. Reese wanted her lips there. First, though, her eyes had to take in all of her. They lowered to Kellan's flat stomach, which she'd seen before, but never in the light like this.

There was something new about this, despite Reese having seen, touched, and kissed that skin already. Her palms pressed into Kellan's flesh just under her breasts. Kellan spread her legs on instinct, giving Reese more space as she knelt between them. Reese lowered one of her hands to use her fingertips to graze the light brown curls at the apex of Kellan's thighs. Kellan's hips jerked almost imperceptibly at the touch. Reese slid forward on her knees and leaned forward just enough to press her center to Kellan's.

She parted Kellan's folds first and then parted her own before pressing further into Kellan's flesh. She placed both hands on either side of Kellan's shoulders and leaned into her as she rocked her hips forward. She felt Kellan's wetness mingle with her own instantly, and her clit throbbed as it pressed to Kellan's. Kellan's arms went to Reese's ass. She pushed Reese into her further as they worked a slow rhythm into a much faster one. Reese's lips hovered just above Kellan's, but neither made any effort to kiss the other. They merely exchanged the air back and forth as they let out hard and fast breaths matching their pace. Reese's arms had always been strong, but due to her lack of consistent activity, they weren't as strong as they had been. She could feel the slight tremors in her muscles as she continued to drive her center into Kellan's.

Both of them were incredibly wet, which normally she loved, but she was having difficulty holding herself up while continuing the rapid movement she knew both their bodies craved. Kellan's hands moved from her ass to Reese's hips. She lifted herself up, spread her legs just a little further, and used her hands to guide Reese's hips into her while Reese lifted up off her arms and placed her hands on Kellan's shoulders. She rocked into Kellan as Kellan held her in her straddling position. Reese felt the rippling muscles in Kellan's upper arms as Kellan slowed their pace and took one of Reese's nipples into her mouth. Reese gripped the back of Kellan's head to encourage her more.

Reese was close to coming, but her breathing had slowed with Kellan's pace. She knew it wouldn't take long. When her clit slid against Kellan's with a little more pressure than before, she sensed her orgasm was about to overtake her. She squeezed the back of Kellan's neck unintentionally. Kellan nipped at her flesh while her hands gripped Reese's hips tighter and moved her faster. Reese had never been handled so roughly yet so gently and lovingly at the same time. In her past relationships and dalliances with women, she'd usually been the more dominant in bed, but Kellan was taking the lead. Reese decided she liked that just as her orgasm ripped through her.

Kellan came moments later. Reese felt the sweat on Kellan's back as she continued to help Reese move against her to ride out their shared climaxes. Reese leaned down and captured Kellan's lips just as she determined Kellan's orgasm had begun to fade. She pressed Kellan back to the ground and slid her fingers quickly inside her. Kellan gasped first before she moaned. Reese thrust hard as she used her free arm to hold herself up while her lips remained connected to Kellan's. Kellan's muscles clenched around Reese's fingers, and she thrust harder and deeper.

"You're so tight," Reese said.

"It's been–" Kellan tried, but finished with two back-to-back moans followed by a near yell, "Reese!"

Kellan's hands were clenching Reese's lower back as she came again. Reese continued her pace. Her eyes met the shaking arm holding her above Kellan, and she wondered how it felt for other people. She could tell her arm was tired because she could feel the shaking. She knew she was exhausted because she'd hiked all day, and there was soreness. She recognized the soreness, but the pain that others felt that told them to stop doing something wasn't present. She knew the gash on her arm would be causing someone else pain, but there was nothing for her. There was nothing except Kellan coming beneath her. Her bright blue eyes were closed. Sweat droplets covered her hairline. Her nose was scrunched in an adorably sexy way, and her mouth hung open as she attempted to ride out this moment of bliss. Reese slowed when Kellan's grip loosened and her eyes opened. Reese stopped moving inside her in that moment because the beauty of Kellan's satisfied gaze caused her to get distracted.

"I needed that," Kellan said and then laughed.

CHAPTER 24

"WHAT ARE YOU GUYS going to do?" Remy asked.

"I don't know. We keep saying we're going to talk about it, but then we don't," Reese offered as she tossed the football into the back of Remy's car.

They'd played their last game of the year, and it had been a cold one. Reese had played, but her shoulder had started bleeding again, thanks to a run-in with Dave in the end zone. She hadn't noticed the pain, but she had noticed the blood on her shirt. Kellan had taped her back up, but she'd decided to sit on the sidelines for the rest of the game. She'd watched Kellan say goodbye to everyone just in case she didn't get a chance to see them before she left. She was currently talking to Morgan and Kinsley by Kinsley's car while Reese and Remy were packing up Remy's. Ryan and Dave were loading a cooler into Dave's truck. Reese closed the door and leaned her back against it.

"Time's kind of running out," Remy reminded. "You guys exchanged some pretty big words, little sister. Also, some bodily fluids." She wiggled her eyebrows and shoved lightly at Reese's uninjured shoulder.

"Gross." Reese crossed her arms.

"I bet it wasn't gross last night though." She stuck

her tongue out for a second, but then her face turned serious. "You told her first, didn't you?" she asked.

Reese and Kellan had driven from the trailhead to Kellan's cabin where they'd cleaned up and gone immediately to the beach for football. During the few water breaks, Reese had confided in Remy that she and Kellan had made love and that they'd shared *the* words as well. Unfortunately, they'd not been alone enough for Reese's satisfaction to talk about the other words she'd exchanged with Kellan the previous night.

"How'd you know?"

"You seem different today, and not in that way where people say you have sex and you look different after. You do look different because of that as well. You're finally satisfied, I'd wager." She winked and then turned serious again. "But you're also lighter somehow. That can't just be because you told each other how you feel or because you finally had sex."

"I told her before. I told her I loved her first, and then told her about it."

"And?"

Reese looked over at Kellan, who was hugging Kinsley. She turned back to Remy and smiled widely.

"Nothing's changed. She doesn't look at me any differently or seem to worry more. When we were hiking down this morning, she didn't do anything differently than she'd done in the past. She didn't charge ahead and cleared the path to be extra cautious, and she didn't try to overcompensate by letting me take the lead this time. She just walked ahead like she'd always done. She didn't ask me how I was fifteen times or ask a million questions about what I can feel and what I can't feel."

"Like mom used to do?" Remy laughed.

"Yeah, she used to ask me if I could feel the blanket over me when we were little, remember?"

"She didn't understand it back then." Remy smiled at the memory. "None of us did. I never knew if you could feel things. We used to hold hands all the time as kids, and I remember wondering if you could actually feel my hand."

"I remember." Reese laughed lightly as she watched Kellan hug Morgan. "When we were together last night, it was right after I told her. I worried she'd be so gentle and worry about whether or not she'd hurt me and I wouldn't know."

"Like you wouldn't even know she was doing anything to you?" Remy chuckled.

"Right." Reese smiled and watched Kellan head over to Dave and Stacy. "But she didn't."

"No?"

"She…" Reese searched for the right words. "Handled me."

Remy burst out laughing. Reese shoved her to get her to knock it off. Dave, Stacy, and Kellan had all turned to see what was going on. Even Morgan and Kinsley had heard them as they prepared to leave.

"Handled you?" Remy whispered as she recovered.

"I can't talk about this now," she whispered back.

"You're blushing, Reese." She pointed at Reese's reddening cheeks.

"I am not," Reese argued.

"It was that good?" Remy took a step closer and whispered again.

"Hey, babe," Reese greeted Kellan, who approached from behind Remy.

"Hey." Kellan moved right past Remy to Reese's side. "I've said all my just in case goodbyes. Are you ready?"

She placed a hand on Reese's abdomen over her shirt, and Reese felt it in her bones. They hadn't made love that morning. They'd been cutting it close to make it to football. Her body craved Kellan's touch again. She knew she was likely blushing for the second time in only a couple of minutes. Remy was smirking at her as she, too, must have realized what Reese was thinking about.

"Are we still doing dinner?" Remy asked with a lifted eyebrow.

"Yeah... no," Reese replied before Kellan had the chance and pulled on Kellan's arm as she started to walk away. "We're staying at Kellan's place tonight."

"Bye, Remy," Kellan said while being pulled by the hand toward her car. "See you later."

"No, you won't," Reese said.

***

"We're on the floor," Kellan stated. "We seem to have a thing with having sex on the ground."

"Not my fault you couldn't wait until we got to the bedroom." Reese kissed down Kellan's abdomen, enjoying the feel of the skin beneath her lips.

"You're the one on top of me," she retorted.

"Are you complaining?" Reese asked as she kissed the inside of Kellan's thigh.

Before Kellan could respond, Reese's tongue licked from her entrance to the very tip of her clit, returning to its origin point right after. She slid her tongue inside Kellan while lifting Kellan's hips with her hands on her ass. Kellan sucked in a breath while Reese's tongue moved in and out. Her hips jerked up when Reese's tongue met her clit and flicked it before Reese sucked her into her mouth.

After Reese had pulled Kellan into the car so they could head back to the cabin for some privacy, they'd barely made it inside before she had Kellan's shirt and sports bra off. They'd bumped into the coffee table on the way to the sofa. Kellan had tripped over her sweats as she'd tried to get them off quickly. Reese had caught her in time, but they'd ended up on the floor. Kellan had torn at Reese's clothes, and Reese had settled on top of her.

"Reese," Kellan uttered and spread her legs wider.

Reese had been waiting all day, and if she was being

honest with herself – much longer, to be with this woman this way. Kellan's breasts were in her palms. She squeezed them as Kellan climbed higher. She tweaked at Kellan's nipples and pinched them as Kellan came in her mouth. Reese slowed her strong strokes until Kellan's body released its tension, and then she slid on top of her.

"That was…" She stared down as Kellan opened her eyes. "Beautiful."

"That was amazing," Kellan expressed. "Seriously, that was…" She wrapped her arms around Reese's back and flipped them over.

"Whoa!" Reese laughed when she realized she was now underneath Kellan, who had her trapped beneath her weight, with her arms on either side of Reese's head.

"I was thinking I'd make us dinner now. What are your thoughts on that?" Kellan asked as she rubbed her center against Reese's.

"What? No way," she objected.

Kellan gave her a playful laugh before kissing her.

***

"Reese, we should talk."

"I know, but I don't want to talk right now. Can't we just sit here and enjoy the fire, go to bed, make love, and pretend like you're not leaving in a week?"

"I don't think so." Kellan didn't want to have to say. "It's not that far. Once I get back, I'll try to get my schedule and see which weekends I have to work. We can schedule a trip for you there or one for me here when I'm free."

"I have a fall break next month. Well, it's like six weeks away. I can go there then. I don't know what you normally do for Thanksgiving, but Remy and I were planning on having it here and inviting our friends. Can you come? If not, I can do the day here and drive there or something so we can have the weekend. We should probably figure out Christmas and New Year's Eve, too. I want a midnight kiss with you, and there's this party we usually go to here. Could you come?"

"Six weeks?"

"Huh?" Reese lifted her head to look at her. "Babe, are you crying?"

"No," Kellan lied as a slow tear ran down her cheek. "Six weeks, Reese?"

"That's just when my break is, but you can come here before that, or I can drive up after school on Friday." She paused. "Kell, how often did you think we'd be able to see each other?"

"I don't know. It's just – hearing six weeks and thinking that I won't see you for that long – got to me." She lifted her arm from behind Reese and leaned forward, clasping her hands together. "I just found you."

"Baby, I know." Reese rubbed her back. "I can't get away every weekend though. I have Remy here, and my friends, and–"

"Your whole life?"

"No, not my whole life." Reese stilled her hand. "You're not here, or at least you won't be soon."

"I know."

"I have a job on the weekends too, sometimes, remember? I volunteer at the visitor center. I know it's just volunteer work, but it's important to me because my mom did it, and it was important to her. I've been skipping a lot of it already because you're here, but I do normally work there every weekend."

"I can come here on the weekends when I don't have a shift. I'll go down to one job."

"Can you afford that?" Reese asked.

"It's mainly to try to pay back loans faster, but yeah, I'll have to budget closely. It'll be worth it though. I want more time to see you." She turned her head to Reese. "I love you."

"I love you, too." Reese let out an exasperated sigh.

"I guess we should feel lucky that you don't live further away. A few hours on the road isn't as bad as a flight to the east coast."

"What happens when it becomes too much?" Kellan asked. "When you're supposed to come here, but you're too tired after a long week at work; or it's my turn, and I have to pull a weekend shift unexpectedly?"

"We'll make it work," Reese insisted.

"I don't want to make it work, Reese. I want it to work."

"Every relationship takes work, Kell," she countered.

"Yes, and this just adds to that work."

"You're worried we won't last?" Reese sat back and removed her hand from Kellan.

"No, that's not it." Kellan turned to her on the sofa, placing her leg underneath her body. "Reese, I've had relationships, but I've never experienced something like this."

"Like what exactly?"

"This feels so right to me." She took Reese's hand. "I thought things were right in my past relationships. I guess we all do. That's why we date people as long as we do. But I've never felt how I feel about you."

"Not even with Keira?"

Kellan couldn't tell by her expression and tone if Reese was asking her seriously or in jest. Kellan leaned in and placed her forehead against Reese's. She let go of her hand so she could place it on her cheek instead.

"Not with anyone."

"Then, we'll be okay, Kell. If it matters this much to both of us, we'll be okay."

CHAPTER 25

IT WAS THURSDAY, and that meant she had one more day at the vet clinic here and only a few more days with Reese before she'd have to return home. While she and Reese had spent nearly every night working out their visit schedule through the end of the year, she'd tried to keep herself focused on the present and the fact that she and Reese were together now. They'd made love every free moment, as if they could store up the feelings and sensations of their experiences for their upcoming time apart.

"How do you like your sandwich?" Dr. Sanders asked her after she took her first bite of the roast beef she'd ordered at his suggestion.

"It's great."

"This is my favorite place to grab a quick lunch. It can get busy during the summer and winter, but this time of year, the locals get it all to ourselves."

"I can see why it would get busy." She took a drink from the styrofoam cup that contained her peach iced tea.

"I wanted to talk to you about something, Kellan. I know we've only just met, and that you're leaving in a few days, but I was hoping you'd be coming back soon because of Reese."

"I will. We've planned out the rest of the year. I should be back next month. But it's just for the weekend. Did you need help in the clinic?"

"A bit more than that." He slid his untouched plate toward the center of the table, placed his elbows down, and clasped his hands together. "I need a replacement."

"Replacement for what?" She focused on his brown eyes with near white, bushy eyebrows above them.

"Me," he answered. "I'm sixty-eight years old. My

wife has put up with me for forty-five years. She's given me three children, who are off living their lives with my five grandchildren. Despite my attempts, none of them appear interested in taking over the clinic. My oldest son is a nature photographer and travels the world, my middle daughter practices law. My youngest is almost done with medical school in Portland, but he's content to practice medicine on humans." He chuckled a little. "I don't have anyone I can leave the place to. I don't want to just sell it. I will if I have to, but I'd like it to remain a vet facility. If I sell the building, the new owner can turn it into anything they want."

"And you want me to take it over?" Kellan asked.

"I've still got another six months or so in me, but Elizabeth wants to travel. She's retired. She's been waiting on me to do the same. I've watched you work, Kellan. I think I can trust you with these patients and the people that bring them in. I've watched you taking looks at the reference materials to ensure you're doing the right thing and just to learn. I'd like to teach you more if I can, and I'd like to offer you a job."

"A job?" Kellan lifted both eyebrows.

"Well, at first. You'd work *with* me until I retire. We'd make sure you understand the business parts. I'd connect you to the accountant and suppliers. If things work out as I suspect they will, I'd give you the keys, and you'd run it for me."

"But you'd still own it?"

"Just until you could afford to buy me out. We could do a lease to own if that would work for you. I'm not concerned about the money, but I do believe the process should be handled legally and properly."

"Dr. Sanders, I don't know what to say." Her hands were clasped in her lap. "I have a job. I live in San Francisco."

"I don't need an answer today. That's why I was hoping you'd be returning soon. I thought we could meet and talk then, once you'd have some time to think it over."

"What would happen to the place if I don't take it?"

"I suppose I can try to find another vet to take the place over. There are a couple that might be interested in adding a new location or maybe even one that wants their own practice."

"They can probably afford to buy it from you faster than me."

"Probably. But I've worked with you, Kellan. I like you. I'd trust you with my practice. I've known Reese and Remy forever, and if they trust you too, that makes this an even easier decision."

"I can think about it?"

"Of course. Take your time. I'd like to make a decision about what to do next at the beginning of the year though."

"Okay. I understand."

As Kellan put her car in drive to head to meet Reese after they'd locked up the clinic, she still couldn't believe that she'd come to Lake Tahoe to get over a broken heart and had somehow managed to fall in love with a beautiful woman, and, perhaps, had even found a job. She couldn't wait to talk to Reese about this. She thought about how she could go back to the city and think further about it while they continued building their relationship. When she came back to Tahoe, she'd talk to the doctor, and they'd make a plan for her to start working there officially. The thought of leaving the city she'd always lived in didn't scare or intimidate her as she'd expected it should have. It felt right. It felt like everything in her life had led her here.

***

Kellan's right hand moved to the back of Reese's neck, and Kellan pulled her back for more. Reese obliged. Their tongues met and danced slowly until Reese gave in and moved to lie on Kellan's side. Kellan was in a t-shirt and shorts while Reese had put on a pair of sweats to go with her tank top. Reese pulled her shirt over her own head and tossed it aside. Kellan stared at her breasts and the points of her nipples while Reese slid a hand inside Kellan's shorts under her panties. Kellan lifted her own shirt up to her shoulders but couldn't remove it because Reese's hand was already between her legs, stroking her clit through her wetness. Kellan's head went back slightly as Reese leaned down and kissed her breasts before sucking a nipple into her mouth.

"I want you," Kellan whispered.

Kellan hadn't told Reese about the potential job opportunity yet. She knew she needed to take some time to think it over before she filled her in. She didn't want to get Reese's hopes up. When she'd arrived at Reese's, the woman hadn't given her much time to tell her anything. She'd had her against the front door the moment Kellan had closed it behind her. They'd managed to make it to the bedroom without bumping into anything before Reese practically tossed her onto the bed.

Kellan searched with her right hand until she could slide it into Reese's pants. Reese slid up a little to allow Kellan access. As Reese stroked her, Kellan found Reese's wet center and cupped it. Reese bucked into Kellan's hand and into the mattress beneath, as she turned slightly so her stomach was now to the mattress. Reese's hips rocked up and down against Kellan's hand while Kellan absorbed the intensity of Reese's touch against her clit. Reese slid two fingers inside Kellan as her hips continued to move against Kellan's hand. Kellan angled her own two fingers at Reese's entrance. Reese shifted and slid herself onto them. Kellan waited for Reese to start moving again, and when she did, Reese's fingers inside of Kellan picked up speed. Kellan's orgasm was building, and as Reese took her pleasure from Kellan's hand and her own hip-grinding, Kellan came on a particularly hard thrust.

Reese continued to move quickly against Kellan's

hand, but as soon as she realized Kellan had come down from her explosion, Reese lifted her own body up, forcing Kellan's hand from her pants, and moved off the bed. Kellan wanted to say something. She knew Reese was close to coming. She needed to watch Reese's orgasm take her away if she was ever going to settle down herself. Before she could utter a word though, Reese was at the end of the bed, tugging on Kellan's shorts until they were on the floor along with her panties. Reese moved between her legs and sucked her into her mouth. They both moaned at the contact as Kellan spread her legs further. Kellan's clit was so close to coming, she wasn't sure how much more she could handle.

She opened her eyes and lifted her head slightly to watch Reese take her with her mouth when she noticed Reese's one hand on her right hip and the other between her own legs, moving back and forth. Reese was getting herself off while making Kellan come, and Kellan couldn't handle it. She came when Reese sucked her fully into her mouth, and Kellan watched Reese's trembling arm stroke between her legs. She couldn't see anything more than the arm movement, but it was enough to take her over the edge. And over the edge she went, slamming to the ground of an earth-shattering orgasm while her right hand held Reese's head in place. Moments later, Reese's mouth tightened around her clit again, and her sounds told Kellan what was about to happen. Reese's hips jerked feverishly as her hand continued its work. She came as she still sucked on Kellan's clit. When Reese finally stilled with her hand still inside her own pants, she lifted her head, and still desire-filled eyes met Kellan's blue ones.

"Is that what you wanted?" Reese kissed the inside of her thigh.

"Yes," Kellan breathed out.

Reese slid her hand from her pants and stood. Kellan watched her go into the bathroom, heard the water in the sink running for a few minutes, and stayed completely still as Reese made her way back into the bedroom. She watched as Reese put her shirt back on and reached for Kellan's to help her lower it back over her torso. She separated Kellan's shorts from her ruined underwear, searched the bag Kellan always had on the floor of the bedroom to find their replacement, and tossed them to Kellan.

"Now, I'll order us dinner." Reese kissed her lips.

Kellan could still taste herself on Reese's lips, despite her attempts to clean up. She couldn't believe Reese had just completely blown her mind. Reese headed into the kitchen while Kellan stared up at the ceiling, still trying to get her heart rate to slow to something resembling normal. She heard a strange almost smacking sound followed by a loud thud coming from the other room.

"Reese?" Kellan waited for a response. "Reese?" She sat up. "Hey, are you okay?" she asked and sat up further. She tried to peer out from her position on the bed, but the kitchen was around the corner and Reese didn't appear to be in the living room. She turned to the left toward the kitchen and saw Reese on the floor. "Reese!" She rushed to the kitchen where Reese was lying on the floor on her stomach. Her face was turned toward Kellan, and her eyes were closed. There was also blood on her forehead. "Baby!" Kellan kneeled beside her. She didn't want to lift her head in case she'd injured her neck or spine. She touched the wound on her forehead, which appeared to be a cut delivered in her fall. She noticed a small bit of blood on the counter in front of Reese. "Reese! Wake up!" The wound on her forehead was still bleeding and somewhat heavily. She reached for a rag hanging from the stove and used it to staunch the blood. She placed two fingers on Reese's neck and felt a slow pulse. It was too slow. "Hold on, babe. Hold on. I've got you. It's okay," she said those words of comfort to herself more than to Reese, who was unconscious and couldn't hear her. "Reese, I love you. It's okay."

CHAPTER 26

KELLAN HADN'T SLEPT since Thursday night. It was now Saturday night. She also wasn't sure she'd eaten anything more than the snacks Remy and Ryan had forced on her. She'd been told several times that she should go back to the house and rest. They'd let her know if there was any change. She'd yet to leave the hospital. Morgan had gone to the cabin to grab her clothes to change into. Remy had been by her side in the waiting room whenever they weren't allowed in Reese's room. Ryan had only left to bring food for them, knowing they probably wouldn't eat it. Morgan had moved three plastic chairs together and made a bed for herself. She was currently attempting to nap while Remy and Ryan were speaking softly to one another. Kellan watched him comfort his girlfriend. Kellan missed Reese more in that moment. She needed her to help ease her own worries.

Reese had been in a medically induced coma since they'd brought her in. The doctors had run test after test to try to determine how this could have happened. Friday afternoon, they'd known the fall Reese had experienced in the kitchen had likely been caused by an infection she'd sustained when she'd cut her arm. They'd had her on antibiotics since she'd arrived. Kellan hated herself for not insisting harder that Reese see a doctor. The cut had been more than just a cut. She'd known that when she'd bandaged her up that night.

The cut had opened again and again. There was no telling what kind of bacteria could've entered, and because Reese didn't feel the irritation that normally came with infections, she wouldn't have known the signs. Kellan should have paid more attention. Hell, Reese should have paid more attention. She should have seen the doctor because only Reese knew her body and understood the reality of her condition.

The wound on her forehead had been deep and required several stitches, but her brain had swelled. The doctors wanted to keep her unconscious until the swelling decreased enough for it to be safe. In the meantime, Kellan, Morgan, Remy, and Ryan could only wait and pray. Kellan had never been a person who prayed, but she'd pray now if it meant Reese would be okay. She'd pray now if it meant she'd wake up soon with a smile on her face, telling everyone it was just a silly accident and she was fine. Kellan's stomach lurched at her, begging her to eat something. She was certain the entire waiting room had heard the sound, but no one moved. She leaned her head back against the plastic chair and heard it creak.

Her phone buzzed in her pocket. She pulled it out to see a text from Keira. She'd had a couple from Greene and Hillary earlier that day, asking when they could expect her tomorrow night. They wanted to bring dinner by her place and catch up with Emma and Joanna. She hadn't replied because she didn't know what to say to them. She'd texted her boss to tell her she wouldn't be back on Monday after all because she wasn't leaving Reese like this. The way she felt right now, she never wanted to leave Reese. She turned her phone off and returned her stare to the clock on the wall.

"She's back in the room now if you want to go in." The doctor entered the waiting room. "Tests are done for a bit at least. Oh, one at a time right now, okay?" he added.

"You go first," Kellan told Remy.

"I'll just check on her and come right back." Remy moved without waiting for a reply.

Kellan wanted more than anything to see Reese now, but Remy was her sister. They were twins. She knew how strong their connection was and that Remy had already gone through this once.

"How is she?" Kellan asked the doctor as he made his way over to sit across from her in a plastic chair.

"She's the same. But we're monitoring everything, and the moment something changes, I'll let you know."

"What's going on?" Morgan woke up and sat immediately in her chair. "What happened?" Her eyes got big when she saw the doctor.

"She's the same," Kellan calmed her. "No change."

"Is that good or bad?" Morgan asked the doctor.

"We still have–"

"Doc, tell me honestly. Don't give me any bullshit. She's my best friend and Kellan's girlfriend." She pointed at Kellan. "She's Remy's twin sister. We need to know."

The doctor looked from Morgan to Kellan. She nodded as she held her breath.

"It's not good news." He lowered his head and lifted it a moment later with more resolve in his expression. "The swelling hasn't gone down as quickly as we would have hoped. The plan is to keep her in coma for at least another day. If we don't see any change, we'll run some more tests and talk other options."

"Like what?" Morgan asked what Kellan wanted to know.

"Surgery."

"Brain surgery?" Kellan asked.

"We'd remove a part of the skull to help relieve the pressure. It's called a decompressive craniectomy. It's not the only option, and we're not there yet. If we get to that point, I'll have to discuss the options with Remy. She's her next of kin." he explained.

"Of course," Kellan replied.

Remy would be the one making decisions for Reese if it came to that. Kellan had no say in any of it. She was her girlfriend and had only known Reese for a month. Was it less than a month? When had they met? When exactly was their first date? She couldn't remember anything right now. Her only thought was of Reese lying there unconscious and possibly having to undergo a brain surgery. It seemed like only an hour ago that they'd been making love, with Kellan feeling optimistic about their life together.

"I have to go. I'll stop by later if there's anything new to report, okay?"

"Can I stay with her tonight?" Kellan asked.

"No, Kellan. I'm sorry. Honestly, I think it would be good for someone to take you home. All of you should get some rest."

"I don't think I can," Kellan said.

"I'll make sure she heads home, doc," Morgan offered as she stood.

"I don't have a home," Kellan stated.

"Of course, you do." Remy entered the room and headed toward her. "It's with Reese." She sat next to Kellan. "Go in and say goodnight to your girlfriend. Ryan will drive us all back to the house. Morgan will stay with us tonight, right?"

"Yeah," Morgan agreed.

"We'll all take care of each other until she gets better."

"I'm cooking us all dinner tonight," Ryan said. "We need to eat something solid."

"I'll call around to everyone when we get there and give them an update," Morgan added.

"Good. We've got a plan. Right, Kellan?" Remy placed a hand on top of Kellan's.

Kellan turned to look at her and almost couldn't stand the sight of her. She looked so much like Reese that it hurt to see her.

"Right," she acquiesced and stood.

"I'll get the car and bring it around," Ryan offered.

"Morgan and I will wait here," Remy said.

Ten minutes later, Kellan was in Reese's room. She made her way slowly to the bed. Reese's eyes were closed. Kellan realized she hadn't seen them in two days. She nearly cried at that, but the breathing tube and ventilator being used to control the amount of oxygen and carbon dioxide going to and from Reese's brain was what caused her tears to fall. The doctor had explained that blood carried fluid into the brain and also took up space in the head; it was important to optimize how much entered Reese's brain. Too little would lead to a lack of oxygen, and too much would take too much space and raise the pressure. The buildup of carbon dioxide and lack of oxygen both caused blood vessels in the head to raise the pressure, too. It was all very medical and important, but to Kellan, this was her girlfriend. Her hair was matted against the white of the pillow behind it. Her hands were at her sides, and she looked so pale. Kellan sat in the chair next to the bed and took Reese's hand. She leaned forward and kissed it.

"Babe, they won't let me stay here tonight." She squeezed Reese's fingers and prayed Reese would squeeze back. "Morgan is very stubborn, and so is Remy. They're making me go back to the house, but I'll be back first thing tomorrow morning. If anything happens, the doctors will call. I'll be right here, okay? I'm not leaving you. I won't leave you." She let her tears fall freely. "Reese, please come back. I've waited so long to find you. This can't be the end of us." Kellan wiped her tears from her face and stood up. "I love you." She leaned forward and kissed Reese on the forehead next to the bandage that covered her wound. "I love you, Reese."

***

"You settled in?" Morgan asked as she sat on the side of the bed next to Kellan.

"I'm okay," Kellan told her. "Thank you."

"Sure." Morgan stood. "I'll say good night then."

"You can stay in here. You don't have to sleep on the couch."

"I can't, actually," Morgan commented. "Reese and I used to date, remember? I haven't been in this bed since then. I don't really plan on sleeping in it again."

"Oh." Kellan looked to the side of the bed where Reese normally slept and clenched her jaw. "Is it weird that I'm in here?"

"No, it seems about right." Morgan smiled an awkward smile. "It seems like such a long time ago that I was jealous of her because of you and somehow also jealous of you because of her. Doesn't it seem like such a long time ago?"

"Given what's happened since then, I'd say yes," she answered.

"She's my best friend in the world. She has been forever. I don't know what I'd do without her. Last year, I thought I was going to lose my girlfriend, and that was hard, but the hardest part wasn't that. It was that I was going to lose my best friend."

"She's going to be fine."

"She has to be," Morgan replied.

Kellan didn't want to sleep for fear she'd miss news of Reese, but her eyes closed due to the immense exhaustion. A few moments later, she was out.

CHAPTER 27

W<small>HEN</small> K<small>ELLAN</small> <small>WOKE</small> <small>UP</small>, Reese was lying on her side of the bed, staring at her phone. Kellan's eyes went wide because Reese couldn't be here. She was in the hospital. Her first thought was that she was dreaming, but a second later she realized it was Remy.

"Hey." Remy turned to see that she was awake. "I just called the hospital, and they said the swelling has gone down a little."

"What? Really?" Kellan sat up slowly. "Are they taking her out of the coma?"

"Not yet." Remy tossed her phone on the bed. "I sent Ryan to get us coffee and something to eat. Morgan is in my shower."

"It feels weird, being here without her," Kellan confessed.

"She'll be okay."

"How can you be so sure?"

Remy leaned back against the pillows and clasped her hands over her stomach in the same way Reese often did.

"Last year, when she got sick, it was bad. It was really bad there for a few days, and I'd already lost my parents. I didn't know what I'd do if I lost Reese, too. She's told me many times that she thinks I'm so strong for going through all that and coming out on the other side, but I don't think so."

"What do you mean?"

"It's hard to explain how this twin thing works to other people; and, sometimes, I don't understand it myself. I don't feel her pain or anything but, sometimes, it's like I can understand what she's going through. Last year, I could sense things I didn't tell anyone about. Reese doesn't even know. I sensed she was going to be okay. I can't explain it scientifically or medically, but I knew she'd recover."

"And now?"

"Now, I sense the same thing. I don't know how. I don't know when, but I know she's going to be okay."

"I hope you're right."

"Of course, I'm right. I'm always right," Remy joked and nearly jumped out of the bed.

***

"My God! Kellan, are you okay?" Hillary asked her as Kellan sat alone in the waiting room at the hospital while they ran more tests on Reese.

Remy, Ryan, and Morgan had gone to the hospital cafeteria for dinner, but Kellan wasn't hungry. She'd eaten the pastries Morgan had brought them for breakfast, and she'd had half a sandwich at lunch. That was about all she could stomach for the day. She'd gotten a few more texts from her friends and finally determined that she needed to give them an update about the fact that she wasn't returning as planned. The moment she'd connected with Hillary, she'd revealed everything she'd intended to keep to herself.

"She still isn't awake."

"I'm so sorry, Kell. Do you want us to come there? I can get someone to cover my classes. I don't know about Greene, but she could probably move some things around."

"No, there's nothing you guys can do."

"But you're there alone."

Kellan was alone in the room, but she hadn't felt alone the entire time she'd been in Tahoe. Even prior to meeting Remy at the market and before she met Reese and got introduced to all their friends, she still felt better because she was in Tahoe. She'd always loved this place. She'd considered it a home away from home and had returned as often as she could. This trip was different, and it was different because of Reese but also because she loved these people, too.

"I have people here," Kellan returned. "Reese's sister and her boyfriend are here. Her best friend is here. Others come in and out but can't stay the whole time." She sighed.

"If you change your mind, I'll be there, Kell. We all will be," Hillary insisted. "I'm so sorry about this."

"Me too. I'm so in love with her, Hill. I've never been more in love with anyone, and I've known her a month. It's not enough time." She let her tears fall and resisted trying to catch them. "It's not enough time."

"Kellan, it never is," Hillary replied sympathetically. "I've felt that kind of connection once before, and I thought it was forever. I thought I'd found my soulmate. And when things were good between us, it didn't matter how much time we had together. It was never enough."

"And when things got bad between you two?"

"Even when we'd fight back then, there was no one else I wanted to fight with like that, because I knew it was us against the world. We'd always work it out."

"And then you didn't?"

"Life happened; we separated. It was terrible and lonely. I hated it, but it was for the best for both of us. I hope I'll find the person I'm actually supposed to be with one day. But, Kellan, even when I do, there will never be enough time. That's why it's so important to make the time we do have count."

Kellan knew Hillary was right. She also knew she needed to get out of this hospital waiting room for at least a few minutes. Reese would be getting more tests done for at least another hour, and she'd been at the hospital since seven in the morning. She'd wanted to stay the night last night, but Remy and the doctors had insisted she go home. She'd objected but had been overruled. She'd slept again in Reese's bed without Reese beside her, and it had been cold.

She made her way to the automatic glass doors that opened to the outside and slid her hands into the pockets of her jacket. She moved to sit on the bench where she'd seen a couple of smokers congregate before, which she now had to herself, and breathed the fresh, cold air into her lungs. She held it there for a moment before releasing it and then repeated the same actions again and again.

"There you are!" Ryan rushed through the doors a few moments later.

"What's wrong?" Kellan stood quickly.

"You need to come back inside," he said but offered nothing else before rushing back into the hospital.

Kellan guessed he wanted to get back to Remy's side as quickly as possible, which could only be bad in Kellan's estimation. She rushed toward the waiting room. When she arrived, she saw Morgan with her head in her hands, but there was no sign of Remy or Ryan.

"What happened?" She moved toward Morgan.

"She crashed," Morgan stated without looking up. Kellan could tell she either still was or had been crying. "I don't know."

"What?" Kellan more or less fell into a chair across from Morgan. "What do you mean you don't know?"

"We came back up here, and the doctor walked in and told Remy something. She ran to Reese's room. Ryan and I stayed here. Remy came back to tell us she'd crashed and they were trying to revive her. She sent Ryan to get you and then she ran back to the room." She lifted her head enough to say and then lowered it again. "I thought she was getting better."

"I'm going back there." Kellan stood.

"You can't. Ryan's not even supposed to be back there, but he went for Remy."

"I'm going back there," Kellan asserted. "I can't leave her alone, Morgan. I won't."

She made the hardest and longest walk of her entire life as she proceeded down the now familiar path to Reese's hospital room. When she got there, she couldn't hear anything coming from inside it. She pressed her palm to the wall to hold herself up because no noise could not be a good thing when someone's heart was failing. Her own heart was racing as she pushed off and took a few steps into the room. When she arrived, the emptiness of the space was both a relief and a concern. Reese's hospital bed wasn't there, which could only mean that they'd moved her. Kellan left the room and walked down the hallway in the opposite direction of the waiting room. She found a nurse at the nurse's station and approached her.

"Can you tell me where Reese is?"

"You shouldn't be back here."

"Please!" she yelled and could no longer contain her emotions. "Where's Reese?"

"Honey, I don't know." The nurse placed a tentative hand on Kellan's forearm. "Why don't you have a seat over here? I'll find out for you, okay?"

Kellan didn't respond. She didn't want to have a seat either, but she'd do it if it meant the nurse would help her find her girlfriend. The woman walked her behind the desk in the alcove to their right and sat her in one of the rolling chairs before she walked off. The beige and off-white walls closed in on Kellan as she waited and waited. The nurse returned an eternity later and knelt by Kellan's chair. Kellan couldn't breathe. She couldn't think. She couldn't speak. The nurse's eyes showed fear. Kellan could only assume at the meaning behind that glance. Her chest heaved in and out as the woman muttered something to her. She couldn't hear the words though. She could only see the woman's mouth move, as if she were in a silent movie. Then, it went dark.

CHAPTER 28

"SHE'S AWAKE." Morgan's voice was coming from Kellan's side. "Kellan?"

"What happened?" she asked with a groggy voice she didn't even recognize as her own.

"You passed out. You were dehydrated and exhausted," Remy replied.

Kellan opened her eyes further and lifted her head to see Remy at the end of the bed and Morgan on the right side of it.

"What happened to Reese? You should be with her." Kellan moved to sit up, but Morgan placed a hand over her own and stopped her.

"They are."

The voice sounded even groggier than her own and came from her left. She turned to see Reese lying in a hospital bed identical to her own. Her gray eyes were open. Her face was turned toward Kellan.

"Reese?" Kellan sat straight up, throwing Morgan's hand aside. "You're okay?" She hung her legs over the bed and Remy came around to that side.

"Hey, hold on there. You have an IV in you." She helped Kellan steady herself.

"Lie down, Kell," Reese said in that still groggy voice.

Kellan moved with Remy's help to Reese's bed a few feet from her own. The IV pole moved on its wheels with her.

"How are you? What happened? I love you. I thought I'd lost you. God, I love you, Reese." She let it all out along with a few tears as her hand cupped Reese's cheek.

"I love you too," Reese replied and turned her head into Kellan's hand.

"She's still a little out of it," Remy told Kellan. "And you should be in bed. The two of you have reached your limit of hospital visits in this relationship. Understood?" Remy placed a hand on Kellan's shoulder. "Unless it's because one of you is popping out a kid or something."

"Remy!" Morgan exclaimed. "Come on, let's give them a minute. Kellan, do you want a chair?"

"Yes, please."

Morgan pushed the chair from the corner in between their beds. Kellan sat down, holding Reese's hand now and intertwining their fingers while she stared into Reese's eyes.

"She's not out of the woods yet," Remy told Kellan.

"How long was I out?" she asked Remy but didn't look away from Reese.

"It's Monday." Remy lifted her phone from her pocket. "And it's three in the afternoon."

"What?" Kellan turned her head toward her, finally. "It was Sunday night."

"It was. Now, it's Monday afternoon. The doctors thought it would be best to let you sleep after they got you hydrated. You woke up around six this morning. Do you not remember?"

"No, I don't." Kellan tried to recall waking up but couldn't remember anything after the nurse's blurry face and soundless speech.

"You're okay. But they wanted to make sure you rested. You haven't exactly been taking care of yourself. You'll just need to be discharged. They'll probably want some blood work and maybe to feed you."

"I'm not going anywhere." She turned back to Reese.

"Obviously." Remy chuckled. "But at least then you

can stay in here as a girlfriend and not as a patient," she informed. "My little sister here, on the other hand, will be a patient for at least another few days."

"Great," Reese grumbled with sarcasm, and Kellan smiled at her.

"How do you feel?" Kellan asked her. "Or is that a dumb question?"

"Why would that be a dumb question?" Morgan asked, and Kellan remembered Morgan was in the room.

"I think you were right," Remy said. "Let's give these two some time alone." She moved to the other side of Reese's bed and squeezed her hand. "I'm going to find Ryan. He's calling everyone to update them. We'll be in the cafeteria, getting a late lunch, okay?"

"Okay."

"Have them find us if there's any change?" Remy looked at Kellan, who nodded. "Be back soon. I love you, little sis."

"I love you, big sis."

Once they were alone, Kellan ran a hand over Reese's other cheek. Her hair was still matted to the pillow. There was still a white bandage on her forehead. She had lines and cables coming from nearly every body part, it seemed. But, to Kellan, she was perfect. She was awake. She was talking. She was perfect.

"You're awake," she muttered in disbelief.

"I love you too, you know?" Reese said with a small smile.

"I know." Kellan nodded, and a tear trickled down her cheek. "What happened? I came looking for you, and you were bad, Reese. I thought you'd–"

"Hey, I'm still here. And I'd love a kiss from my girlfriend," Reese interrupted.

"Should we?"

"Of course, we should," she said.

Kellan lifted herself up slightly and kissed Reese's dry, chapped lips. She held her own lips in place for as long as she could stand before she separated them.

"I love you."

"I'm sorry," Reese started. "I should have gone to the doctor. I just didn't think there was a problem, and not because of the no pain thing." She reached for Kellan's hand. "It just seemed like a regular old cut."

"I think it was a combination of things," Kellan said. "You had an infection. We weren't exactly taking care of ourselves. We'd stayed up practically every night."

"Oh, I remember." Reese smiled a bigger smile this time. "I miss that."

"Me too," Kellan agreed. "You were exhausted. You fell."

"And hit my head on the counter. That part, Remy told me about. I don't remember it. She said you found me."

"I did. I came here with you."

"I'm sorry, Kellan. I should have just gone to a damn doctor."

"I'm just glad you're okay. You are okay, right?" Kellan questioned and suddenly felt that she needed to know every detail of what had happened while she was out.

"I'm okay. Not officially okay, technically, but I'm okay."

"What's that mean?" Kellan leaned in.

"Remy can probably give you all the details later, but what I know is that I had pressure in my brain. I was in a coma."

"Yes, for days." She remembered what Reese had looked like with that ventilator and breathing tube, and it made her angry and sad at the same time.

"And my throat is still raw from that damn tube. That's the second time I've had to be on one of those things."

"And the last," Kellan stated.

"And the last," Reese agreed. "I don't remember

anything. The doctor told me that they were treating me with antibiotics for the infection but that I reacted to something and my heart stopped. They were able to revive me." She gulped. Kellan wondered how scared Reese must be, to know that her heart had stopped and that she had almost died again. "They fixed the combination of meds I was on and are running more tests to see what happened, but it's likely I'm just allergic to one and never knew it. It happens with people like me sometimes."

"God, Reese!" Kellan ran her hand through what she could of Reese's hair. "I was so scared."

"I'm sorry, babe." Reese tried to move, but Kellan placed her hand on Reese's stomach to stop her. "I just want to hold you."

"You will. When you're out of here and better."

"The swelling went down enough for them to pull me out of it late last night. I woke up midday. Remy had you brought in here with me. Imagine how scared I was to wake up after all that and find you in a damn hospital bed next to me."

"I'm sorry, too?" Kellan gave a sympathetic look.

"The doctor said I have at least a few more days in here. Maybe I can go home by Friday. They have to see how the antibiotics work, and they're monitoring the swelling, too. It's down, but not gone."

"I'll get myself checked out of here as a patient and just be here as your girlfriend then. I'm sure you'll be bored of lying around soon. I can ask Morgan to pick up some stuff from the house. Your phone is there. I can get some magazines from the gift shop and—"

"Kellan?"

"Do you want your computer? It's still on the coffee table. No, you don't want your computer. You just came out of a coma."

"I want you."

"You have me. I'm here." Kellan squeezed Reese's hand.

"That's all I want, okay? I don't need anything to keep me occupied. I love you for being here the whole time. But Remy said that's how you ended up in that less than sexy hospital gown. You overdid it. So, I want you to get discharged when the doctor says it's okay, and then you'll go home."

"Reese."

"You'll go home, Kellan. You and Remy will take care of each other. Ryan and Morgan will help. Eat a real meal and get some sleep. Come back tomorrow morning. I'll be asleep soon anyway. The nurse was in right before you woke up and said it's almost time for my medicine." She paused as she considered something. "How long can you stay before you have to go back to the city?"

"I called work and told them what happened. I can stay however long you need me."

"Kell, how long can you *afford* to stay?"

"However long it takes, Reese."

"Baby, I love you, but you have to go home eventually. You'll be back in a few weeks anyway. Stay until I'm discharged, and maybe a night or two after, but then you have to go home."

"You are my home."

"How were you still single when I met you with lines like those?"

"I heard you were awake," the doctor said. "How are you feeling?"

"Which one?" Kellan questioned.

"You first."

"I feel fine," Kellan replied.

"That's because you got a good night's sleep and fluids. Eat something, and if you're still feeling okay, I'll have you discharged."

"Sounds fair," Reese said. "Can I get the same deal?"

"Absolutely not," he answered. "You're improving though, which is good news. Your latest scans show the swelling is almost gone, and the new combo of meds we have you on seems to be knocking out the infection, according to your blood work."

"That's great." Kellan turned back to Reese. "When will she be able to go home?"

"Not so fast. We've still got a way to go before I'm comfortable with her being anywhere other than here, but it is good news. I must also inform you that it's time for your medication and a break from all this company."

"Meaning me?"

"You're still technically a patient. You just need to go back to your bed. I'll have someone bring you an early dinner. Remy and the others, though, should wait outside."

"Good luck telling her that," Kellan remarked.

"Eat, like the doctor says, and then take my sister home." Reese squeezed her hand. "I'll be asleep anyway."

"I'm agreeing only because I don't want to stress you out," Kellan said and stood.

"Hold on there." The doctor approached and wrapped his arm around Kellan's waist to help her stand.

"Watch those hands, doc. That's *my* girl."

CHAPTER 29

"KELLAN, HOW ARE YOU? I heard about Reese and heard you were in the hospital as well," Dr. Sanders said when she entered his office on Thursday afternoon.

"Reese is still in the hospital, but she's improving. They're hoping she'll be released tomorrow."

"That's great news. Elizabeth and I sent flowers."

"We got them. Thank you. That was very sweet of you."

"I assume you'll be staying here for a bit until Reese is settled?"

"I'm staying until Sunday. She's already told me I have to go back then, or she won't let me stay at the house." She chuckled. "I have an apartment back in San Francisco that's collecting dust. And I've been wearing the same clothes over and over for the past month because I didn't plan on being here this long. I need to get back to work."

"Is this a goodbye then or just a goodbye for now?" he asked as he set down the file he'd been reading when she'd entered.

"For now, I hope. I know you're busy, but I did want to talk to you about the job. I haven't talked to Reese about it, but I am considering it. Is it still on the table?"

"Of course. I'd love to talk to you about it more. I'm sure you don't have the time now, but when you return, we can meet."

"That sounds great. I'd like to keep this as a possibility from her for now. She's still healing and not completely out of the woods yet. I don't want to give her anything else to think about; good or bad."

"I understand."

"Dad, I'm going upstairs." A woman stood in the doorway.

"Oh, Riley. Come in here and meet Kellan." He stood up behind his desk. "Kellan, this is my daughter, Riley. Riley, this is Kellan Cobb. I mentioned her to you the other day."

"Right. Hi, Kellan. It's nice to meet you." The woman was a little taller than Kellan and had sable-colored hair with eyes that near-matched. "I've heard a lot about you from my father."

Kellan shook Riley's hand and gave her a smile.

"I hope good things."

"All good," he answered for his daughter. "Riley is in town for a visit."

"I was going up to the apartment to try to get some work done," she said to her father.

"She insists on staying in the apartment when she visits, even though her bedroom is always available at the house," he said to Kellan but looked at his daughter, who must have looked like her mother because Kellan saw almost no resemblance to the old man.

"There's an apartment up there? I saw the stairs, but I never thought to ask."

"It's an old building. My old practice was a few blocks down. I bought this building about ten years ago to expand," he began. "When I bought it, we originally thought about renovating the upstairs and renting it out. We renovated it but mainly used it for storage until a few years ago. Now, the kids use it when they come back if there's not enough room for everyone at the house. It's a two-bedroom. Riley oversaw the remodel and benefits from it when she stays."

"It has a garden tub," she offered Kellan as if in explanation for why she'd prefer to stay there instead of at her parents' house.

"You could always move back here and live there, dear," Edward told his daughter.

"My work is over an hour away in good weather, dad," she reminded.

"There's law to practice everywhere, Riley," he countered.

"I should go." Kellan suddenly felt very out of place in this family conversation. "I need to get back to Reese." She turned to Riley. "That's my girlfriend."

"I know Reese."

"Right. Small town," Kellan remembered.

"Last I heard, she was still dating Morgan Burns. I guess I do need to come around more." Riley turned serious. "Dad told me she was in the hospital, though. I hope she's okay."

"She's on the mend." Kellan smiled at the truth of that statement. "But I should be getting back to the hospital. I promised her mint chocolate chip ice cream, and I need to pick some up on the way."

"It was nice to meet you," Riley said.

"You too."

"Kellan, we can talk when you visit," Edward offered.

"Can we maybe meet sooner?" she asked.

"Of course."

"I'll call you?"

"Sounds good, dear."

***

"Reese, I swear to God, if you ever do this to me again, I will kill you myself." Remy threatened her sister as she helped her into her wheelchair on Friday evening.

"I promise, I will do everything in my power not to

end up back at this hospital again." Reese gave her a light laugh.

"Or any hospital."

"Or any hospital unless Kellan or I is popping out a kid. That's what you said, right?"

"Right." Remy nodded as she began to push the wheelchair toward the hallway.

"Where is my girlfriend?" Reese asked.

"Right here." Kellan stood in front of her as they exited the room. "I was just pulling the car around. It's right outside."

"Hi, babe." Reese smiled at her and lifted her head expectantly so that Kellan could lean down and give her a gentle kiss. "Well, I guess that'll have to do," she teased.

"You're still healing," Kellan reminded. "And we're not doing anything until you're fully healed. I won't make the same mistake again."

"Again?" Remy asked. "Did you two have such good sex, it caused my sister to pass out?"

"The car's right outside." Kellan avoided that question.

"She's ready to roll." Remy pushed the wheelchair a little further into the hall. "And all yours," she added and stood aside.

"Thanks." Kellan moved behind the chair and began pushing Reese down the hall.

"Ryan and I are staying at the house tonight just to make sure you're all settled in and everything, but we'll stay out of your way if everything's okay. I'm sure you two will want your privacy."

"It's fine, Rem. I kind of like the idea of all of us being there tonight. Maybe tomorrow night, though, Kell and I could have the place to ourselves? It's her last night," Reese requested.

"She just said you're not getting any until you're fully healed. And according to the team of doctors that treated you, that's another couple of weeks just to be safe. You need to pay attention to them, Reese," Remy demanded as she walked beside Reese. "I mean it. You're not like the rest of us, poor saps, that know when we don't feel well, so we know when we feel better. You need to take the full two weeks to heal, go to every doctor's visit in-between and then whatever follow-ups they tell you about."

"Fine. Fine," Reese agreed.

"Maybe I should–" Kellan began.

"No, Kell. You're going home. As much as I want you to stay forever, you have a life back there and a job that pays you money." Reese placed her hand on top of one of Kellan's that was on the handle of the wheelchair. "Besides, now it's only a couple of weeks before I get to see you again, since I was in the hospital for so long. In a way, it was good I got sick. I don't have to miss you for as long."

"That's not funny," Kellan and Remy both chastised at the same time.

***

"You should be in bed," Remy scolded her on Sunday morning.

"I'm so tired of being in bed," Reese responded and lowered herself on the couch.

"Yes, but today is the last day your girlfriend is in town for a while. Shouldn't she be waking up beside you about now?"

"She did a few minutes ago," Reese told her and rested her head against the back of the couch. "She's brushing her teeth and stuff. I told her I'd make her coffee. She told me I would not make her coffee. So, we compromised and decided you would make us both coffee."

"Joke's on both of you because Ryan made us a pot of coffee before he went on a run," Remy returned. "I will get you a cup though." She stood, made her way into the kitchen, poured Reese a cup of coffee just the way she liked it, and returned to place it on the table in front of her. "How are you?"

"Healing-wise?"

"Kellan-wise."

"Trying not to think about it." Reese leaned forward slowly and picked up the mug. She held it between her hands and stared at the fireplace beyond the coffee table. "In a way, I'm lucky she's still here, since she was supposed to leave last Sunday, but-"

"But you didn't actually get to spend any real time with her all week?"

"Exactly." Reese took a hesitant sip of her coffee. "I think I scared the shit out of her, Rem."

"You scared the shit out of all of us."

"I know. But you and Morgan know the drill. Well, *you* know the drill. Morgan went through this last year though, and so did Ryan. This is all so new to her. We've been together less than a month, and I've already told her the story of one coma, and she had to witness another."

"Extraordinary circumstances, though, Reese," she reminded.

"Are they, though?" Reese glanced at the closed bedroom door and lowered her voice. "This is my life, Rem. I get hurt, don't realize it, and end up in the hospital. I don't want to keep putting her through this."

"But you're fine putting me through it?" Remy chuckled at her.

"You're my sister. You don't have a choice." She took a longer drink from her coffee this time.

"She doesn't either."

"Of course, she does. She's going to go back to San Francisco, spend time with her friends and her family, get back to work; and she deserves to have someone she doesn't have to worry about like this."

"Reese, has she said something to you like that?"

"What? No."

"What's making you talk like this then?" Remy took a drink of her own coffee out of her matching mug. Their mom had purchased them both brown coffee mugs with the letter R on them in white a few years ago, in Reno. "She loves you, Reese."

"I know she does."

"You do, but you don't. You didn't see her when you were out, little sister." Remy sat her cup down next to Reese's on the coffee table. "She literally passed out from the anxiety of possibly losing you."

"See? This is what I'm talking about. I can't keep putting her through this."

"You don't have a choice, baby sis. She loves you. It comes with the territory."

"But, with most people, it's just the normal stuff. With me, you have to check me every day to make sure I didn't hurt myself and failed to notice."

"Somehow, I highly doubt Kellan's going to mind getting free looks at your entire body on a daily basis." She lifted an eyebrow. "Reese, you love her. She loves you."

"She's going back soon."

"And you're worried she'll forget about you or something? She's coming back in like three weeks."

"Maybe she won't, though."

"You want to run scared now? Is that it?" Remy pressed. "You pulled this crap with Morgan, but I thought Kellan was different." She stood.

"She *is* different," Reese nearly yelled and then glanced at her bedroom door again.

"Then, act like it," Remy told her. "Don't push her away because you're scared she might leave you when she's given you no reason to think that."

"Quiet down. She'll hear you."

"Maybe she *should* hear me so she knows what a big wuss her girlfriend is," Remy suggested. "Better to learn that now instead of later, right?"

"Knock it off."

"Are you really going to push her away?" She sat back down next to Reese.

Reese thought about what Remy was saying. She hadn't thought about pushing Kellan away when she'd woken up next to her that morning. She'd thought about how beautiful Kellan was. They'd hardly even kissed since Reese had gotten home, and she'd missed every touch they'd shared. She'd decided that, even though she wanted Kellan like crazy, she needed to listen to the doctors. It did help that Kellan had refused to put out until she was given the all-clear, but not nearly enough. She'd seen Kellan fresh out of the shower on Saturday. It had taken everything in her not to devour her on the spot.

She hated the fact that Kellan was leaving later that day, but she believed she was doing the right thing. She wasn't pushing Kellan back to the city. She was pushing her to get back to her life; to the life she'd left behind for a quick two-week trip to Tahoe that had turned into an over-a-month one and had gotten a lot more complicated. Reese was being practical. Kellan had a job to get back to.

"Hey, I was promised coffee." Kellan emerged from the bedroom, wearing a pair of well-worn jeans, tennis shoes, and a black long-sleeved shirt. She dropped her bag by the door of the bedroom and made her way toward the sofa. "Hi," she greeted as she leaned down, giving Reese a peck on the lips.

"Coffee's in the kitchen," Remy directed.

"Thanks." Kellan made her way toward the kitchen.

"So?" Remy asked Reese softly. "What's it going to be, baby sister?"

CHAPTER 30

"ARE YOU SURE I CAN'T STAY?"

Kellan asked Reese as they stood in front of Kellan's Jeep.

"I'm sure." Reese had her arms around Kellan's neck and her face pressed to it. "I want you to, though. You know that, right?"

"I do. I also understand why you're making me leave," Kellan explained and tightened her grip on Reese's waist.

"Call me when you get back? And tomorrow when you get home from work? And maybe text me in the morning so I know you woke up, and–"

"Reese, I'll call you when I get in. I'll call you tonight when we're both about to go to sleep. I'll text you when I wake up every day, if you want me to. I'll text you when I get to work and when I leave the office, and again when I get home. I'll call you before I'm about to go to sleep every night." Kellan kissed Reese's neck just below her earlobe. "I'll do whatever it takes for us."

"Now, you're making me sound clingy," Reese said and felt the ripples of Kellan's laughter as they continued to embrace. "I love you."

"I love you."

Reese hesitantly pulled away and said, "I promise I'll follow all the doctors' orders."

"I know you will, because Remy will tell me if you don't." Kellan gave her a playful glare. "But please do what the doctors say because *you* want to be safe and healthy, Reese. Don't do it for Remy or me or anyone else."

"I will."

"You can't be reckless anymore, because you went and fell in love with me and made me fall in love with you. You have to consider me now, too," Kellan warned.

"I know. Remy is probably putting those hideous rubber bumper things back in place as we speak," she said regretfully as she held onto Kellan's hands between them.

"Babe, if you don't want those things, get rid of them."

"You just told me to—"

"I told you not to be reckless. And you won't be; I know that. It's your life though, Reese. If you don't want to take those extra precautions, just take the regular kind of precautions for yourself. I love you. I trust you."

Reese smiled and squeezed both of Kellan's hands at that comment. Only a few people in the world had ever known about Reese's condition. She believed she'd been right not to reveal it to everyone, as her mother had also thought, but she also knew she'd been right in sharing it with Kellan. Reese loved her mother, her father, and her sister more than life, but none of them had ever just allowed her to be without the added worry. None of them had said the words Kellan had.

"Oh, I almost forgot." Reese reached into the back pocket of her jeans. "I noticed you didn't have one of these on your car. I actually got it a while ago, when you were leaving the first time. I thought I'd hang onto it until you actually left." She held out a bright blue bumper sticker. "I had this line I was going to give you before all this happened."

"A line?" Kellan chuckled.

"Yeah, just remember that I thought you were leaving after two weeks. We had just met. I didn't know where this was going. You'd mentioned having a kind of open leave of absence. I was going to hand this to you and tell you I wanted to keep Tahoe blue," Reese explained with a slight blush creeping on her cheeks.

"So, you were going to give me a bumper sticker saying that?" Kellan smirked at her but also had a look of confusion on her face.

"No, I was going to ask you to stay longer. I was going to tell you I wanted to keep Tahoe blue and look into those eyes of yours." She moved in and pressed her forehead to Kellan's, closing her own eyes in the process. "Your eyes are the most beautiful blue I've ever seen. I want to look at them every day, Kellan." Kellan took the sticker from Reese's hand. "One day?"

"One day what?" Kellan asked, keeping her forehead pressed to Reese's.

"One day, do you think I'll get to wake up to you every day?" Reese asked, and with her heart in her throat.

"You want to wake up to me every day?"

"Yes."

"Then, yes," Kellan said in a hushed whisper. "One day." She leaned in to capture Reese's lips.

It was a slow kiss that Reese knew Kellan was using to show her exactly how she felt. Reese hoped her kiss back was doing the same in return. It was the most they'd been able to share with one another in over a week. Reese wanted more, but she'd wait until Kellan returned and she had a clean bill of health. She'd wait for that visit, the one after, and the one after that. She hoped that Kellan would keep her word and that one day, they'd be able to wake up to one another every day.

"Get on the road. I don't want you driving in the dark." Reese pushed at Kellan's shoulders lightly before wiping a few stray tears off her cheeks.

"I'll call you when I get there," she repeated.

"You better," Reese chided and hoped it was covering the intense sadness that had overtaken her when she pulled entirely away from Kellan's body.

Kellan stripped the sticker from its paper backing, moved to the back of the car, and returned sans sticker. She handed Reese the paper with a smile and climbed into her car. Reese watched as she backed out of the drive and turned the Jeep onto the street. She noticed the bright blue of the bumper sticker begin to fade as Kellan drove further and further away until she was completely out of sight. Then, Reese started to cry and held her hands to her face.

"I've got you." Remy was beside her, and Reese turned into her arms. "She'll be back soon, Reese."

"I wanted her to stay," Reese finally admitted. "I didn't want to ask, but I wanted her to stay."

***

Kellan didn't call her friends upon her return. Maybe that made her a bad person, but she wasn't ready to see anyone. She wanted to take care of everything she had to in the city so she could get back to Tahoe in three weeks and, more importantly, get back to Reese. She'd been back for a week already, and she'd kept her promise to Reese. She'd texted and called. They'd talked on the phone nightly and video chatted whenever possible. Kellan wanted evidence that Reese was indeed improving and was happy to see that the bandage on Reese's head was gone and her stitches had been removed. Reese had also gone to the doctor twice, as ordered, and had only good news to report.

Kellan missed her like crazy. She found work helped to keep her mind on her patients and not on Reese, but getting back into things at the clinic and going home to her apartment every night just didn't feel right anymore. She'd decided to work the weekend to help keep her mind off things and to prevent the temptation to go see Reese from taking over. She was worried she'd pack a bag and hit the road. Reese was still healing though, and Kellan had things to take care of.

Her sister joined her for dinner Sunday night, which was out of the ordinary, but Kellan suspected her parents had asked Katie to check on her. They weren't a close family, but they were still blood. Kellan had welcomed the visit, though, because she had something she wanted to talk to Katie about and felt it would be best in person. Now that Katie was out of school and looking for a job, it seemed like the timing was right for this conversation.

She listened to Katie talk about the night she met her boyfriend, Gordon, and saw her eyes light up. She listened as her sister talked until it was her turn. Then, she filled Katie in on Reese. She mentioned working for Dr. Sanders and enjoying the experience. Then she got to the thing she wanted to talk to her sister about. If Katie said no, Kellan would still figure it all out. But Katie saying yes would make things a lot easier and would allow Kellan to bring her plan to fruition faster.

Her entire life leading to her trip to Tahoe had been in slow motion. She'd done all the right things. She'd gone to school, had friends, and even girlfriends. She'd graduated and gone to work before going back to vet school when she'd been able to afford it. All of that mattered, but it wasn't until she arrived in Tahoe and met Reese Lee that her life finally felt like it had real meaning. She wanted fast motion now, and she hoped it would all work out the way she wanted and needed it to.

CHAPTER 31

"YOUR TEST RESULTS are good, Reese. I think we can safely say you're in the clear. Your infection is gone, your cut has healed nicely. You'll have only a small scar, which is great news," her doctor told her after her exam.

"That *is* great news," she agreed as she sat in the chair off to the side of the exam table.

"I understand you wanted to talk about something else too," she said as she sat on the stool and wheeled closer to her.

"That trial you've mentioned before? Is there still a chance I can get in?"

"I believe so. I'd have to contact the specialist to confirm. But your condition is so rare, they tend to jump at the chance to have more participants. I thought you weren't interested."

"Recent events had me thinking about things."

"Your fall?" she guessed.

"The consequences from it, mainly."

"You know this might not make a difference?"

"I do, yes," Reese told her. "I think I should try something. If there's a chance it might work, it could help me know when I've hurt myself, right?"

"That's the idea." The doctor sighed. "You know it means you'd be able to feel pain. If it works, you will feel when you hurt yourself. That's both good and bad."

"I know. It's one of the reasons I didn't want to do it before," she admitted. "I was afraid. Most people don't even worry about this stuff, and I'm worried about a paper cut. I've never felt when I got one, but I've seen others get them. And their initial reaction is always one of pain." She laughed lightly. "It's so silly, but I'm afraid of feeling what that's like."

"I've had a few in my day. It's not too bad." The doctor shrugged.

"I'd like to start as soon as possible. I don't know what I need to do."

"I'll make a few calls and get you in the group. Keep in mind that this is a clinical trial. That means there's a control group and a placebo."

"So, I might not even get the real deal," Reese remembered the specialist's statements from their video call. "I know."

"And you'll be required to do work. You'll have to ensure you take the doses regularly and report symptoms and changes you experience."

"I can do that."

"I'll get the process started. There are two options: there's the spray, and there are the injections."

"The injections have shown better results, right?"

"They have so far, yes. But you'd have to have someone at home give them to you daily; more than once a day in the beginning. I assume Remy will do that for you?"

"She's volunteered."

"I'll have some paperwork for you to fill out. I'll work with Stanford to get the medication sent here. I'll administer the first injection for you to show you how it needs to be done."

"Thank you."

"I think this is the right move, Reese. Not just because it's a medical trial that will help others with your condition. If there's a chance that it works, it means injections regularly – which is not fun, but it also means a longer life expectancy for you."

"That's why I'm here." Reese smiled at her.

**

"So, how did it go?" Remy asked.

"You still up for jabbing me with a needle every day for a while?" Reese asked as she tossed her keys on the kitchen counter.

"Really?" Remy asked excitedly from her position at the dining room table.

"What am I missing?" Morgan turned from her position on the couch.

"Hey, Mo," Reese greeted. She hadn't realized Morgan was there when she'd entered, but Morgan's questioning glance gave her an opportunity, and she decided it was time she took it. "Can we talk?"

"You and me?" Morgan asked.

"Maybe we can go for a walk or something."

"Everything okay?" Morgan stood.

"Everything's great."

"Okay." She walked toward Reese. "And will you explain why your sister sounded so happy about jabbing you with needles?"

"Yes." Reese laughed as she ushered Morgan out the door. "I'll be back."

"Ryan's bringing dinner," Remy informed and returned her glance to her laptop. "Morgan picked up burgers."

"Bacon burger for me?" She turned to ask Morgan as she closed the door.

"Of course." Morgan smiled. "Who's your best friend?"

"You are, Mo."

"Good. Now, tell me what's going on." Morgan stepped off the porch, and Reese followed. "Side path?"

"Sure." Reese nodded toward the path off to the right of the house that led nowhere of interest but went on for about a mile on fairly even terrain.

"How was your visit with the doctor?"

"I'm all healed up, off the meds, and the infection is gone."

"That's great news, Reese." Morgan smiled over at her as they walked and entered the path between the rows of trees.

"But there is something I've been keeping from you that I shouldn't have," she began. "You deserved to know this a long time ago."

"Know what?"

"I have a condition," Reese confessed. "It's called congenital analgesia, and it's the reason I keep hurting myself and not realizing how badly."

"Congenital what?" Morgan stopped walking and turned to her.

"Analgesia. It means I can't feel pain."

"Wait. What?"

"I was born with it. Not many people know. I haven't told anyone. Well, my doctor knows. Remy knows, obviously."

"Kellan?"

Reese gulped and looked up at one of the tall trees that had already started to lose its leaves. The greens of summer had given way to the oranges, reds, and browns of autumn. Much sooner than she was prepared for, winter would be upon them, and the beautiful colors would turn to white.

"I told her, yes."

Morgan sighed and looked back in the direction of the house before taking a few steps that way. Reese realized she could potentially lose her best friend over this.

"I should be mad." Morgan stopped and turned back. "I should be pissed off at you, Reese. We dated for three years."

"I know."

"And you never thought to tell me even before that? We were friends, Reese."

"I know."

"And then we were together; and you fell. You were in the hospital. I thought you were dying."

"I know," Reese said again.

"Stop saying that."

"What do you want me to say?" Reese asked.

"Why didn't you tell me?" Morgan asked.

"I didn't tell anyone."

"Until Kellan. You can't say it's because she's your girlfriend, because *I* was your girlfriend."

"Because she's the one, Morgan." Reese stared into Morgan's eyes. "I knew it when I met her. I don't know if I told her more because of that, or because she was always leaving and going back to the city, or for another reason entirely. I just know that I want to be with her forever. When I realized that, I knew she needed to know." She looked quizzically at Morgan. "You said you *should* be mad at me."

"Should be, yeah. But I can't be, can I? You're just getting over another major injury and, also, you're my best damn friend, Reese."

"I'm sorry I didn't tell you sooner. My mom didn't want anyone to know when I was growing up. She was always afraid people would treat me differently. And since I'm a twin, she didn't want Remy getting special treatment. She'd be able to play at recess and the teachers would keep me off to the side or something like that. She thought it was important that we were treated equally. It's a hard habit to break, not telling people," she admitted. "I kept it up because it was easier. Most of the time, the condition is just inconvenient. I get a scratch and don't know it. I bump into a table and get a bruise, but I don't feel anything. I've just had a lot of bad luck recently."

"Bad luck? That's what you call it?"

"I fell last year. I didn't know how bad it was, but the surgery to fix it was what caused the real problem, remember? Had that not been the case, I would have had a broken ankle and moved on."

"And this time?"

"This time, there was an infection that I didn't notice. That was my fault. And I feel terrible because I made all of you go through that again."

"Yeah, that *was* terrible." Morgan nodded. "And now? What do you do?"

"What do you mean?"

"I mean how do you protect yourself from this happening again?" Morgan took a few steps toward her. "What do we do to help you?"

"Nothing, Mo. I just have to be careful."

"Fuck that," Morgan stated defiantly. "There's no cure, or you wouldn't still have it. But are there treatments? Is there something people around you can do? Watch you closely or something?"

"No, there is no cure. There aren't treatments exactly, but there is a clinical trial. That's what I was talking to Remy about. But, Morgan, you don't have to watch me more closely. I can take care of myself," she said, and Morgan went to argue. "I know what's happened recently makes you think otherwise, but I've learned my lesson, Morgan. It won't happen again. I don't need a more watchful eye on me to take care of myself."

"I have to be able to do something, Reese," she pled, and Reese recognized it as her friend feeling as if she couldn't protect her.

"You can just be my best friend." She shrugged a shoulder. "Morgan, that's all I need. Remy can help with the trial. I will be more careful every day. You can just be my friend."

"That's all?" She lifted an unsatisfied eyebrow.

"That's so much, Mo." She took Morgan's hand. "You have no idea how much I just want you back in my life as my best friend. I want all this crap behind us. I want to move on with you knowing everything."

Morgan looked down at their linked hands and seemed to consider Reese's statements for a moment before she looked back up and gave Reese a smile.

"Fine. But I draw the line at hearing about any bedroom details between you and Kellan. That's going to be weird for a while."

"Deal." Reese laughed and pulled Morgan in for a hug.

CHAPTER 32

"WHEN ARE YOU GETTING HERE?"
Reese asked before even saying hello to Kellan.

Kellan laughed in response as Reese stood from her sofa and paced in her living room.

"Hello to you, too." Kellan's laugh continued.

"Babe, I love you, and hello back, but when are you getting here?" she asked with a wide smile on her face.

It had been three weeks since Kellan had left the lake, and Reese missed her terribly. Kellan had been working a lot of hours at the clinic and had been incredibly busy recently. They'd still had their calls and text exchanges, but it wasn't the same as being together in person. Kellan had promised her she'd leave work early to hit the road and they'd have a near full weekend together. Reese also didn't like the idea of Kellan being on the curvy and somewhat dangerous roads around the mountains as one neared Tahoe in the dark at the end of a long drive.

"I actually need you to do something for me. You're at home, right?" Kellan asked her with a hint of something mischievous in her tone.

"Yes. Why?" Reese's eyes brightened, as did her smile, and she rushed to her front door, swung it open, and made her way out to the porch. Then, her smile dimmed as she glanced around. "You're not here."

"Did you expect me to be?" Kellan asked.

"You can't ask me where I am and then not be right outside my door, waiting to surprise me like in all the romantic comedies, Kellan. Everyone knows that."

"Oh, I'm sorry." Kellan laughed again.

"Please don't tell me you had to cancel your trip. I don't think I can wait until Thanksgiving to see you," she said, thinking about the holiday that was several weeks away.

"I'll be there. I just need you to run an errand for me, if you can."

"An errand? How romantic," Reese said sarcastically and went back inside the house, closing the door behind her.

"Will you do it if I promise you sex later?" Kellan chuckled.

"You're giving me sex later whether I run this mystery errand or not. It's been over a month, Kellan," she stated seriously. "You're giving me sex all weekend. We're doing nothing else."

"I can't even eat to keep up my energy?" Kellan's smile could be heard through the phone.

"I'll allow regular meals," Reese replied with a smirk. "To be taken in bed."

"That's kind of you." Kellan still laughed.

"Do you know how long it's been?"

"You just told me," she reminded.

"No, since I've done anything," Reese whispered, despite being alone in the house. "To myself."

"Reese, you can't talk like that right now," Kellan whispered back.

"Why not? Where are you?" Reese changed the subject.

"Will you run that errand for me?"

"You're infuriating," Reese replied with gritted teeth. "But I will do whatever you want me to if it means you'll get here."

"Can you go to Dr. Sanders at the vet clinic? He has something I need."

"Dr. Sanders?" Reese leaned against the counter. "What does he have?"

"You are annoying sometimes. Please just go to the clinic. I promise everything will make sense."

"Fine. Fine. But you either better be at that damn clinic with a good explanation or you better be meeting me next door at that Italian place with really expensive wine and their famous tiramisu, or I'm going to be pissed off, Kellan Cobb."

"I understand the terms." Kellan chuckled.

***

Reese arrived at the clinic a little after five in the afternoon on a Friday and was surprised to find it still open. She knew Dr. Sanders kept odd hours here and there when needed for the animals, but she suspected there was something else going on if Kellan had asked her to come here. Reese had been to the clinic a few times when Kellan was working there. She knew the layout well. She entered through the front door while staring over at the busy Italian place next door, still half-hoping that Kellan was there. She also didn't want Kellan to be there because she didn't want their reunion to be in a public place. She planned to kiss that woman long and slow when she first saw her again and wanted that to be in private.

"Reese, good to see you," the receptionist greeted her upon arrival.

"You too. I'm here to get something for Kellan from the doc," she replied as she leaned slightly over the high counter of the desk. "Do you happen to have it or know what it is?"

"Oh, I don't. He's in his office, wrapping up for the day, if you want to go check with him though."

"Thank you." Reese gave her a wave as she moved

around the desk and through the door that led to the back of the clinic.

She made her way pass the small break room where she'd shared a cup of terrible coffee with Kellan once and then saw the doctor's office door open. She knocked on the doorframe when she saw him hunched over, writing something in a patient chart.

"Reese, how are you?" Edward asked her when he looked up.

"I'm good."

"I heard you were out of the hospital and doing much better. I'm glad to hear it." He closed the folder in front of him.

"I am. And thank you for the flowers. Thank your wife, too. That was very kind of you."

"Oh, of course. It was the least we could do. We would have visited as well, but we figured you had enough people crowding around you."

"I did, yes." She laughed.

"That's the sign of a good person, Reese. Having all those people surround you when you need them most is the sign of a good person," he insisted.

"I hope so," she said and felt bad about wanting to steer this conversation in a different direction. "Listen, I'm sorry to just stop by like this, but Kellan said you had something she needed. She didn't tell me what, but she asked me to come by and get it. She's due in town later tonight."

"Oh, right." Edward smiled and pulled out a drawer. "Here you go." He stood and held out one of those yellow, interoffice envelopes with the red string acting as a closure. "Everything's in there."

"Oh." Reese took the envelope and knew her disappointment had to be showing on her face.

Kellan really had just needed her to run an errand. The envelope was thick enough and had weight to it. It was likely filled with papers, which made no sense to

Reese, but it probably had something to do with the time Kellan spent working for Dr. Sanders. Maybe it was a paper they were looking to publish together on a particular treatment or some kind of legal document Kellan had to sign to work at the clinic that they never got around to signing before. Reese held it to her chest.

"Disappointed?" he asked with a lifted eyebrow and a slight smirk.

"That obvious, huh?" She let out a short laugh. "I guess I thought there was more to this errand than there really was. She told me it would make sense, but this is just an envelope, and I'm merely her errand girl."

"Sorry to mislead you. It really is just an envelope with some paperwork for Kellan. She can tell you the rest when you see her." He seemed to remember something. "Oh, I forgot. She actually left a few of her things in the office she was borrowing. Nothing of consequence, but would you mind taking it to her? I have a new doctor starting on Monday, and they'll be using that office."

"No problem."

"Great. There's a box on the desk."

"It was good to see you," she told him and lowered the envelope to her side.

"You too, dear. Don't be a stranger."

"I won't." Reese left the office, and the man sat down in his chair.

She turned to give him a wave before heading down the hall only a few feet and noticing the door to Kellan's borrowed office was closed. She reached for the knob with her free hand and opened it. She expected to find the old office she'd seen before, with its old and overly large wooden desk and two chairs in front of it that had been borrowed from the lobby. There had been a bookshelf behind the desk and off to the right and a small window that only showed the alley between this building and the restaurant next door. She expected to see a box of Kellan's belongings on top of that old desk, but what she saw instead was Kellan leaning her butt against that desk, holding out a single red rose.

"Hi, baby," she said with the widest of smiles on her face.

"Babe," Reese let out, dropped the envelope to the floor, and moved immediately into her.

Kellan wrapped her arms around Reese's waist, and Reese's went to Kellan's neck. She placed her head on her shoulder and breathed in Kellan's familiar and very missed scent. Reese squeezed her harder before she kissed her neck several times in rapid succession while Kellan vibrated against her in laughter. Reese pulled back and, without waiting for an explanation, captured Kellan's lips in a heated kiss. Kellan complied easily and moved her mouth against Reese's quickly until Reese recalled her plan to kiss Kellan long and slow. She detached their lips for a moment and ran her hand under Kellan's hair at the back of her neck. She brought Kellan's mouth back to her own and kissed her slowly. Their tongues met. Reese moaned. With one hand in Kellan's hair, she used the other to slide under Kellan's shirt. She rested it there for several moments before she began walking them backward toward the door of the office. She reached frantically for the thing and closed it behind her. Kellan pressed her against it while she locked it and ran her hands up and down Reese's sides.

"God, I missed you," Kellan stated between kisses.

"Show me," Reese told her.

"Not here." Kellan pulled back with shock on her face.

Reese heard three things in rapid succession from outside the office; each one made her smile grow wider. She heard the door to the doctor's office close, she then heard him say goodnight to his receptionist, and the receptionist said she'd follow him out. Then, she heard the sound of the front door closing.

"Yes, here," Reese said.

She'd been waiting. She was done with it. She unbuttoned Kellan's jeans and lifted at Kellan's shirt.

"Hold on." Kellan chuckled and halted Reese's hands.

"Babe–"

"I promise, you can do whatever you want to me soon, okay? Just listen for a second."

Reese stilled her hands on the hem of Kellan's shirt but gave it a tug.

"Fine. But this better be good."

"Do you like this place?" Kellan looked around the office and returned her eyes to a glare Reese knew she recognized.

"This office? You're asking me about this office?"

"I am asking what you think about this office, yes. I'm asking you this because this office is now my office."

Reese let go of Kellan's shirt. Despite still having her back against the door, she leaned as far as she could back farther to take in Kellan's face.

"What do you mean?"

"I start work on Monday. This will be my office," she revealed with a hesitant smile.

"What? You work *here* now?" Reese pointed to the floor with both hands. "You can't work here and live in San Francisco," she said.

"I know that." Kellan's smile grew. Her hands went to cup Reese's neck. "I live here now."

"What? Where?"

"In this building, actually," Kellan answered.

"Kellan, you're speaking in riddles. Or at least they sound like riddles, because you live and work in San Francisco, so you can't possibly live and work here."

"Reese, I quit my job in San Francisco." Kellan held onto Reese's face now, as if that would help focus her attention. "Babe, Dr. Sanders made me an offer before I left the first time. He offered me the chance to not only work here with him but to potentially take over the business from him when he retires next year. I was going to talk to you about it, but the accident happened. I knew I wanted to be here; and not just be here with you or because of you, Reese, but because I love it here. I loved working here with Dr. Sanders. I can see this place in the future. I could see remodeling it and adding onto it. I love your friends, and I think they've become my friends. Morgan has texted me like ten times that she wants to hang out when I'm here. I felt at home here. I felt at home for the first time in my entire life. I love spending time with Remy and Ryan when it's the four of us. I love how you two are as sisters. I love just being able to be a part of that sometimes: watch how you two care about each other." Kellan paused as Reese let out a few happy tears. She wiped them away with her thumbs. "There's an apartment upstairs. It's fully furnished. Riley stays there sometimes. You know Riley, right?"

"Yes," Reese replied.

"I'm renting it from Dr. Sanders. It's a two-bedroom, so Riley can still stay there, but it'll be mine for a while."

"Until you move in with me?" Reese asked.

"That's my plan, yes." Kellan smiled and kissed Reese's forehead. "I sublet my apartment to my sister, Katie. She wanted something in the city since she's looking for jobs there and also just started dating someone that lives there. It worked out perfectly. She's going to take over my rent until the end of the lease, so I can afford to move."

"When will you? When are you moving?" Reese asked.

"I left everything there. I already moved."

"You're here now?" Reese gulped. "Permanently?"

"Yes," Kellan replied and leaned in. "I hope that's okay."

"It's definitely okay." Reese smiled back at her. "You live here now?"

"I packed what I could and drove here this morning.

All my stuff is upstairs." Kellan glanced over at the floor where Reese had dropped the envelope. "That was mainly an excuse to get you here for my surprise, but it is also my rental agreement for the apartment that I've already signed. And this is the key." She reached into her pocket of the still unbuttoned jeans and held out a single key. "Actually, this is your key. Mine is already on my key ring."

"My key to your place?"

"Yes."

"But what about all your other girlfriends? Do they get keys too?" Reese asked in a tone she hoped conveyed there was more behind those words.

"They do not," Kellan replied and leaned in. "Only you get a key. Only you get to come over whenever you want, slide into bed with me, and do whatever you want."

Kellan slid the key back into her front pocket. Reese followed the movement of her hand until she met Kellan's eyes again.

"Take me upstairs now."

Kellan's eyes darkened at Reese's demand, and she asked, "Why wait?"

Reese's eyes lowered again. Her heart thundered in her chest. It had been so long. She wanted this woman like crazy. She loved her like crazy. She loved this surprise like crazy. Kellan was here. She was here permanently. They wouldn't have to plan holidays together or decide which one would visit the other. She no longer had to worry if the complicated nature of a long-distance relationship would cause too much stress for them. She could just stare at Kellan like this. She could touch her and not worry about it being the last time until they saw one another again. She could slide her hand into Kellan's pants, feel her wetness, and make her come in her new office before they went up to Kellan's new apartment and made love all night.

Kellan came when Reese stroked her with one hand while holding Kellan against her with the other one. She came again not long after as they made love on the floor of Kellan's new living room, with Reese above her. She came again in her new bed after that, with Reese under, and with Reese coming on Kellan's fingers that were buried inside her. She came again in the shower, with Reese on her knees and hot water delightfully assaulting their skin. And she came later that night, after they'd gone to that Italian restaurant, had some really good wine, and shared an amazing tiramisu.

EPILOGUE

"I'M HAPPY FOR YOU, KEIRA. That's amazing news," Kellan said as Reese lay with her head in her lap.

"I've got four new clients. I can barely handle it all myself," Keira explained. "I've got to hire already, and that's crazy to me. Just a few months ago, I was considering moving back in with my parents."

"And now you have a thriving business and a girlfriend who wouldn't be happy with you relocating." Kellan smiled at her friend.

"How are you?" Keira asked. "When are you coming back for a visit?"

Kellan had been living in Tahoe for months now. She made it through the winter by getting acclimated at the new clinic. She went to the holiday events as Reese's girlfriend, and they celebrated the New Year together. She said goodbye to Dr. Sanders in April – when he was ready to leave the place in her hands – and hello to Riley, who had decided to move back to South Lake after all and start her own law practice in town. Kellan had come to enjoy having Riley as a roommate in their now shared apartment. Riley was funny and smart, and she kept all the common areas clean. She was also hardly home, because starting up her own practice took a lot of time and effort. Kellan mostly didn't mind it, though.

It was now July. She'd been at the helm of her vet practice for over two months now and felt very comfortable making the decisions. She'd hire another doctor soon and begin part of the remodel with the lobby area in August. She was also very close to celebrating her one-year anniversary with Reese, and while she ran her fingers through Reese's hair, she thought about their future together.

"I don't know, Keira. Things are hectic here. I miss you guys, I do. But I'm about to hire another doctor and add at least another two to my staff. Plus, I'm running adoption events for local shelter animals on the weekends when I'm not helping Reese at the visitor's center."

Upon hearing her name, Reese looked up at Kellan and smiled.

"Say hi for me," she said.

"Reese says hi," Kellan told Keira.

"Tell her hi back from me, but that I'd actually like to meet her in person one day," Keira said.

"I will." Kellan chuckled.

Reese gave her a confused expression but turned her attention back to the TV. They'd been watching an old movie when Keira had called.

"You happy, Kell?" Keira checked.

"I am, yes." She ran her hand through Reese's hair again. "You?"

"Well, I miss one of my close friends, but other than that, I am very happy. Emma is amazing. The business is starting to kick ass. Oh, have you talked to Macon recently?"

"Not for a while. Why?"

"She's been spending a lot of time with Joanna lately."

"Emma's co-worker?"

"Like, *a lot* of time."

"Is Macon Greene going to settle down?" Kellan laughed lightly.

"Joanna's straight."

"Is Macon Greene going to get her heart broken?" She frowned.

"I don't know. But, let's just say, when Joanna's hanging out at bars on weekends – it's with Macon and us, usually, and not with some guy on her arm."

Kellan laughed again and moved her hand to Reese's stomach where she scratched lightly. Reese turned her head to face Kellan again and gave her a look that told Kellan she should probably hang up the phone soon.

"Ask her to invite me to the wedding," she teased.

"You'd have to come back to the bay for that."

"You know I'd come back for her wedding, your wedding, or Hill's wedding to that girl from the coffee shop she still hasn't spoken to."

Keira laughed this time. Kellan ran her hand up Reese's body to cup her breast, causing Reese to turn over onto her back and look up at Kellan expectantly. Kellan squeezed her nipple hard, and Reese made a face.

"Ow," Reese exclaimed.

Both she and Kellan froze.

"Keira, I have to go. Can I call you back?"

Reese shot up. Kellan's hand moved from under her shirt. Kellan hung up the phone and tossed it onto her sofa.

"Did you feel that?" Kellan asked.

"Yes." Reese turned so that she was sitting up on the sofa. Kellan turned toward her, sliding her leg underneath her body. "It hurt, Kell."

"I'm sorry," Kellan said on instinct, because she never wanted to hurt Reese. But then, she remembered. "Also, that's pretty amazing." She smiled at Reese.

"Do it again?" Reese turned her body slightly toward her. "Please."

Kellan smirked and decided she should comply with her girlfriend's request. But instead of merely tweaking her nipple with her fingers again, Kellan lifted Reese's tank top and pulled it off, tossing it to the floor, before she moved on top of Reese. She kissed Reese first before sliding her hand to Reese's breast and cupping it again. She massaged it while moving her lips to Reese's earlobe, sucking on it. Reese moved beneath her until Kellan's thigh was between both of her own. Kellan lowered her lips further to Reese's collarbone and kissed, nibbled gently, and sucked while her thigh lowered against Reese's center.

"Is this what you had in mind?"

"Not exactly. But don't stop." Reese lifted her hips to meet Kellan's thigh.

Kellan lowered her hips further and pulled Reese's nipple into her mouth. She sucked on it as she massaged Reese's other breast. She pressed her thigh to Reese's center, knowing it would be more than enough to get Reese started since she was only wearing a pair of thin white panties for their now usual night where they'd Netflix and chill. Riley had gone out with friends tonight and would be gone until well after they'd retire to Kellan's room. She decided they could have at least one round on the sofa before going into the bedroom to continue. She ran her hand down Reese's stomach and slid into her panties, feeling her soaked flesh.

"God, baby. How long have you been like this?" she husked against Reese's breast.

"All night," Reese replied as Kellan dipped between her folds.

Kellan stroked her and sucked on her breasts until she entered her fully and used her thigh to add pressure to her thrusts. Reese peeled at Kellan's boy shorts until they were down at her knees. Kellan shook them slightly further down and lowered her center onto Reese's thigh. Reese made no attempt to touch Kellan, knowing by now that Kellan loved coming this way; riding Reese's thigh.

Kellan thrust into Reese as she ground down against her. Reese encouraged her by massaging Kellan's ass and pressing her down more. Kellan was gliding on Reese's skin. She'd grown wet the moment she'd touched Reese, and as she felt Reese clench around her fingers, she added another one on the next thrust and took Reese over the edge, following right behind her with her lips around Reese's nipple.

As they both caught their breath, Reese's grip loosened. Kellan slid out of her, keeping her hand on Reese's sex for a moment longer before moving out of her panties and hovering over her. She kissed her long and slow. Reese's hands slid up and down her back, matching that pace until Kellan separated their lips, lowered her mouth, took Reese's nipple between her teeth and gave it a soft, testing bite. Reese made no sound. She bit slightly harder, and Reese only rubbed her back more. Kellan bit just a little harder.

"Ow," Reese exclaimed, and Kellan pulled up to stare down at her.

"Yeah?" she asked with hopeful eyes.

"I felt it. It hurt."

"Bad?"

"No, not bad, babe." Reese pulled her back down to her lips. "But I felt it."

Kellan kissed her then and pulled her own shirt over her body, tossing it on the floor somewhere next to Reese's. Reese had gotten into the clinical trial. They'd started with the injections a few weeks after Kellan had moved to Tahoe. They started out with four injections daily, which had taken a toll on Reese physically and mentally when nothing happened at the beginning. That had gone on for over a month, so Reese and Kellan both worried she'd been placed on the placebo.

The doctor told them to keep at it though, for the sake of the trial if nothing else. When the injections went from four to two for the following few months, Reese still showed no signs and completed the trial believing she had been placed on the placebo. When the specialist told her they were switching her to the nasal spray though, Kellan had known Reese had been on the real drug then. The specialist was trying another delivery mechanism for the strong drug combination to see if it would have any effect. Reese used it several times daily for the next several months. While she was lucky there were no negative side effects and that she'd been relatively healthy, she also wasn't showing any signs of positive results. They'd all but given up on the trial.

Reese hadn't felt any pain during any of the exams or any of her own pokes and prods at home. Kellan had no explanation for why Reese would feel pain tonight and no other night. The drug dosage hadn't been increased nor had she taken more than the required dose. It may have simply been the last time Reese had taken it, the drug had broken down the last of the barriers to Reese's nerve, registering the pain, or it may have been something else entirely.

"You're going to the doctor tomorrow," Kellan told her when Reese laid down on top of her.

"Yes, I am," she agreed. "But we're not talking about that anymore tonight."

"No, we're not. I think we should talk about something else."

"What's that?"

"I think you should ask me to move in with you."

"You do?" Reese laughed as Kellan kissed her neck.

"I do, yes."

"Because you bit my nipple and I felt it?"

"Because we love each other and Remy is moving in with Ryan. I'd ask you to move in here, but I'm renting, and you own." Kellan leaned up and placed her hand on Reese's heart. "I love you."

"I love you," Reese told her. "I was going to ask you to move in on the anniversary of our little island trip," she confessed. "You've now ruined my surprise." She pulled Kellan's hips back down. "I'll forgive you, though, if it means you'll move in sooner."

"How kind of you." Kellan played with her earlobe. "When will Remy be out?"

"Next weekend. She and Ryan closed on their new place yesterday."

"What will we turn her old room into?" Kellan asked as she kissed Reese's jawline.

"A nursery," Reese told her.

Kellan lifted up to stare down at her once more, with those bright blue eyes showing immense happiness in their color.

"Yeah?" Kellan smiled.

"Well, one day." Reese rubbed her hands over Kellan's back.

"One day," Kellan agreed.

Made in the USA
Monee, IL
04 November 2021

81450823R00157